The Aura Answer

PSYCHIC SOLUTIONS MYSTERY #5

PATRICIA RICE

One

"Look at this, just look!" Short, blond, and normally serene, Gracie flung a stack of colorful paperbacks on the plastic protecting the bed from slimy, shredded wallpaper remnants.

Evie was supposed to be the one with ADHD, not her cautious school-teacher sister. From her perch on the ladder, Evangeline Malcolm Carstairs studied the cute covers of kittens and snow-covered houses with bloody knives on the porch and assumed they were cozy mysteries. Even a non-reader could work that out.

What did mysteries have to do with anything? Maybe Gracie wanted more for Christmas? Given that a tree had crushed the roof of her sister's bungalow shortly after Thanksgiving, Gracie really didn't have a place to put more books.

"*Annnd?*" Evie returned to scraping flocked wallpaper from the guest bedroom of Great-Aunt Val's Victorian.

The house belonged to their aunt, but Evie had been appointed caretaker. The structure was genuine late 1800s, the décor, pure 70's clutter. Living here alone since Val married and moved to Atlanta, Evie had never cared about the muddle. Except, this past year, her life had taken a few drastic turns, and more space was required. Someone had to take charge, and as chief dog walker and useless ghostbuster, she elected herself.

She hadn't realized once she removed decades of old boxes and furniture that the walls would be quite so hideous.

Gracie—legally Grania Malcolm Carstairs Jenkins, but Evie's self-effacing sister wouldn't claim that grandiose moniker—pointed at the colorful books as if they were alive and squirming. "In every one of those books—the heroine *inherits a house*. What's with this business of inheriting a house from complete strangers or unknown family members? Maybe we should look for bones in the attic and write about them!"

Evie sort of got where Spacey Gracie was coming from. Having to beg for housing from her dysfunctional sister in an already over-crowded household had upset Gracie's tidy, home-loving Cancerian nature. Gracie wanted to be snuggled up in her neat little bungalow for Christmas.

But Evie wasn't much of a reader, so she dismissed the rant. "I think we have to knit or bake to qualify as book detectives."

"Or renovate old houses!" Gracie shouted, gesturing at the paper-pocked walls. "Pris bakes. I sew. That ought to count. You can renovate the house."

"Thought that was what I was doing." Evie studied the half-stripped wallpaper. Whoever had put the stuff on meant it to last forever. "Aren't those books all about librarians dropping dead because the mayor wants to turn the library into a nightclub. . ."

Gracie glared.

Oh right. Evie had already had former Mayor Block arrested and thrown in jail on land fraud, after she'd uncovered the murder of her ward's parents by one of Blockhead's contractors. But she was the furthest thing possible from a librarian.

"Fine. You can be my Watson. Write my stories. Make me pretty and smart and sound like I know what I'm doing. You have over two weeks of Christmas vacation to do it in." Evie put down her scraper when her phone warbled "I Got You Babe." Everything in this house was old, including the ring tones.

Jax didn't even greet her. "You'd better come down to the courthouse and persuade your mother to picket somewhere else. There's an ugly counter-protest group gathering, and some of them are armed. Apparently Block has called a news conference."

Normally, Jax's voice thrilled Evie to her toes, even after all these months together. But this was her fiancé's angry, frustrated lawyer voice. She vaguely recalled he was representing the current mayor in some war over zoning and licensing at the courthouse today, and her mother was supposed to be there supporting their cause. Mavis had her reasons for getting involved, although they tended to be more emotional than logical.

Why would former Mayor Block be holding a news conference? Shouldn't he be in jail? *Irrelevant, Evie, focus.*

"If Mavis has the whole coven with her, I'm unlikely to be much influence, unless they're singing Christmas carols," Evie warned. "I can kill a carol in two minutes flat."

Her mother's friends weren't actually a coven. Malcolms might be called witches by the ill-informed and superstitious, but her family simply had extra abilities others didn't recognize as normal. Evie saw ghosts. No witchcraft there. And the people who frequented her mother's Psychic Solutions shop for herbal remedies and tarot reading simply had different fantasies than men like the former mayor with his delusions of power.

Labeling her mother's friends as libtards and tree-huggers for protecting a pond and family cemetery from development might be a stretch, but the *coven* did consider their job of defending nature seriously. The mayor had paid the price for seeing dollar signs and ignoring angry constituents.

Poor Jax had spent his teenage years in city suburbia, with normal parents and country club memberships and yachts. He was still adapting to Evie's rural neighbors.

"No Christmas carols that I hear." Jax sounded decidedly not merry. "Even the bell ringer stopped. I can't see if one of the guns held him up."

"Protesting zoning with guns seems a little. . . out of context?" she suggested, hoping he was exaggerating.

He sighed in exasperation. "Judge Satterwhite chose today to consider your ex-mayor's plea to be let out on bail on some sort of holiday leniency. Judge Rhodes is hearing Larraine's zoning case in the other courtroom at the same time. If I were paranoid, I'd call the timing collusion. The conspiracy nut-jobs are still screaming that Larraine stole the election. These aren't just local loudmouths, and this really isn't about zoning. Pry Mavis and her friends out before someone is hurt."

Oh crap, if the mob wasn't about zoning, it was about hating on their new Black transgender mayor. Former mayor Block might be a thief, but he was white and male. Of course all the rubes wanted one of their own back. Evie started down the ladder. "Mavis *knows* things. She must have known the crowd would turn ugly. She's not protesting, she's standing guard over her soul sister."

On the other end of the line, Jax cursed more colorfully than she did. "The sheriff doesn't have enough men to hold back a mob. And I don't think a lot of old people waving signs will help."

Holding the phone in one hand, Evie swiped sticky paper off her overalls with the other. "I'll see what I can do, but your best option is smuggling Larraine out. Mavis and Company will follow her."

"We're working on it, but there are news crews all over—*Larraine, get back!*"

A loud crack sounded through the phone before the line went dead.

That crack had sounded an awful lot like a gunshot.

"Jax?" Alarmed when she received no answer, Evie shoved her phone in her pocket and rushed for the door. "Riot in progress. Gotta go. You can be the renovator who solves mysteries," she shouted back at her sister. "I don't have time."

"You have wallpaper in your hair!" Gracie shouted back.

TRAINED IN COMBAT, JAX REACTED INSTINCTIVELY AT THE FIRST LOUD CRACK from above and shoved the current mayor toward Reuben. Acting as bodyguard, the ex-Marine and computer nerd pushed Larraine against the wall, providing a six-foot shield of muscle.

In a downpour of plaster to the second-floor rotunda, the courthouse ceiling collapsed.

Jax yanked short, white-haired Judge Satterwhite out of the raining chunks and back toward his courtroom while trying to see through the dust cloud descending on the melee of the news conference in the center.

Who had Block? He'd been at the podium. . .

A female reporter shrieked. Jax watched in disbelief as a stuffed comforter—sleeping bag?—plunged through the opening in the ceiling, landing smack on top of the former mayor. The bag must have contained something heavier than feathers because Block crumpled. Whatever it was, was small. Block was large. This did not compute.

Ancient plaster thickened the air while cameras rolled, and reporters shouted into microphones. After checking to be certain nothing else plummeted from above, Jax abandoned Satterwhite to his courtroom and the mayor to Reuben's care. Beneath the gaping hole, he joined the sheriff and his deputy in pushing the crowd back. The collapsed former mayor was now hidden by the gruesome sight slipping from the sleeping bag.

The slight male body was pretty obviously a corpse, even if the stench wasn't as strong as it might have been had it been midsummer and not December.

At a nod from the sheriff, a female Jax didn't recognize dropped to her knees to shove aside the filthy comforter and examine Block, who wasn't moving, cursing, or blustering as any normal man might had a corpse fallen on his face. Had he had a heart attack? Block was in his sixties, stout, and under a lot of stress. Jax prayed he was alive.

Still in his robes, Judge Rhodes warily appeared in his courtroom doorway to assess the situation. Younger and more athletic than white-haired Satterwhite, he wisely retreated from the reporters.

Wearing one of her quieter dark wigs and a sedate suit for her meeting with the judge and town council, Mayor Larraine Ward didn't scream but watched warily from behind Reuben. The same couldn't be said of a news reporter shouting into her microphone about dead bodies.

Out of habit, Jax tried to count heads, but it was impossible. This was a busy courthouse with two courtrooms in use and a news conference in progress. Whoever had scheduled the former mayor's hearing at the same time as the current mayor's conference had an evil mind. The entire town council—all Block supporters—had brought their own cheering sections and were now crowding around their downed leader.

Outside, a mob shouted for Block's release. . . *Crap.* Block didn't look to be going anywhere soon.

Jax stepped in front of a news camera. The sheriff had the same thought and began gesturing for the news crews to be removed. They protested.

"The man is due some privacy," the sheriff shouted. "Put down your cameras."

The woman examining Block shook her head sadly and stood.

Shit, crap, hell, unmerry Christmas. Jax couldn't see the bodies clearly through the mob and the sleeping bag, but he was pretty damned certain the crack he'd heard before the corpse fell hadn't just been the ceiling. If there was any chance at all that Block had been shot. . .

The mob outside was demanding Block's release from custody and rein-statement. If the news of his death got out, shouting would escalate to a real riot. Larraine's life could be in serious danger. Not to mention Evie's mother and the rest of her. . . coven. Although he was pretty certain there were more than thirteen old hippies out there swinging signs protesting Block's release and supporting Larraine's zoning law—counter to everything the mob wanted.

The sheriff shouted orders to clear the area around the bodies in the center of the rotunda and set up a perimeter, making it official. Not one body—two.

As if the mob had already heard the news, a howl of fury bellowed from below.

Jax gestured Reuben toward the door of the courtroom they'd vacated only moments ago. "Judge's chambers. Lock it."

Shaking his head, his former military intelligence officer pointed upward, confirming what Jax had suspected. "Active shooter. I'm going in."

He was no longer Reuben's commanding officer. When Larraine didn't countermand his suggestion, Jax held up a hand to make him wait and reached for his phone. It rang before he could open his contacts.

"The state better be sending riot gear," Evie's voice spoke in his ear.

Damn, he regretted calling her down here, but if her mother was out in that mob. . . At least neither of them were inside the courthouse. They both despised Block and would be instant suspects. "How do we get into the attic?"

Evie had grown up in Afterthought and knew everything, even when she shouldn't.

"On second floor there's an employee-only closet that ought to be locked but probably isn't. Look for pull-down stairs in the ceiling. Attic's full of guano. Wear a mask. Why?"

"No time to explain. Get your mother out *now*." While Larraine took her elegant self into the courtroom with the white-haired judge and several bystanders, Jax gestured at Reuben, indicated the employee door, and pointed upward. "The scene is about to go ballistic."

Reuben jogged off, a tall black nerd in a business suit, wearing a topknot and tribal scars. People hurriedly stepped out of his way.

"Is Larraine okay?" Evie demanded in his ear. "Because Mavis is down here talking burning brooms, and you really don't want her going there. She's screaming about black clouds forming."

Shit. Mavis's black clouds were always an ill-omen, if only because she made them so. "Have her march the brooms up Main Street, away from the courthouse. Larraine is fine, but no one else will be unless we distract the mob." Jax was making this up on the fly as he jogged back to help Sheriff Troy control the scene.

He was quite positive that Block hadn't died from corpse assault.

"I like the way your mind works, honey sweetikins. Stay safe and wait for the fire engines." Evie shouted at someone and cut off.

Evie never called him pet names. She was upset. *Fire engines?*

He probably shouldn't encourage Mavis's rare rages, but he hoped that would divert Evie, at least.

Knowing what Jax had sent Reuben to do, the sheriff scowled, but two deputies and a bailiff were barely enough to threaten news crews into standing back, much less the entire town council, Block's lawyer, and some powerful supporters. Someone had to look for a shooter, and Rube was trained.

The shouts outside became bellows as the mob crashed through the front doors. The old courthouse only had a few security guards and a metal detector that wouldn't stop anything but wheelchairs. At least the employee Christmas tree in the hall below was artificial and couldn't burn.

At the escalating chaos, Troy hurriedly escorted the rest of the council members after Larraine into Judge Satterwhite's chambers. Jax gestured at the bailiff, and he herded the reporters and bystanders across the hall, toward Judge Rhodes' courtroom. Rhodes didn't emerge from his office to object. The TV news crews resisted. Block's lawyer and a big man in cowboy boots shouted protests. Jax didn't care.

The deputies taped off the dust-covered bodies. Jax didn't recognize the tattered corpse and didn't give Block a second thought once he realized not much of him could be seen. He'd testified against the former mayor but had never known him personally as Sheriff Troy must have. The older man looked grim, but he simply did his job, slamming the courtroom door after the reporters and placing a bailiff in front of it.

Unfortunately, no man could hold back a riot.

Jax stuck in his earbuds and grabbed a roll of yellow police tape. He hit his cell contact for Rube's security partner, Roark, and started down the stairs with the roll.

Roark answered with a curt, "Where are you and where do I need to be?"

Jax tied tape on the lowest baluster on the first landing. Security still held the mob trapped at the roadblock of the metal detector. They couldn't see him at this angle. "Reuben in attic. Mayor in judge's chambers. I'm taping off stairs. Evie should be encouraging Mavis to march down Main Street. What do you see?"

Roark lived with Jax's sister about a mile out of town, but the beauty of a small town like Afterthought was that anyone could be anywhere in minutes. Communication was key.

"I see flaming brooms," the Cajun replied in what sounded like awe. "They are actually marchin' through da middle o' town with *flaming brooms*. Dozens of old ladies. A few doddering gents. Couple on motor scooters. They're swinging the brooms at. . . Holy shit, they just set someone's hair on fire!"

Jax groaned. Evie hadn't been kidding. "As long as they're in the middle of the street and not breaking into the courthouse, we're good. This place is a tinderbox. Evie mentioned fire engines?" Jax created a spiderweb of knotted yellow tape at ankle and knee height up the stairs and tied it all off on top. They'd need to cut each and every strand to get past the trap without breaking a few necks.

One of the deputies had grabbed a second roll of tape and was preparing the back stairs the same way.

"Both da sheriff's cars out front. No more manpower arriving except ladder truck pullin' in the parking lot on the side. Let me get back to you. I gotta punch this *couillon*." Roark's voice cut off.

"Are you carrying?" Troy shouted over the cries below. He'd brought out one of the news photographers to take the photos his forensics team would have taken had they been able to get inside.

"Ricochet factor, nope. Are the state cops on the way?" Jax entered a courtroom and tugged at one of the antique wooden benches. It weighed a ton but wasn't bolted down, so he began dragging it into the rotunda.

Troy joined in, and they hauled the barrier to the front stairs. "It could take the state hours to organize, if only out of sheer obstinacy. The governor hates Larraine. We have a few cars coming in from Charleston. I've called for fire hoses."

"Smart move. Mavis is setting hair on fire."

Troy snorted but didn't comment on Mavis. He'd known her for a lifetime.

Jax continued as they returned for another bench. "The ladder truck arrived. Can we evacuate people before they bring out the hoses?"

"If they're not afraid of heights. You got a disguise for Mayor Larraine? Because if that mob sees her. . ." Troy helped him position the second bench at the back stairs.

Jax understood. Larraine was nearly six feet tall in heels and not exactly a shrinking violet. He punched up Reuben's number. "Finding anything?"

"Shooter's gone. There's a trapdoor exit onto the roof and an old fire escape. Someone's been living up here. Looks like work is being done on electrical. Floorboards are ripped off. Gaping hole where our corpse must have been sleeping on the insulation between the rafters."

He'd process that at a later date. "Do you think you can get the mayor down a ladder truck without anyone recognizing her?" Jax positioned the bench across the stairs and looked around for more obstacles.

"Judge's robe. I'll be right down."

Gunshots fired below. Screams, cursing, and smashing glass—the mob must have breached the metal detector. Shouts of "Free Mayor Block!" echoed up the stairs.

Had the former mayor been alive, he'd have been grandstanding for his supporters right now and the mob might have retreated. This mob had been planned.

Jax glanced at the bodies surrounded by yellow tape. He'd like to shout back *Bring a coffin and you can have him.*

Instead, he took the police baton the sheriff handed him and waited for the first of the mob to stumble over his spider web.

Two

"YOU YANKS REALLY KNOW HOW TO THROW A RIOT." NICK GLADWELL, stranded British marketing expert, knew he'd crossed into foreign territory when he accepted the flaming broom his ginger-haired hostess shoved into his hands. Against the darkening December sky, the fiery twigs looked more like a hand warmer than a threat. "Has anyone told you that you're wearing paper in your hair?"

His lawyer's significant other ran a hand through her tangled curls and grimaced. Short and nicely rounded, Evie was cute and fierce when she was angry. Nick, thankfully, preferred his women long, lean, and sophisticated. Not that he expected to find city sophistication in the South Carolina cotton fields where he currently moldered.

He had to find other ways to amuse himself. Flaming brooms hadn't been on the agenda, but he was open to new experiences.

"We need to clear the more vulnerable out of harm's way." Evie gestured at a gray-haired bundle of quilted nylon waving a wooden sign heavy enough to be a weapon. "The sheriff will unleash water cannon if this escalates."

"Escalates? Any more of these brooms and they'll burn down the whole damned town! Or at least that dried-out Christmas tree on the lawn." He swung the glowing twigs over his head but the flames didn't change. He scowled at the weirdness.

"Fake fire. Don't ask. My mother has a cigarette lighter torch in hers that can do real damage though, so stay out of her way." Evie worriedly watched the mob swirling around the evergreen decorated in childish ornaments and blinking lights, then winced at a high-pitched male scream from the mob.

They both glanced in that direction.

As if to confirm Evie's warning, flames licked at the long, scraggly, gray beard of a shrieking man in a camouflage jacket. A stout woman with flaming broom marched away in a swirl of colorful shawls and caftan while bystanders doused the beard with water bottles, some with great glee and little accuracy. He'd be a popsicle by nightfall.

"My word, she's ferocious, although face hair that ugly deserves torching." Saluting Evie, Nick waded into the fray, waving his fake fire to separate sign-swinging seniors from rude fellows carrying hatchets and tire irons.

He whacked a few rioters using machetes to hack branches from the sun-dried evergreen. Evie was right. Even the paper decorations didn't suffer from his weird broom, but the ogres with beards retreated warily.

At some point, Nick decided the signs were more useful than non-flammable brooms, and he made a trade with a senior whose arms were giving out. He pointed her off after the rest of the torch parade, then used the sign-post to flog a saber-wielding bounder in a helmet.

He was a dealer and a marketing expert. He knew how to trade and talk. The warrior thing was new, but he was bored and eager to create an impression.

One couldn't really make an impression in a mob without suitable armor and weapons, but his tweed coat was more stylish than fur vests and camouflage. Little old ladies *listened* when he directed them out of danger with an air of authority. If, in the process of clearing their escape, he bashed a few hard heads, who noticed?

He was feeling quite righteous by the time the massive Cajun he knew by the ridiculous Scots name of Roark pointed to a fire engine and halted Nick's sign-swinging. "They're coming down. Help me move them somewhere safe."

Who was coming down? The gods? Certainly, whatever. Following Roark's direction, brandishing his sign post horizontally with both hands to clear a path, Nick worked his way around to the relatively open area by the emergency vehicle. He had to poke a post into a burly thug or two who took objection to their progress, but he'd dodged worse in pub brawls. Took him right back to his youth, if only there were a beer waiting at the bar.

Apparently, they were using the ladder truck to evacuate the courthouse upper floor. Jolly good fun. Along with the firemen, Nick assisted a motley lot off the big red truck, including a couple of judges in black robes. Always good to be seen on the right side of the law. A few reporters, janitors in overalls, and a bunch of prosperous-looking old white men in rumpled shirts and ties joined the precarious descent from the upper story.

Once safely in the parking lot, most of the business suits peeled off and headed down a side street, muttering and cursing. Nick wasn't familiar enough with the town to know where they went, but he knew people well enough to recognize a clique when he saw one. He desperately needed a job. He should probably follow the money.

That's how he'd reached this crossroads in his life. He liked having money. But right now, he wasn't too fond of the people who had it. Or pretended they did. He needed to adjust his people radar.

Roark shouted, gestured, and led the remainder of the escapees down an alley. Nick decided to stick with the person he knew. Presumably Jax's friends wouldn't lead him astray.

A few journalists bearing news cameras and microphones peeled off and ran down Main Street to risk their necks in the melee. Intent on breaking and entering, the howling horde ebbed and flowed up the courthouse stairs as they found entrance through windows. Nick winced as a bunch wielded the Christmas tree as a battering ram. More glass smashed.

"Is there anyone else in there we need to rescue?" he asked once he realized they were leaving the action and escorting the judges and the remainders to the safety of Jax's law office.

No one answered. Oh well. He hung on to his sign, just in case.

Once inside the quiet lobby, one of the black robes shrugged off the billowing garment and handed it to a short, distinguished man in a suit. "Thank you, your honor. I appreciate the loan." She brushed the lint off her blue skirt.

Nick blinked, recognizing the flamingly gay transgender mayor the mob was out to kill. He resolved never to be mayor of a small town if the last mayor had been thrown in jail and the other was a target for a mob. It was impossible to please everyone.

Another of the suits, incongruously wearing cowboy boots, glared at the mayor in surprise, muttered imprecations, and marched out as if offended by the company. Nick gathered he wasn't one of Larraine's fans.

Roark gestured for the mayor to follow him upstairs, but she knew her own mind and began shaking hands with the few people who hadn't departed, apologizing for the *altercation* and checking to see if they were okay.

When she arrived at Nick, Larraine Ward met him nose to nose in her in four-inch heels. "Mr. Gladwell, so glad you're still with us! I do hope none of your family was caught up in this unfortunate episode."

His *family* were all in a Charleston jail awaiting trial on murder, kidnapping, theft, and assorted other sacrileges. If they'd been inside, he'd have set fire to the courthouse himself.

"Jax and Rube are in there," Roark answered for him. "Troy, two deputies, and a few more reporters." He turned to Nick. "Evie and Mavis?"

"Marching uptown with a bevy of aunts and flame throwers. Shall we rescue reporters next or let them suffer?" Despite the press essentially being his bread and butter, Nick had no particular fondness for them.

"Dante and Priscilla!" Mayor Ward abruptly cried. "They aren't marching with Evie, are they? I'm supposed to meet with them tomorrow about the restaurant."

"They're Christmas shopping in Charleston," Nick reassured her, edging toward the door. "I'm a wee bit concerned about the flaming brooms though. If you're all hunky-dory. . ."

"You go on. Reuben will have my head if anything happens to Miz Ward." Roark gestured at two men now carrying their black robes. "Your honors, would you like to come upstairs with the mayor? Jax has a mini-bar."

Nervous around officialdom, Nick preferred to wait outside. His phone rang, and he used that as an excuse to exit along with the other escapees who weren't invited upstairs.

"The children!" Evie's sister Gracie cried in his ear. "They've quit working on the parade floats for the day, and others are leaving play rehearsal, and Main Street is blocked. What on earth is going on?"

Nick had only a vague concept of where things were. He stepped into the street and glanced to his left, in the opposite direction of Evie's house and the mob.

Far down the hill, children were dashing from a big brick building that was most likely the school.

Painted hordes of savages smashing glass, brandishing tire irons—and the student-decorated Christmas tree—swarmed the road through town.

Well, hell of a merry Christmas, peace-to-all example that set.

"Water cannon," he remembered. "Don't take Main. I'll see what I can do from here."

~

Terrified, idling her aging Kia off Main, Gracie checked on her six-year-old in the backseat. Aster seemed content to watch people running down the streets as if their pants were on fire. Thank heavens she was too young for after-school activities.

Things like this didn't happen in sleepy Afterthought! That was the whole entire reason for living in this backwater where she knew everyone and felt safe.

Swallowing her fear, Gracie began calling people she knew near the school. After verifying a mob surrounded the courthouse and blocked Main, she formed a map in her head. Praying, she maneuvered back streets and lanes, trying to work around the courthouse area to reach the school.

She was supposed to be looking after Loretta, Jax and Evie's eleven-year-old millionaire ward. Thunder, lightning, and swarms of locusts would probably rain on their heads for a thousand years if any harm came to their precocious Indigo child.

Gracie had to admit, Loretta was a very unusual child, even for a Malcolm.

"Mama, look, it'th Thanta Clawth," Aster cried, straining at her car seat to watch out the backseat window. "It's lots of Thanta Clawtheth! And Cwismas trees! And thnowmen!"

Aster's missing front teeth produced an exercise in elocution.

Winding through the city parking lot that had once been the trailer park her mother lived in, Gracie halted before exiting into the road in front of the school. Afterthought was a rural town, the seat of a tiny county consisting of cotton fields and little else. The two-lane into town wasn't big enough for two tractors side-by-side, but it had a gravel shoulder parents used for parking when picking up their kids.

Today, in the middle of that road, students gathered around a veritable wonderland of flashing Christmas lawn decorations. Unable to drive through the colorful barricade, cars stopped along the side of the road, spilling parents and children. Men in red Santa hats scrambled around the ornaments, stringing blinking lights they'd plugged into. . . Gracie strained to see, but a dozen cords ran in different directions, and she gave up.

Against the lowering clouds and late afternoon gloom, the colorful lights were probably a wise idea. If the sheriff didn't have enough patrol cars to cordon off the mob-filled streets, this was a much jollier method.

She parked the car and helped Aster out. She wouldn't be able to find

Loretta from this distance, not with the crowd forming around. . . a cart manned by a jolly Pakistani elf in green hat, handing out candy.

"Don't take candy from strangers," she muttered under her breath as she looked both ways and plunged into the fray. Although she knew Mr. Patel owned the produce market nearby, he wasn't exactly a real elf.

The younger children recognized her and shouted her name. She'd been a teacher for years and knew them all. She hugged one of her students and scoured the crowd for familiar—adult—faces.

Sirens wailed uptown. A boom box playing holiday music boomed louder. She recognized the band director standing on a folding chair and waving his baton to direct his caroling chorus.

Gracie wished she'd brought her reindeer antlers. . . *But there was a mob burning down the courthouse.* Was this playing while Rome burned?

She had to hold Aster back while she scanned faces for Loretta. Her adopted niece found her first.

"Aunt Gracie! Do you think it will snow? We want to do a snow dance!" Garbed in festive red and green to clash with her purple glasses, Loretta waved a candy cane, happy in her own protected world, for the moment.

Gracie knew she should be grateful that the children were shielded from the ugliness uptown, but her cautious nature could see ten thousand opportunities for disaster.

"Where did all this come from?" she asked, preventing Aster from reaching for the candy. Pied pipers and trickster tales flashed alarms in her mind.

Loretta waved vaguely. "Everywhere. My music teacher carried the school's snowmen over. Some of the moms brought lights. I think Evie broke into the hardware store. She said Henry should pay for his treachery. I don't know what she meant, but Mr. Gladwell is trying to blow-up a reindeer."

Gladwell—Nick. He was behind this? He'd been the only person she could reach earlier. He was a stranger here. How had he—

She watched with incredulity as a twelve-foot Rudolph slowly unfolded above the barricade while a tall, Nick-tall elf wearing a red hat over his dark hair pumped his fists in triumph.

More sirens—this time from outside of town, coming up the highway but too far away to be seen. Emergency vehicles wouldn't be going slow.

Oh dear.

She handed Aster over to Loretta. "Hop in the car, please. We have to clear the road."

Her niece looked disappointed, but the kid was smart and caught on quickly. She grabbed Aster and started shouting at her friends to move back to the gravel edge.

Gracie dived into the crowd, yelling over the boom box at the teachers and mothers she knew, working her way toward the candy cane cart and the towering Rudolph.

"Police!" she shouted over the kiddies singing "Up on the Housetop."

Mr. Patel heard and hurriedly shoved his cart toward the edge of the road. The Nick-sized mad elf working on the inflatable decoration apparently couldn't hear her. He jumped up and down like a little boy as Rudolph reached full height, just missing a string of lights that might have decapitated the enormous balloon. All around, children cheered and clapped and the boom box rang louder.

Gracie ripped plugs out of extension cords, bumping aside ornamental snowmen. "Police!" she kept shouting—until she pulled the cord on the boom box and silence descended.

Uptown, howls, sirens, and smashing windows filled the once cheery party atmosphere. She felt like Scrooge as she cleared a path through the barricade.

Flashing strobe lights in the distance broke the early twilight. Even the demented elf caught on. In seconds, Nick had grabbed the centerpiece of his roadblock and shooed the rest of the children out of the road.

By the time the state cops screamed by, the party had dissolved. Snowmen and Christmas trees melted into the darkness, leaving candy wrappers blowing in the breeze.

Gracie's phone rang. She didn't have to look to know who it was. She could see Evie on the other side of the road.

"Buzz killer," Evie said without rancor. "Good thinking, though. The Brit is our kind of nuts."

"Yeah, because we need more nuts. You broke into Hank's hardware?"

Evie waited for the last police car to scream by before crossing the street. "If you'd seen what his cronies did to the courthouse, you'd have set fire to Hank. Mom almost did. I did him a favor by helping her steal Rudy and a few elf hats instead."

Wearing her hair tucked up inside one of the elf hats, Evie stopped to help Nick fold up the big balloon. Gracie shoved her phone into her pocket. She'd long ago quit arguing with her insane family.

Nick dissolved into the crowd hauling snowmen back to the school. Evie dumped the folded reindeer into Gracie's arms and handed the box of elf hats to Loretta. "Leave them in the alley behind Hank's and then it's just vandalism, not theft. He can call his insurance company. I have to go back to the courthouse. Jax is still in there."

She vanished into the crowd, leaving Gracie holding her stolen goods.

Nick arrived with a collection of orange extension cords. "Have a vehicle? We can decorate the hardware store!"

She almost bashed him over his pointy elf head.

Three

STILL WEARING THE ELF HAT TO CONCEAL HER CONSPICUOUS, FIERY HAIR, EVIE cased the courthouse from the safety of the fire engine parking lot.

The state cops had all gone inside to drive out the invaders with bull-horns and weapons. The firemen were busy controlling the hose as they inundated what remained of the mob on the front stairs. They didn't have anyone to spare to stop Evie as she swung up on the truck and onto the extended ladder. They'd moved it back from the second story window but hadn't considered the rusted fire escape.

It was like swinging from her childhood bedroom window to the pine tree, she told herself as she reached for the ancient iron rungs. Jax would kill her, but he was busy risking his own life fighting off rioters. She knew her man well. She loved him with all her heart and soul, but like any man, he had flaws. Well, so did she.

As a kid, she'd climbed around the courthouse roof any number of times. It was practically a high school tradition to sneak up here to smoke or neck. She'd never tried the rusty fire escape, but it held her just fine.

Up on the housetop reindeer pause. . . Climbing over the parapet onto the roof, she couldn't pry the stupid song out of her head that the kids had been singing.

Once there, though, she started having second thoughts about crime scenes. The news snippets she'd seen from the courthouse had sounded ominous. Bodies did not fall through ceilings without reason.

She visually searched the roof but saw nothing dangerous. Good thing she was wearing overalls. She was going to be filthy. Decades of crud littered the rubber sealant over the flat portion of the roof, with scuffs and footprints everywhere. She'd just have to add hers as she crossed to the door in the cupola. A lot of the disturbance looked fresh, and she assumed Bertie had moved in for the winter.

Down through the chimney goes good St. Nick. Stupid earworm. She'd have to wear earplugs at the Christmas concert.

The dust on the metal steps into the attic was trampled. Not daring to disturb evidence, she stuck to the edge, just in case. Someone had left the attic stairs lowered, and she continued down to the second floor to peer around the door into the storage room. Seeing only brooms, she pulled off her felt hat and stuffed it into one of the many pockets of her flannel-lined vest, then opened the closet door into the second-floor rotunda to peer out.

Even her multi-tasking brain had trouble processing the chaos on the other side. An unholy din echoed from all corners and two floors. Shouts, screams, a few gunshots, which raised her pulse rate to heart attack city. From this angle, she watched in horror as Jax stood on a heavy bench, swinging a wicked baton. Without hesitation, he walloped a guy carrying a machete, toppling him backward down the stairs into a crowd of people pushing up. He appeared to be bleeding from a cut on his hand and another near his temple, and she swallowed hard. At least he was still upright and fighting.

Grabbing a fire extinguisher from the back wall, she edged the door open a little more. In the middle of the hall, a circle of yellow tape flapped around what appeared to be a dust-and-plaster covered sleeping bag with legs and partial heads. They weren't moving. Dang, so very not good. Did that shaggy blond mane belong to Bertie?

She didn't have time for sorrow. Inching out at a shout from behind the door, she brandished her fire extinguisher weapon. Near the sleeping bag, Reuben wielded a metal chair and bashed a couple of skinheads. They had knives. That made them villains in her book.

Singing "Ho, ho, you didn't go," she aimed, pointed, and sprayed their bald heads.

The thugs shrieked and stupidly scrubbed at their eyes. Whooping, Reuben took advantage of their temporary distraction. The computer nerd was tall and lean but packed a lot of muscle. He grabbed the back of his opponents' shirts, knocked their heads together, and heaved them headfirst over the barricade at the back stairs. They landed squarely on top of a few of their comrades who were trying to clamber upward.

"Up on the courthouse, click, click, click." he shouted, adapting her refrain. Jumping on a bench blocking the stairs like Jax, he swung his chair in time to the beat, knocking back a few laggards attempting to climb past their fallen comrades.

Bullhorns below warned the state cops had taken over the first floor.

Looking gray and weary, Sheriff Troy gave Reuben and Evie a look that probably ought to kill, but he merely confiscated the fire extinguisher and handed it to a deputy.

Evie shrugged and dashed into the closet for a first-aid kit. When she returned, Jax was sitting on his bench, wiping his bloody head with a hand-kerchief. The intruders had vanished from the stairs, crawling back into the woodwork like the cockroaches they were.

"Up on the housetop, yeah, yeah, yeah," she sang, settling beside him and opening her kit. "How many bullets did your skull stop?"

He let her dab antiseptic around the wounds but didn't answer. Her heart quit freaking out once she decided the cut was bloody but not mortal.

The sheriff was on his phone and radio at the same time. Evie kept a wary eye over Jax's shoulder, but the state cops were hauling away any remaining pests on the stairs. The dangerous obstacle course of yellow tape fluttered in a breeze from below.

"Bertie smells less fresh than usual," she commented. Given her weird gift for ghosts, she really didn't want to look back at the pile circled with police tape. She fixed a bandage to Jax's head, then reached for his bleeding hand.

"Bertie?" He held her fingers rather than reveal his palm.

"Albert Walker. I wonder if he'd have turned out differently if he'd been called Al. How can anyone demand respect when called Bertie?" Evie knew all about longing for respect, but she'd had better resources than poor Bert.

"You know him?" Jax finally opened his hand so she could staunch the nearly dried cut. She didn't think it would need stitches, but she'd like to knife the jerkwad who'd done this.

"Everyone knows Bertie. He's a good guy, really, with a good family. But he has. . . had? . . . learning problems. I remember kids taunting him, because they did that to me a lot."

"Which is why you learned martial arts?" Jax closed his hand around hers again.

"Well, it was that or ask for a flaming broom." She grinned and dabbed at the cut. "Bertie. . . wasn't a fighter. He was an artist."

The sheriff put down his phone and crossed the hall to check on Jax and scowl at Evie. "What the damn hell are you doing up here, Evangeline?"

"Playing Florence Nightingale, naturally. Do you have any injuries, good sir? And what happened to Bertie?" She plastered a bandage over Jax's hand and turned to study the sheriff she'd known most of her life.

Troy wasn't tall but hefty and didn't look too battered. "Jax here took the brunt of it," he said with grudging respect. "Where's your mother?"

"Setting beards on fire, of course. They may be roasting marshmallows by now, I don't know. I had to help Gracie divert the kids from Main Street and couldn't join the fun. Bertie?" she reminded him.

"Forensics team on their way. I'm going with overdose for now." Troy nodded at Jax and headed over to check on the backstairs.

"Bertie's an addict?" Jax hugged her shoulders and began picking wallpaper out of her hair. Between the hat and the damp air, her curls probably looked like a hurricane had twisted them. Every so often she blew them straight, but it took work.

"Yeah, has been for years. It's pretty sad. ER gave him painkillers after he got beat up pretty badly in high school. He hated Special Ed classes, so he dropped out, did manual labor wherever he could, sold a few sketches, tried to help his mom. But he liked the drugs. You know the story. He wouldn't go home and offend his family and ended up homeless. He never hurt anyone." Grimacing, Evie turned to face the body. *Bodies*?

She avoided opening her third eye, not wanting to see Bertie's spirit. He'd never had much of one when alive. She'd like to grieve for the misunderstood artist and not deal with his ghost. "Who is that under him?"

"Arthur Block. The judge just let him out on a reduced bond. Block called a news conference. At first, I thought maybe Bertie attacked him, but your artist has been pretty obviously dead for a while." Jax stood and helped Evie to do the same. "We need to let the forensics team up."

Block? Mayor Block was dead?

Unable to process news that enormous, she helped Jax push the bench aside, then took scissors out of the first aid kit to cut the tape remains on the stairs. After that news, she *really* did not want to see ghosts right now. Block hadn't been an evil man, she didn't think, not like Paul Clancy, his right-hand toady had been. Clancy's ghost had been demonic as hell.

Not evil, maybe, but the former mayor hadn't been a particularly nice man either. He'd certainly hated her and had done his best to break up her relationship with his son in her younger years. She'd been more in love with Toby's Harley than Toby, so she didn't hold a grudge, just wariness.

Her grief wasn't for the former mayor but for his son's loss. "Sheriff, have you called Tobias? I think he's been living in his father' s house these past months."

"I have someone going out there and over to the Walkers. We've been otherwise occupied until now," Troy said dryly as he crouched down to examine the debris from the ceiling.

"Open water bottle." Reuben joined the sheriff, toed a plastic gallon bottle, and studied the ceiling. "Soaked the plaster."

"Bert fell on Mr. Block and killed him?" Evie asked in incredulity.

"Allergic reaction to the stink?" Reuben asked wickedly, studying the person-sized hole in the ceiling.

She threw tape at the top-knotted nerd but it only fluttered to the floor. "Bertie was living in the trailer park when Block condemned it and had the park razed. He's been homeless since. But I'm pretty sure he wasn't in any condition to choose plastering the mayor."

A fitting end, though, don't you agree?

Refraining from rolling her eyes, Evie grimaced, reluctantly opened her inner vision, and located a gray shadow lingering near the closet door —*Bertie*. Talking to a dead man was never a good idea in public, but she hated to be impolite. She patted Jax and left him sprawled on the bench. Pulling out her phone, she ambled over to the spirit.

"Fitting for Block or you?" she asked, pretending to talk into the phone.

Both, I guess. Did I actually kill him?

"Don't know. What happened to you, do you remember?" In her experience, spirits seldom did. She hastily checked her cell battery. They also tended to drain her phone.

The gray shadow shrugged. *Fell asleep. Didn't wake up.*

"No one came to visit you up there?" Well, she didn't need battery juice if she was only pretend-talking, but she probably ought to call and check on Loretta soon.

Bertie's ghost flickered nervously. *Friends.*

"Friends who brought you drugs?"

Maybe. He vanished.

"Bertie?" she whispered. "Are you still here?"

He didn't reply. She sighed, but her battery was draining rapidly. She called Loretta. "Are you good?"

"I'm watching Aster. Aunt Gracie is mad about stealing stuff. She's scraping wallpaper. Stealing for a good reason isn't bad, is it?"

"Stealing is *always* bad. We just *borrowed* a few things and returned them. I'm sure Hank wouldn't have wanted anyone hurt by a mob and would have been happy they were used in a good cause, if he'd been around to ask." But the hardware store owner had probably been up here in the courthouse with the rest of the town council, standing as character witness for the former lying, thieving mayor. "Is Pris back yet?"

"She's mad, too, and cooking everything in the refrigerator, I think. It's not feeling very Christmasy."

"My battery is about to run out. Why don't you put on a Christmas cartoon movie for Aster and the twins and ask if you can run over and buy some candy canes for the tree? I'll be there as soon as I can. We can play Christmas music and finish the decorating."

Loretta's late parents had not been a frivolous, kid-friendly couple. Evie wanted to give her ward the Christmas Loretta never had as a rich kid, the kind with sleigh bells ringing and ho-ho-ho in every corner. This was not a good start to the season.

As she put her phone away, Jax greeted the forensic team ascending the stairs. Her lawyer man had an uncanny ability to know everyone in official-dom, even though he'd lived here for less than a year.

She didn't have much time before they kicked her out.

Steeling herself, Evie concentrated on what little she could see of Toby's dad. She owed her old boyfriend that much.

Ghosts didn't usually manifest immediately after death. Bertie had apparently been deceased for a few days, Block, only a few hours. But the former mayor's spirit lingered. He hadn't moved on. She could see an unhealthy brown and a bit of yellow and green, not his usual colors. But she couldn't associate them with any chakra since she couldn't see much more than his feet.

Spirits normally lingered because they'd left something undone. After her last experience with one who clung to her. . .

She really didn't want Block's disagreeable personality focusing on her. Before the sheriff could throw her out, she crossed back to Jax. "Let's go home."

Four

Avoiding family chaos, Jax had dropped Evie at home earlier and gone back to his office to verify the mayor and the judges had escaped safely. He'd grown accustomed to thinking of Evie's old Victorian as home, except these days, it had become some kind of mad boarding house. But he had to go in sometime. He parked his Harley beside the carriage house and let himself in the back door.

Entering the warm kitchen, he savored the aroma of fresh-baked cookies. Evie's cousin Priscilla removed a baking sheet from the oven while instructing his cousin Dante's twins in decorating with icing. They were only five. The results were predictably disastrous.

But after the day he'd spent, children, cookies, and baking were a welcome relief. Snatching an undecorated ginger snap, avoiding Pris's towel swat, Jax aimed for the stairs, hoping to make himself presentable before dinner.

He couldn't slip past the eagle eye of his ward. Loretta flew out of the front parlor dangling a particularly disreputable tin angel.

"This needs to go on top and we can't reach it!" she cried. At eleven, she was practicing for her adolescent drama years.

Childish laughter, women's voices, and a professional chorus warbling "We Three Kings"—probably from the aging tape deck—spilled into the hall from the parlor. Jax had wanted to wash up and remove his bloody bandages first, but he couldn't deny Loretta's plea.

She was so not the pig-tailed, uniformed, boarding school nerd she once was. Today, she wore a hokey red Christmas sweater with a blinking Rudolph on front, probably purchased in a thrift store. Her purple glasses frames were practically falling off her nose, and artificial snow adorned her messy, shoulder-length, brown hair.

He took the dented angel with a bent halo. Evie was teaching him to show affection, so he squeezed Loretta's shoulder as they entered the parlor. His adoptive parents hadn't been much on hugs, so he was rusty but learning.

Evie teetered precariously on a battered stepstool, trying to replace a dead bulb in a string of old-fashioned Christmas lights. In bright green leggings and an equally ridiculous red sweater that clashed with her sunset hair, she looked like a sexy elf.

Crossing the room, lifting her off the steps, and relishing soft curves, he asked, "Is there nothing in this house under a half-century old?"

"Me," she replied chirpily. "I *like* these old bulbs. They're traditional."

"So are candles, but I don't see you hanging those." Kissing her cheek, he set her down and climbed the precarious stool to shove the treetop up the angel's. . . gown. Angels probably didn't have asses. "Is this pathetic creature the Malcolm version of the Nature Goddess or are you trying to prove to your neighbors that you're good normal Christians who believe angels come with broken wings and tattered gowns?"

"We are not arguing what makes a Christian tonight." Evie handed up the replacement bulb. "Tell us what happened to Mayor Block before gossip balloons into conspiracy theory."

At her question, the music snapped off mid-alleluia. No longer focused on his assigned task, Jax noted the entire family had gathered—Evie's mother, aunts, cousins, and even her sister Gracie with her daughter. This was serious business.

They'd all been marching in the streets earlier. They looked like an innocent collection of homemakers gathered around the tree now. There was nothing innocent about them—except maybe Gracie and her daughter. The schoolteacher did not often participate in the rest of the family's mischief.

He should be wary that none of these women had husbands or fathers in their lives. They were strong women who forged on without men, not dainty Southern belles who needed to be protected. He wasn't entirely certain how he fit in except as occasional muscle.

"Aster, honey, why don't you help the twins decorate cookies?" Catching his expression, Gracie ushered her daughter out of the room.

Evie kissed his scruffy jaw, handed him a candy cane, and brought him back to the question. "Someone shot Block from the attic, didn't they?"

Shaking off his weird thoughts, Jax hugged her and leaned against the mullion window frame to study the decidedly lopsided evergreen. Sometimes, the world looked better through blinking lights.

"Yeah," he admitted. "Weird angle, lucky shot, but it definitely came from the attic. Your homeless Bertie made too much of a mess up there to distinguish footprints. Sheriff is testing for fingerprints."

"In guano?" Evie made a face.

"Doesn't the attic have a floor?" Evie's veterinarian cousin asked. Iddy was usually too buried in work to join the family festivities, so the women were seriously worried.

Unlike the rest of her family, Iddy was tall, lanky, and black-haired, but she was definitely a Malcolm. She talked to animals. He checked, and even the Siamese cat had abandoned the box of lights to twist around Iddy's ankles and appeared to be listening. Her blazer pocket squirmed, and a tiny furry kitten head peered out. At least she had left her raven home or it might be perching where the angel sat.

Jax tried to soothe their fears. "Contractors apparently lifted the floorboards to replace cannister lights and haven't put them back. Working theory is that the shooter used the hole from a missing fixture to aim through. But he did so over Bertie's body. Bertie must have taken advantage of the absent floorboards to place his sleeping bag on soft insulation next to the hole and probably fell asleep with the top off his water bottle. It leaked and soaked the aging plaster for days, and when the gun went off, the reverberation caused the entire section to cave."

"But the killer didn't fall through?" Iddy asked, apparently trying to picture it.

"He would have been kneeling on the floorboards. Most people know better than to touch insulation or kneel on plaster," Jax explained, trying not to question the mental state of homeless Bertie out of respect.

"Well, it's a good thing Larraine was safely in the judge's chambers." Mavis lit an evergreen-scented candle. "They'd either have shot her or accused her of murder."

Larraine had been standing near the former mayor at the time of the shot, preparing for her turn to speak, but Jax refrained from correcting Evie's mother. Their flamboyant new mayor had definitely not shot Block.

"You have no good reason to become involved," he warned. "No one is accusing anyone of anything. Now, if I may be excused, I'd like to wash before dinner." He hesitated, remembering the baking sheets of cookies. "Pris *is* fixing dinner, isn't she?"

"Eventually." Checking her phone, Evie waved away his concern. "And you may be wrong in your thinking. Tobias just offered a hundred thousand reasons for finding his father's killer."

Jax groaned. "Evie, you *really* don't want to be involved, not even for a hundred grand. Block knew a lot of shady characters and owed a lot of money in the wrong circles. He's not an innocent needing justice. I'm surprised his son has the money to offer."

Surprisingly, Mavis agreed with him. "It's Christmas, Evangeline. Let this one go. It's not as if you're making any money off this detective business."

"*Au contraire, ma mere.*" Evie beamed and scooped up Psycat to prevent him from climbing the tree. "Bella's insurance company rewarded us for finding the killer of the company's CEO, and one of Dante's archeological organizations paid us well for catching artifact thieves. Reuben and Roark are eager to earn more. They have a reputation to build."

And way too much time on their hands. Jax needed to have a word with his gung-ho friends.

But Evie was right in her own way. They all needed money. They had talents that normal officialdom couldn't bring to the table. And sadly, the world possessed way too much hatred and greed and too many guns for Evie's fledgling *Solutions* Agency to ever lack business.

He was just terrified Evie would die trying to find justice—as his parents had.

∿

NICK WHISTLED A MERRY TUNE AS HE CARRIED THE ANTIQUE MAPLE BEDFRAME out to the carriage house. "A little refinishing, and this thing could bring in some cash," he told Jax's towering Italian cousin. The family Victorian accumulated more strays than a pet shelter. Nick didn't feel too out of place mooching on their goodwill. He had lots of company.

Dante flung the ancient twin-size mattress into the back of Evie's Subaru to take to the dump and slid back the carriage house door. "A *lot* of refinishing and you could turn Evie's entire household into an antique store. I'm gathering our hostess isn't much into sanding and staining."

"And her family isn't much into giving up their furniture. They're hoarders, is what they are." Nick carefully arranged the bedframe pieces along the wall with the cartons of who-knows-what accumulating in the empty space.

At any given time, the family could produce vintage clothing from the last century, original rock albums from the sixties, and board games probably dating back to the 1800s. The ivory chess set and mahogany dominoes alone would pay the groceries for a month or more.

Not having money made him mercenary. He'd become used to ready cash these last years.

"You have to admit, it's handy not having to buy anything to move in here. It's just a matter of rearranging until we have what everyone needs. That tiny bed had to go." Dante stretched his back. He'd apparently been sleeping with his feet dangling off the end of the small bed until his leg had healed enough to take the stairs to more suitable quarters—hence the frenzy of redecorating.

"And there are still how many more bedrooms packed with this paraphernalia? Plus an attic? They all need to have larger houses of their own." Nick admired the gilded, ornate collection of picture frames that had accumulated along with the cartons. He didn't admire the photos and paintings inside them, but he was no art expert.

"We all need our own homes," Dante agreed. "But I already have one stuffed full of the same rubbish in Italy. All valuable for museums but worthless for modern use."

"Hotels, restaurants." Nick absently poked through a carton of wrapped ceramic figurines. "Huge business decorating with antiques and collectibles. I used to work with a chain that hunted through antique stores for their décor."

He'd lived on the knife's edge of poverty too, but those had been his student days. He'd learned how to mix with the movers and shakers since then. Once this damned trial was done, he'd have to go back to London, work through his contact list, get back in the groove. Poverty wasn't his thing.

"Huh, send them my way if they ever come to Italy. I'd love to have LED lighting and closets instead of armoires and floor lamps." Dante headed back to the house, uninterested in the cold dark garage.

Nick followed. "If my family had ever owned anything except cheap junk from a dustbin, I might have gone into the antiques business."

"Don't the Brits have enough of those already? You're better off in marketing. Everyone needs marketing." Dante still limped a little as he climbed to the back porch. The archeology professor had cracked a shin bone back before Thanksgiving and was using his inability to climb around caves as an excuse to hang out here a little longer.

Nick figured his real excuse was trying to entice Priscilla back to Italy with him and the twins, but that wasn't any of his business.

"Yeah, but I'm good at recognizing the expensive pieces and selling them for top dollar to the right people. Just having a store isn't enough. You have to know how to market the inventory." Nick hesitated on the porch. He wasn't family. He'd been sleeping in the cellar man cave as Jax's guest. He felt intrusive joining in whatever family festivity followed dinner.

"C'mon, if we haul enough furniture, they'll feed us Irish coffee and cake. I'm thinking there hasn't been a man around this house in decades, and they're taking advantage of us while we're here, but I'm good with that." Dante held open the screen door and gestured Nick inside.

The little blond schoolteacher was putting supper dishes away. Nick was glad she wasn't his type either—he was a bit of a bounder, and she was a freaky neat mother of a six-year-old.

She glanced over her shoulder at them. "Would either of you be interested in taking Pris's truck and rescuing my daughter's clothing chest from my house? Now that you've moved some of those cartons out of our room, there's space for it."

Dante frowned. "Shouldn't you have moved everything into storage? A hole in the roof can't be good for your furnishings."

She dried her hands and shrugged. "They cut the tree off the roof and covered the hole with a tarp. I can't afford storage while the contractors and insurance company argue. I've brought over our winter clothes and bedding, but Pris is using the only other small dresser for the twins. It's hard for Aster to dress herself out of boxes."

"I'll go for the heavy lifting," Nick offered, grateful that Jax's family had taken him in while he wasted away waiting to give evidence against his family and former employer. "But I'm trying to be legal these days. I don't have an international permit to drive."

Priscilla emerged from the pantry with jars of canned fruit. In the few weeks Nick had known her, she'd worn her mouse-brown hair striped in red, purple, green, and orange. Tonight, he saw the streaks were naturally a dramatic silver, emerging from a widow's peak and flopping over her eyes. She was taller than Gracie, but still far from the stylishly lean London sophisticate Nick preferred. And she only had eyes for Dante.

"You go to the auto club in Charleston, show your passport and license, and get a permit." Pris unloaded her jars on the butcher block and dug underneath for bowls. "Besides, unless you run over a policeman, no one in Afterthought will stop you if you're driving my truck. They know better. But

Gracie should go with you. She can load up a few other things while she's there."

"All right, then, I'll go if I have company. With my luck, the neighbors will report me as a thief otherwise. Let me go down and grab a coat." Nick headed for the door.

"I'll look after Aster. You're the one who needs to go, Grace." Pris unloaded her implements on the counter. "And Dante, we need you to reach the wallpaper near the ceiling if Gracie is abandoning the ladder."

And that was how Nick ended up driving through the winter night in an ancient Ford truck with a respectable schoolteacher at his side. He had no idea how to converse with a teacher, beyond the snark of his adolescence. The fashion models he usually dated preferred compliments, but he had a notion Gracie would smack him if he said he liked her dimples. She didn't flash them very often anyway.

She directed him to a modest cottage on a narrow, tree-lined residential street. Stacks of the huge oak's tree trunk still sat at the curb. Blue tarp had been nailed over the roof, and plywood covered the windows and doors in front. He drove the truck down the driveway where a child's playground equipment sat untouched by the windstorm that had hit right after Thanksgiving.

She sniffed quietly, and he knew she was crying. He'd probably do the same if he owned a nice little place like this. He climbed out and went around to assist her out. She took his hand but hers was gloved against the chilly night air. He hadn't realized how much he missed skin-to-skin contact. It had been a long drought since he'd moved over here to promote now-defunct boutiques.

She unlocked the back door and led him to a tiny pink-painted bedroom. At her direction, he carried out a white dresser decorated in unicorn stickers. The back of the huge pickup had plenty of room for more.

"That's a nice rocker," he told her, indicating the antique mission oak rocker. It was an American style he'd learned about from the hotel chain. "Why don't we bring that with us?"

She patted it fondly. "It was our grandmother's. I suppose we can find a place for it. I hate leaving it in this cold damp."

They went through the house, looking for bits and pieces to rescue. Most of her furniture was cheap trash no better than his parents had owned. But she had some good quilts and porcelain that shouldn't be left at the mercy of contractors. He didn't know art, but a few pretty pieces had been knocked off the walls. Several of them appeared to be pencil sketches of local build-ings he recognized.

One showed a couple in front of this house. He held it up in the dim light from their flashlights. "Is this you and your husband?"

She added it to the cedar chest they were filling. "Craig, yes. He told me he didn't like nine-to-five jobs and preferred working with his hands. Appar-ently that meant picking locks and hotwiring cars."

Ouch. Nick winced. He had a juvenile record for joy-riding in a moment of adolescent rebellion, a stupid move that had seriously reduced his career opportunities. "Where is he now?"

"Georgia prison. I divorced him after we bought this place, and I discov-ered he was selling stolen auto parts from the garage. Aster never really knew him." She added a few more pictures to a trunk stuffed with books.

Evidently agitated, she insisted on hefting the cedar chest on her own. Nick rushed to help her. The thing was solid wood, crammed full, and should have weighed a ton. He grabbed the other handle. It lifted far too easily for its weight, and caught off-guard, he staggered backward, bumping into a bookshelf—which tilted to cascade books.

"Sh—sugar," she muttered—*before the shelf righted itself.*

Instead of falling on Nick's head as they ought, the books slid neatly to the floor. "*Sugar?*" he asked, still in shock at not being crumpled under his own clumsiness.

"We try not to curse." Without acknowledging the anomaly, the school-teacher hefted her end of the chest as if it were nothing and led him through the debris to the kitchen door.

"Because of the kids?" he asked, just to distract himself. Floating books had probably been an optical illusion. The house might be off its foundation and leaning the wrong way. Lucky him. Those had been some serious tomes on those shelves. The little schoolteacher was a reader.

"Because of our reputation. If a family of witches says *damn you to hell,* and something bad happens to the person they cursed. . . Just imagine it."

A family of witches, right. Yup. Got that. Go with the flow, Nick.

"Should we take the books too?" he asked as they heaved the chest into the truck.

She cast a longing look over her shoulder at the house but shook her head. "Another day, maybe. Evie's house is too crowded as it is."

"There's the bookless library. It just needs shelves." He waited, giving her a chance to think about it.

She climbed in the truck. "Another day. It's not as if I have time to read anyway."

He thought Christmas break started soon, but he didn't argue. She almost reminded him of the golden angel on top of the Christmas tree, a little bent and tattered and needing refurbishing.

He couldn't fix himself, much less anyone else.

Five

"A HUNDRED GRAND." ROARK WHISTLED AND SHOVED HIS HANDS INTO HIS pockets as he gazed up at the brick courthouse the next morning. "How do we even go about sorting through all the people who hated a lying, cheating crook?"

"Not everyone hated him, evidenced by the mob. Just the contractors he cheated. And maybe a lot of little folk he walked all over. Mostly, he wasn't Larraine, so the back-to-the-fifties' contingent wanted his return." Evie kicked at the debris still littering the street from yesterday's riot. Water bottles, cardboard food containers, cigarette butts. . . the street looked as if the senior class had gone on spring break here. "Block wasn't all bad, just greedy and selfish. He did, occasionally, help people."

"By way of helping himself?" Reuben suggested.

Reuben was a Black PhD originally from Miami. Roark was a Cajun MIT engineer with roots in New Orleans. They'd arrived in Afterthought via the military and Jax last spring, back when Block's fraud had come undone. The former mayor had been trying to sell land he claimed belonged to Loretta's deceased parents. R&R, former spies, had helped Evie form the Sensible Solutions Agency, then circumspectly developed relationships here and stayed. They hadn't yet learned all the ins and outs of the town.

"Possibly," Evie acknowledged. "But he helped the school grow and brought the town recognition that got businesses into these historic old buildings. Those aren't bad things."

"You're trying to talk yourself into going in to see if his ghost is there, aren't you?" Reuben studied the boarded-up courthouse as if planning to bomb it.

"Well, Block probably never knew that I talked to the spirits of Loretta's parents and started the investigation that brought him down," she said doubtfully. "But it was my family's land he tried to steal, and he's always despised our weirdness, so I can't imagine his ghost will be friendly, like in our last case."

"A hundred *grand*," Roark repeated. "Reuben and I can make lists of everyone who might have wanted Block dead, but just starting with the trailer park families he evicted, dey're likely to be endless. We can sort through which ones were in town yesterday, but dat will take a while and won't be foolproof. We can break into the sheriff's records and find out who all was in the courthouse, but dat's still likely to be in the hundreds. You're da one wit' da key no one else possesses."

Roark reverted to his origins when excited. That two unimaginative engineers with cynical outlooks actually believed she talked to unseen spirits rallied her a little. They were men of intelligence counting on her woo-woo abilities, just as she counted on their computer expertise to take the information she provided and run with it. It was a good partnership.

"Sheriff won't let me in there," she hedged. "He's not even letting in contractors to repair the damage until he's satisfied he has all the evidence."

"Do ghosts always stay where they die?" Reuben asked with academic interest. "Didn't Loretta's parents wander? And Nick's beauty queen cousin?"

"Loretta's parents had been dead for nearly a year. KK wasn't connected to anything where she died. It's complicated," she admitted. "Spirit energy might linger for generations in one place, but without a body to contain it, it eventually dissipates, just like any energy. Or maybe I should say it concentrates until it comes down to one single purpose—usually the reason it lingered instead of passing on to the next plane. But when it's new, the energy seems to be volatile and. . ." She gestured helplessly. "It's hard to explain. Until Loretta came along, all I did was pass all that dissipating energy to the Great Beyond. I don't really have enough experience with new energy to predict anything."

"So Block might be at the morgue," Reuben suggested. "Or he might have gone home. He might not be in that courthouse."

"But I saw Bertie there, and he's the one who may have seen what happened or know who else was in the attic. Although if experience is any guide, I'll guess he won't give me names. Maybe we should make like good detectives and question the victims' families first, learn a little more about what was happening at the point this all exploded."

"We're strangers, bébé, dey're not gonna talk to us," Roark pointed out.

"With my share of the reward, I could convert the carriage house into an office, *plus* hire a professional decorator." She glared at the courthouse as she talked herself into this.

She knew what she had to do. But it was Christmas. She didn't want to do it.

"The finger-pointing will get ugly shortly," Reuben warned. "Larraine and your family will be on the top of everyone's list of suspects, even if they physically couldn't have done it."

"Larraine was right there. But I think everyone would have noticed if she held a hand with a gun to Block's head." Evie shoved her hair out of her face. Dog-walking had been simpler.

"I'm betting every one of your family knows how to get into that attic. How long would it take for someone to sneak up those stairs, shoot, and rejoin the crowd? Think like the paranoid, bébé. You're targets. You need to solve this."

Evie shoved her chilled hands into her coat pockets, turned around, and headed home. "All right, start on those lists, hack the sheriff. I can't play my hand too soon. I'll send my mother out to console the families and learn what she can. Then we need to figure out how to get me into the courthouse."

Except she probably already knew. Her father was a contractor who had worked on courthouse renovations back before she was born. She was pretty certain the blueprints were still in one of the boxes stacked in the library. And she knew from experience that the courthouse had an underground basement access that had once been a bomb shelter for elected officials back in the 1950s.

Come to think of it, plenty of others probably knew about it too. This was no closed-door mystery. The courthouse was wide open to anyone in the know—which included a lot of the contractors Block had defrauded.

In a far corner of what Dante called the bookless library, Gracie hid in the cracking leather recliner and typed furiously at her laptop. If she focused on the scene she was writing, she wouldn't have to remember last night's embarrassing incident with the Brit.

She'd used her telekinesis. She never used her telekinesis, except in occasional party tricks where no one would notice. She lacked control, and her stupid gift was both useless and dangerous. She'd proved that so many times that she ought to have killed the stupid instinct to use it by now—before she killed a person instead.

She'd almost killed Craig when she'd found out about his stolen goods. He'd been happy to divorce her and give her the house after she'd slammed him into the garage wall. Had he been a child. . . She might have cracked his head.

That had been the final straw. She'd done her best to turn off the instinct since—and to stay calm and focused and not blow off steam. Pouring her fears and frustration into writing seemed a good outlet.

Besides, Aster needed a college fund and her teacher's salary wouldn't provide it. She returned to typing the scene imprinted in her head. . . much more productive than flinging dirty rotten scoundrels against walls.

And then she'd told him they were a family of witches. Really, she wasn't civilized enough to be let out in public.

The male protagonist in the scene took on a strange resemblance to Nick, right down to the Brit accent. She deliberately went back, deleted, and made him a blond, disheveled, Australian over six feet tall. With a beard. And maybe an eye patch. She'd have to think about that.

Spending Christmas break with her family was turning out to be more convenient than she'd anticipated, especially with Pris here. Her surly cousin was a professional caterer and was in her element practicing recipes on a family that would eat anything anyone bothered to cook. And Aster had the twins to play with and male attention for a nice change. Gracie didn't feel guilty stealing a few hours for herself.

Psycat tried to leap on her laptop, but she pushed him into the cushion by her thigh.

Mmmmm the cat muttered in disgruntlement.

"Merry Christmas to you too." Evie and Iddy understood the cat. She'd never tried.

Evie texted asking Gracie to hunt for their father's wooden box when she had a moment. That couldn't be good. Gracie ignored it.

Although it was her sister's silly solutions agency that had given her the idea for this mystery. Maybe she should encourage her.

She almost had ten pages written when she heard the door open. She hunkered down, hoping no one would see her. She needed to end this chapter with a cliffhanger—

A heavy box hit the floor. She finished the sentence before she heard male voices. Dang. They needed to go away. One more paragraph. . .

"If we move this old hall tree to the garage, we can put the shelves right here." Nick's voice.

Gracie groaned. Shelves? He hadn't, had he? It wasn't as if she were moving in here forever. Books were a nuisance to pack.

"Hall tree is sturdier than this cardboard piece of crap." *Dante.*

The Italian count had inspired her as much as Evie's weird stories. Her hero ought to be Italian, but Pris would object. Or worse, laugh.

"Jax has the good shelves in his office." *Nick.* "I saw some nice pieces at the antique place. I could probably trade for the hall tree. They don't make anything this solid anymore. The mirror just needs silvering." The heavy oak scraped against the heart pine floor.

"Use the throw rug under it," Gracie finally said in exasperation, setting aside her laptop to watch them. Psycat leaped down and stalked off in a huff. "You'll ruin the floor."

Holding one side of the wide hall tree, Nick grinned at her. "There you are! I couldn't find you earlier. Dante volunteered to help me move your books and shelves."

She could have asked how he got into her house, or why he would bother, or any of a dozen questions, but she wasn't Evie. That he'd understood the importance of her books. . . shocked her into biting her tongue.

But she couldn't stay silent after all their hard work. And she didn't want to sound indebted for a task she hadn't asked done. Keeping a lid on her emotions was tricky. "I suppose the books will see more use here, should anyone actually decide to read. I think the hall tree is original to the house and belongs to all of us. I'll see if anyone wants to claim it."

While the men placed her *cardboard* shelves where the hall tree had been, Gracie hit the family group text and sent inquiries.

"It's a shame to part with family heirlooms." Dante studied the library as if envisioning his own aging villa. "But a house can only hold so much."

Nick tested the planks of the solid oak library table she'd once used for homework. "The hall tree should be in the hall to catch coats as people come inside, but the armoire out there works better for a large family. The hall tree needs to go to someone who can use it."

Gracie watched an array of thumbs-down icons march down her message screen. "New houses have closets. Even Great-Aunt Val doesn't want it."

"Great-Aunt Val?" Nick inspected the cubbies of an old mahogany secretaire missing the front piece that once formed a desk.

"She lives in an antebellum mansion outside Atlanta. Her antiques are cherry and mahogany and more upscale than plain country oak." Gracie tried to picture this box-filled library with her aunt's delicate cherry, glass-front bookcases and wrinkled her nose. She had more modern tastes. Besides, no one bought print books anymore, except her. For the boxed and illustrated classics she'd so carefully collected, she'd like adjustable glass shelving and. . . Ridiculous.

"Try living with worm-eaten seventeenth century shelving. In the UK, we have lots of grand old piles needing huge old furniture. Here—even your old houses are small in comparison, but there are still some wealthy homes needing good bits to add class. Furnishing with cardboard from China isn't the same." Nick patted the secretaire fondly. "They're hunting for useful pieces like this. You're sitting on some nice cash."

Gracie snorted as Evie sent a thumbs down and a devilishly laughing face. The youngest and last remaining sibling of their grandmother, Aunt Val had appointed Evie as caretaker of this museum, for reasons known only to Val. Evie had no respect for the past—or much else. Maybe Val had *wanted* Evie to clear the place out.

"Looks like, if you're really bored and have nothing better to do, you can trade the hall tree for bookshelves." Gracie hoped that would send them away. Nice bookshelves for her books, in a library she'd never use, made sense in some alternate universe. Right now, all she wanted to do was write.

Nick prowled the library like a sophisticated British antique appraiser on a TV show. His masculine presence itched places she didn't want scratched anymore. Even Dante, the Italian count, came off as a rugged adventurer next to Nick's tailored tweed and sexy saunter. A bit under six feet, broad shoulders, narrow hips. . . he was just the right size, and she longed to add the description to her character on the page.

Dante positioned her cheap shelves on the now empty wall. "I'm supposed to be teaching the twins. I'll help you load and unload, but I'm not good at picking furniture."

"I can't trade off family heirlooms unless I have family with me. Come along, Cinderella, let's go shelf shopping." Nick held out his hand.

Tongue-tied at being abruptly yanked into this, she needed to tell him no. But the possibility of bookshelves and books in the bookless library. . . For Aster and Loretta, she really should do it. Children ought to be surrounded by books, and she shouldn't be selfish.

Still, she wasn't about to touch him. She stood and swept past. "I should probably bring Aster with me. Pris has entertained her long enough."

"She can stay with me and the twins," Dante offered. "Your clever daughter knows her numbers and the twins are eager to imitate her."

Dante was just learning how to deal with his motherless children. She shouldn't discourage his attempts. But riding with Nick in that truck alone. . .

"Dante, help me haul this out," the Brit said cheerfully, running his hands over the oak hall tree. "Grace, do you have a good blanket to wrap around it?"

Before she could find an excuse, Evie sent another text to her alone. MAVIS SAYS BERTIE'S BROTHER IS MANAGING THE BARN. SEE IF HE KNOWS ANY OF BERT'S FRIENDS.

DO I GET A REWARD? Gracie texted back, adding a middle finger salute.

Six

Being new in town, Jax didn't have a long list of clients. But he'd once been an experienced corporate fraud lawyer with a large firm in Savannah. His city reputation and a lot of footwork had garnered him several clients interested in suing former Mayor Block for contract fraud. The cases were small and pretty tame, but every client potentially brought him closer to a wider market.

He now had the unpleasant task of informing his few clients that with Block's death, their cases had become a lot more complicated and indefinitely delayed. Worse, the sheriff would soon be questioning them. Any one of them could have decided to shoot Block in anger, because it had become increasingly obvious that the mayor's assets were stretched thin, and any proceeds from the cases would be small.

He fully expected every one of his clients to drop their suits.

He'd have to go into estate planning and divorce settlements at this rate. Small towns simply weren't a hotbed of corporate fraud, even if Afterthought was within easy driving distance of two cities.

The official business line rang in his outer office. His seriously under-employed receptionist answered, then buzzed Jax. "Tobias Block would like to speak with you."

Jax pondered that for all of half a second, then told her to put the call through. As far as he was aware, he'd never met the former mayor's son. Evie had said Tobias was an ecologist. He'd once led an idiosyncratic protest to save frogs at Evie's family pond. And Jax now owned one of his Harleys after Toby's father sold them all. He doubted this was about amphibians or motorcycles.

After they exchanged greetings, Tobias launched into his request. "My father's lawyers are billing the estate for services rendered. In my limited experience, their bills are higher than if Dad had simply paid back what he owed to all these people. I have no idea of the breadth of his assets and liabilities but assume I'll have to sell off everything. And I need someone besides these sharks to help me."

Swell. So he wasn't a shark anymore. Jax rubbed his forehead and spoke cautiously. "You are aware that several of my clients were suing your father? There is a conflict of interest in my working with you."

"Send them to someone else. I want to play fairly, but everyone in the state probably has a conflict of interest, right down to the judge who shouldn't have lowered his bail and let him out to get killed. If Evie trusts you, I figure I can trust you to do what's right. If you had some reason to murder him, let me know now."

Jax almost chuckled. Evie had said Toby was a bit of a space cadet, but he wasn't dumb by any means. "I didn't know your father, and my clients have only small claims against his estate. I think we can safely assume I haven't been in Afterthought long enough to want to murder him, and once Evie's family established their property rights, they lost all interest in him. If you want to come in, I'll send you a list of records you'll need to bring."

"Thank you. You can tell the sheriff I'm handing everything over to you, and once you see it, you'll know my so-called inheritance is no reason for me to kill my own father." He sounded disgusted.

"I doubt Troy believes you did, but you're the most obvious suspect, and he has to cover all bases should he bring anyone to trial later. But I'll talk to him." Jax gave his new client a few places to start looking, then passed the call to his secretary to set up an appointment.

He texted Evie. **WHAT ARE CHANCES TOBIAS CAN AFFORD MY SERVICES?**

He didn't receive an answer until a little while later, when Evie appeared at his door with the pack of dogs she walked. All well trained by her cousin Iddy, they happily sat where told, tongues lolling.

She hung the leashes on the doorknob and kissed him before perching on his desk like a colorfully feathered bird. Her down vest was a bright blue, and she wore it over another bright red Christmas sweater, this one with blue trees that blinked. The spoon engagement ring he'd given her sparkled as if she'd polished it.

She'd insisted she didn't want a diamond—one more reason he loved her madly. His former girlfriends had been all about what he could give them.

Probably because she saw too much of the spiritual world, Evie had a very loose connection with reality. She was all about what she could give to others. Scary, actually, trying to adjust to a mind that thought in terms of karma.

"Toby and his father were polar opposites. He will pay you out of his salary or sweep floors if he must. Just don't bill him too much because he works for a non-profit. I'm not sure how he'll pay a reward, unless he uncovers his daddy's secret bank account." She picked up the list Jax was making on a legal pad. "Deeds and investments, he might not handle so well. Ask for his father's computers and passwords. Arthur kept everything in cyberspace. I can't call him Blockhead anymore, can I?"

"Rude, since Arthur is now only half a blockhead and dead. Call him Artie. He'll not know—unless you've met his ghost already?" Jax wasn't thrilled with that idea, but he couldn't stop her doing what she did best, so he sat back and admired the colorful elf on his desk, teasing him with her swinging legs—clad in leggings printed in rainbows.

"I stopped at the morgue to see whether *Artie's* spirit energy stayed with his corpse." She tested the new nickname and wrinkled her nose in distaste. "It didn't. I can hope he gave up and passed on, but life is never that simple. Do you know when the sheriff will start letting people back into the courthouse?"

"He ought to be done today unless he finds something major, which I doubt. I was there. I saw what went down. Without cameras filming who came and went, upstairs and down. . ."

Evie shook her loose curls. "Reuben checked. Cameras cover first floor doors and windows, so they can nail a lot of the rioters. Upstairs, not so much. The judges like having cameras on their office doors for security reasons, so if they give the sheriff permission, he'll have footage of Larraine and everyone entering their chambers. News cameras were focused on Block and Larraine, not the ceiling or the crowd. That's about it."

"What we need to see is if anyone went into that janitorial closet with attic access. Without that. . ." Jax shrugged, glad he wasn't a prosecutor.

"Roark says they've run fingerprints on everything. They have lots of smudges and no matches. Reuben and I knew better than to touch anything, except the fire extinguisher. I gave Troy a full accounting of my day, including witnesses, but it was a mob out there. I could easily have slipped inside the courthouse and out at any time." She frowned. "And so could anyone knowing about the basement bomb shelter. I'll hope that's still locked."

Jax whistled. "Bomb shelter? Swell. So the entire town could have been in that attic. I'm guessing you're not the only one who knew about the stairs and shelter." Jax rubbed her thigh. The grim subject kept their sensual heat level muted.

"So everyone in town had motive, opportunity, and means. . . " she said with a grimace. "Although I suppose we don't all have guns. Most of the mob was from out of town and probably armed, but they were the ones who wanted him back as mayor. It's all too weird. If it weren't for the reward, I'd concentrate on what happened to poor Bertie. No one seems to care that we lost a promising talent."

She slid off the desk and scratched a golden retriever's head. "For Bertie, I'll go in."

"Wait for the autopsy," he suggested. "From all reports, it was an overdose."

She didn't look happy. Evie was generally a bouncy, upbeat sort of person. Jax hoped her new *solutions* business didn't take that away.

"Gracie has a whole series of sketches Bertie did when he was off the drugs. You should take a look. He was talented. I hate that he ended up this way." A little light bulb practically lit over her head and she smiled again. "Maybe he's done some recent sketches that would show who his friends were. I'll check around."

In a rush of herbal scent mixed with dog stink, she was off and gone again.

Damn, but he loved that woman. Buoyed by her effervescent spirit, Jax began making calls.

Getting his hands on Arthur Block's financial records could turn the town upside down. He savored the possibilities with anticipation.

GRACIE CLIMBED OUT OF PRIS'S OLD CATERING TRUCK BEFORE NICK COULD COME around and open the door for her. She studied the sagging structure with the big red ANTIQUE BARN sign. Afterthought's inhabitants had never leaned toward the original. *It's an historic building* covered lack of repairs or updates, like fixing a deteriorating roof.

She thought Mrs. Satterwhite, one of Evie's neighbors, owned this place on the outskirts of town, past the school and on the two-lane toward Charleston. The owner must be almost ninety by now.

Nick was already sniffing around the rusty farm equipment outside. She didn't think even his creative marketing mind could find a use for that junk. She aimed for the door adorned with a rusted Esso Oil Company sign.

"World of difference," Nick murmured as he followed her in. "This is fascinating."

"This is junk," she muttered back, scanning the cluttered interior for any sign of a desk or employee.

"Let's scout first," he suggested. "If they don't have anything, we can go into the city."

So not going into the city with a player. . . Gracie headed straight for the walls where taller furniture was buried. "How about this?" She pointed at a pair of cheap pine bookcases. "We can probably buy two for the price of one hall tree."

"You are not putting that rubbish in your beautiful library. Look, the back is cardboard and stapled on." He pulled one out to show her.

He glared at her through dark eyes surrounded by thick short lashes that would make a movie star groan in envy. He even had a cleft in his determined chin. It was at eye level. She couldn't miss it.

Gracie marched away, scouting for furniture without cardboard backs. Her whole house was made of cardboard. What did she know?

Apparently she did know a few things. She spotted an airy set of wood shelving with legs that would elevate the dark library to a lighter, less oppressive mood. Buried behind bed frames and old paintings, the shelves had to be dug out to verify they weren't half propped up by old books.

"Mid-century modern." Nick sounded more thoughtful than chirpy at her discovery. "I hadn't considered that. I'd have thought more Victorian ornate or art nouveau, but. . ." He unburied one of the sections and pulled it back from the wall to examine it.

Didn't look like cardboard to her. And he wasn't totally dissing her selection. Yet.

"May I help you?" A tall, beefy man in a red-checked shirt wound his way through the maze toward them. Brown-haired and round-faced, he looked nothing like his slender, artistic younger brother, but she recognized him. Now she had to practice her detective routine.

"Samuel, good to see you." Gracie smiled her schoolteacher smile. His kids had been in her classes. "How are you doing?"

"Miz Gracie." His face broke into a big grin. "How ya keepin'? What brings you in here? Your sister ready to unload all that junk in your aunt's house?"

"Maybe one piece," she acknowledged as Nick moved more junk to see the other sections of shelving. "I'm so sorry to hear about your brother. Albert was a talented artist."

Sam's grin transformed into a scowl. "We all knew it would happen sooner or later, but Ma's pretty broken up. We thought he'd got clean lately, and that he'd come home for the holiday. He said he had a Christmas surprise for Ma, and I know he's been giving her cash from his new stuff. I useta wanna beat the crap out of Bertie for making Ma cry, but now I wanna pound those dealers."

She patted his arm, sorry she'd upset him. She'd never make a good detective. "Don't we all? I don't suppose any of his friends know who was selling him drugs? Can't the sheriff do something?"

He shrugged. "Bert didn't have many friends left. I figure they're all druggies 'cause he never brought them home. My guess is he traded his surprise for one last crack and did himself in when he realized what he'd done."

Changing the subject, he turned to Nick. "Those came from an estate sale outside Charleston. Some nice wood in there. Might make a decent shelf or two if you take it apart."

Gracie could almost see Nick choking on a violent objection. Or maybe that was her too-vivid imagination. Talking about Bertie and all that lost talent had unsettled her.

"Exactly what I was thinking, sir," Nick finally croaked in that plummy accent certain to make Sam think he'd landed a sucker. "But the ladies are a trifle short on cash. They thought they might trade one of their valuable Victorian pieces for the shelves they need."

All professionalism now, Sammy straightened his bulk. "Do you have a photo?"

"Better, we have the piece in the truck, if you would like a look." Nick started for the door with the arrogance of someone certain he'd be followed.

Gracie would like to smack him upside the head, but Sammy accepted haughty authority. She really needed to curb her irritation. Nick hadn't even said whether her choice was good or not. It didn't matter, she decided. The shelves weren't cardboard, they were pretty wood, and she liked them.

Now that the other junk was out of the way, she could see that there were three separate sections. One of them was actually a kind of secretary, with a pull down desk and a cabinet below. The staggered shelving didn't have sides, but the airy openness allowed ideas to percolate.

She wandered around and found some gorgeous marble bookends. Her boxed classics didn't need much support, but she loved the idea of adding books and pretty ornaments to the shelves. It wasn't as if her tiny library would even begin to fill them.

With all the open space, there might even be room for some small paintings. She poked around the walls where most of the smaller artwork rested on tables, leaning against the wall and each other. In the back, she found a treasure trove of Bertie's sketches, amazingly all framed. Her heart tugged. Sammy must have been paying his brother, then framing the works, and selling them for little more than the value of the frames. The prices were much too cheap for the talent.

Remembering Evie wanted to know who Bertie's friends were, she found a few sketches of card players and men gathered around an old car and so forth and picked out what appeared to be recent ones. In more decent light, she might identify some of these people. She found one where he'd used a touch of watercolor and chose that for herself.

Evie could darned well pay for these out of her reward money. Gracie was texting her sister when Nick and Sammy returned, apparently great friends and having settled on a sum that satisfied both of them.

She added her finds to the invoice Sammy wrote up while his hired hands helped haul the hall tree in and the shelving out. "That was sweet of you to buy Bertie's work," she told him, admiring the watercolor. "I've never seen him use color before."

"That's one of his new ones. He had an artist friend encouraging him. Don't know who he was. Bertie didn't like talking. I was thinking maybe I should take that to Ma and tell her it was his surprise, but I guess I shouldn't lie." He tallied the invoice and charged her for only the bookends. Apparently Nick had made a really good trade.

"Unless your mother knows the people in the sketch, it probably wouldn't help," she said sympathetically. "But if you want it. . ."

He shook his head. "That's Toby Block, Teddy Turlock, the Shepherd boys, and some skank they must have hired. Or maybe she's just one of Toby's do-gooder pals. Don't know why Bertie would sketch that lot. They all think themselves too good for the likes of us. But it's a pretty picture if you don't know them."

Gracie groped for a polite response. "I imagine Bertie's surprise would have been a family portrait, don't you think?"

Brooding, Sammy nodded. "Yeah, maybe."

"Do you know when the funeral will be?"

He shrugged and rang up the sale. "Can't say until the cops release him. We'll probably just have the reverend say a few words over the grave. Pa bought a cemetery lot a long time ago, so there's that covered."

Nick loped up and hugged her before grabbing up the frames. "Perfect! You have excellent taste, Cinderella."

She was too stunned to swat him for taking liberties.

He held out his hand to Sammy before she could react. "Pleasure meeting you, friend. We may do more business in the future."

She took a deep breath, refrained from levitating the frames over the ass's head, picked up the box of heavy bookends, and marched toward the door.

Oblivious to his potential frame-maiming, Nick followed her out. "Those shelves are genuine vintage, Danish-modern *teak*, my girl. You have a brilliant eye! You'll have to fling out all the other clutter in the library and start modernizing the entire house."

Eager to study her acquisitions, Gracie didn't answer but allowed him to open the back of the truck so she could add the heavy box. Then she took the frames and settled in the front seat. She studied the pencil sketch with brushes of color first, the one with the sons of some of the town's wealthiest, most respected families. The Shepherds were farmers and no one thought of them as wealthy like the former mayor's family, but they owned a lot of land.

She didn't recognize the lone female. She was wearing short shorts, so it must have been drawn in summer. Leggy, with a long French braid of indeterminate color, she was leaning over the hood of what appeared to be a vintage Corvette. Teddy Turlock Jr., the son of the local attorney defending the late mayor, sat behind the wheel. Teddy Jr. had been a year or two ahead of her in school, had gone off to Auburn, and she'd lost track of him until he'd recently returned to Afterthought to open a sporting goods store. It must be doing well to afford a car like that.

Nick slid into the driver's seat and studied the sketch from the side. "Deft hand there. Local artist?"

"Bertie Walker, the man who fell through the courthouse ceiling," she said absently, flipping through the other two framed sketches she'd picked up. "He liked to do houses and people together." So the watercolor with the car was doubly unusual.

"They need better frames." He handed them back and started the engine.

"We have a ton in the attic and garage. You can waste a day or two hunting." She identified the people and houses in the plain sketches and wondered if she ought to give them to their families. But apparently, they hadn't liked them enough to pay for them. Bertie always offered.

She returned to the color drawing, and, on a whim, peeled off the paper and cardboard backing to remove the sketch. Bertie had put their names and address on the back of the one he'd done for her and Craig.

He'd done the same here. The woman was Verity Janus, the car was a 1966 Corvette Stingray, and the address was simply the Shepherd Farm. Bertie never added "Afterthought, SC," as if anyone who saw his sketches would know that.

Verity Janus. Where had she heard that name?

Seven

〜✷〜

EVIE GRINNED AS LORETTA PRACTICALLY DANCED INTO THE LIBRARY CARRYING A stack of books to install on Gracie's fancy new shelves.

"Harry Potter will look so good here, and when Aster's old enough, she can read them too." Loretta happily set them in proper order, using the new bookends.

Harry Potter was a bit tattered compared to Gracie's boxed classics. Since Evie didn't plan on opening any volumes, she admired the pretty wood and the cubbyholes in the new desk. "We won't need that ratty old desk in the corner. What can we trade that for?"

"A computer?" Dante asked dryly.

"A television," Jax added.

Electronics, right. Evie snorted and ignored them. She sat on the floor and admired the insides of the cabinet as potential storage for some of the pricey stationery her aunt had collected and no one used for anything except grocery lists.

"If you have the missing drop-down door, I could repair the secretaire and probably sell it for enough to buy a computer or television." Nick examined the battered mahogany. "Probably need a discreet touch-up to bring the best price."

Pris arrived with a tray of appetizers. "Taste these, let me know what you think. Dinner will be ready in half an hour. Have you solved any mysteries today? You'll need the reward if you intend to wire the house for TVs and computers."

Evie kept her head in the cabinet.

"I found sketches of Bertie's friends." Gracie was probably pointing at the display on the table. The old country oak didn't match the fancy teak shelving.

"I talked to Toby Block. He's bringing me his father's computers. Do I get part of any reward or just my usual fee?" Apparently sampling the appetizers, Jax talked while chewing. "I like this. What is it?"

Hoping they were safely past the discussion of what they'd done today, Evie backed out of the cabinet and snatched a few pastries from the table behind her.

"Asparagus tarts with a cornbread crust for the gluten allergic," Pris explained.

Evie noted everyone moved to the other tray with more identifiable crackers. She wasn't fussy. She noshed on cornbread asparagus.

Reuben and Roark were otherwise occupied with their respective partners and weren't present to add their accomplishments for the day. Evie knew the computer geniuses had built lists that included pretty much half the town, but that didn't put them any closer to a killer.

"No mysteries for me." Dante scarfed up half a dozen crackers and answered Pris's inquiry. "I spent the day reading Clifford the Big Red Dog."

"You did not." Pris tasted the asparagus tarts. "You spent at least half the day on Zoom calls with your colleagues, arranging the Etruscan dig on the kids' estate."

Evie wasn't about to enter that fight. Pris wanted to stay here and start a bakery/cafe. Dante wanted to go home and dig ancient bones. They both wanted to stay with the twins. Toss up.

"What did you do, O Great Guru?" Gracie had to ask, kicking Evie where she sat cross-legged on the floor. Darned sisters anyway.

"Visited the morgue, checked auras, this and that," she said vaguely. "Give me that sketch of Tobias and Company. What were they doing on the Shepherd farm?"

"Shooting those accursed hounds, I hope." Sitting on the desk chair, Jax looked over Evie's shoulder to study the sketch Gracie handed her.

The Shepherd hounds were notorious for never shutting up. The brothers were the superstitious sort who probably would have hung witches back in the day. They wouldn't let Iddy train their animals.

"I figure now that their dad is gone, the boys are raising pot out there."

Evie tried to see the face of the woman sprawled stomach down over the Corvette hood, but it wasn't clear. Bertie had apparently been more interested in her rear end in those Daisy Duke's. "The hounds are their early detection system."

The room grew oddly silent. What had she said now? Evie glanced over at Loretta, who was engrossed in the Count of Monte Cristo and not paying the adults a bit of attention. She wasn't eating asparagus either.

"What?" Evie demanded. "It pays better than cotton."

"Hey, Loretta, want to help me finish up dinner?" Pris asked, distributing her uneaten asparagus tarts to the tray with the crackers and cheese. "We can play hide the asparagus in the potatoes."

Loretta jumped up carrying her book and obediently followed Pris out. Evie knew she'd been listening and would know everything by nightfall, but let the protective idiots pretend otherwise.

"*Pot*, my dear dimwit." Jax leaned over and kissed her hair. "Pot, drugs, farm, Bertie, addict."

"Nope, not making any sense. Bertie did opioids, not pot. Taken in moderation, pot isn't any more dangerous than alcohol. Toby was probably out there making the Shepherds ante up for his frog-saving environmentalists. No telling what Turdy Turlock was doing except showing off his Corvette. Maybe he financed their operation." Evie thought about that for half a second. "Although Turdy is a bully who wouldn't let Bertie near his sporting goods store. Huh."

"Have R&R look into the Turlocks," Jax suggested. "If Turlock Sr. was his attorney, Block may have been holding something over his head to keep him on his case once he ran out of land to sell. Could be why Turlock is sending Toby an outrageous bill."

Evie pondered all the possible crimes Block could have blackmailed his lawyer with and decided Jax knew way too much about human behavior to make that probably correct assumption. She calculated the same could be said of the Shepherds. Pot-selling farmers were easy blackmail targets.

"What about this Verity Janus person?" Gracie asked. "The name sounds familiar. Has anyone looked her up?"

Evie pried her phone out of the pocket of her leggings, punched a few buttons, and handed it to her sister. "Charleston artist. Paper just ran an article. She's a tree hugger like Toby. Her mother owns a gallery. Want to visit?"

"Not particularly, no, I can't read auras. Why are we even looking into Bertie anyway? We can assume he overdosed. No one murdered him. Shouldn't you be looking at who wanted Mr. Block dead?" Her sister handed back the phone and returned to arranging her books in some order Evie could never hope to understand.

"A lot of people wanted Block dead once he was of no use to them," Jax said.

"Not everyone would step over Bertie's rotting body to do it," Evie countered. "Not everyone knew that canister light had been removed unless they'd been up there earlier. What are the chances our drug dealer and murderer are the same person?"

No one had a good answer for that.

NICK KNEW NOTHING ABOUT SMALL TOWNS OR KILLERS OR DETECTING. EVIE'S Sensible Solutions team had put his distant cousins in jail for murder, theft, kidnapping, and fraud over the boutique business Nick had stupidly thought genuine. All he'd ever done was promote the product, then hire Jax to force the insurance company into coughing up enough money from a fire to pay off the employees and shut down the stores. He'd never expected to end up as a witness to more criminal acts than it seemed possible for anyone short of mafia to commit.

Well, it was possible his cousins were mafia. He'd been living in York, unaware.

So he was completely useless in determining who might have killed a mayor no one except a redneck mob appeared to like. But he had made his host's family happy by removing an ugly eyesore and trading it for some truly brilliant wall sectionals. The American market lent itself to modern pieces more than the UK. He now knew how to make himself useful while he camped out in their cellar.

Jax's energetic young ward had known exactly where in the attic to find the missing desk portion of the art nouveau mahogany secretaire. So after dinner, he located a rusted dolly in the carriage house. With Evie's permission, and a little oil on the dolly, he hauled the old desk to the huge empty space that could have been a garage, had anyone used it. But carriage doors were too clumsy to open without servants.

He didn't have much in the way of savings, but he had his last paycheck now that the fire insurance proceeds had come through. The supplies for a basic surface touch-up should be easy to find.

Hank's Hardware was only a few blocks from Evie's house. Nick ambled in and perused the stock while the old man behind the counter served another customer. He assumed this was Hank, the owner and city council member who Evie had declared an honest but disagreeable Block supporter.

Nick didn't know how he felt about everyone's belief that his hostess possessed some psychic voodoo for ghosts and auras. But she seemed to have good people instincts. He'd roll with that.

"What can I do fer ya, young fella?" Barely reaching Nick's shoulders, the old clerk had combed his circle of white hair over his freckled head. But he seemed spritely and muscled enough to handle his heavy stock.

"I'd like to restore a few antiques. But lacking professional equipment, I should like to see what you might carry for the task." Nick studied the cans in the likely area of interest, but he was unfamiliar with the American labels.

"You're one of them boarders Evangeline has taken in, ain't you? Her grandmother would roll in her grave if she knew about the sorts living there now. Never would have happened back in the day, but times are tough."

Nick had a suspicion that the old man didn't refer to the Italian count but to Reuben and Roark, one black, one brown, both tattooed and occasionally metaled. But this wasn't his argument, and he bit back any retort. Old people were set in their ways.

With a gnarled hand, Hank took down a couple of colorful cans and handed them over. "You got brushes?"

Nick took the cans and shifted to the brush selection. "I shall assume Evangeline has nothing that isn't fifty years old. Brushes, sandpaper, the works, please."

"Ain't from around here, are ya?" Hank sorted through his stock for what appeared to be the right tools.

"Just visiting." Nick agreed amicably. "Thought small town life might be more agreeable than the city, but crime knows no boundaries, I see."

He didn't know what made him say that. Being helpful should have its limits.

The old man scowled as he carried brushes and scrapers to the counter. "Arthur Block was a good man, did a lot for this town. Can't think that bullet was meant for him. Now shooting those damned reporters makes sense."

"Interesting." Nick set his cans down. "The shooter wanted to stop the press from filming Mr. Block's speech?"

Hank crankily waved a dismissive hand. "Nah, just an old man complaining. Arthur was a good friend. I hope they catch the bastard that did it. Wouldn't put it past shifty Larry to arrange a contract killer to keep Arthur from getting his job back."

Assuming "shifty Larry" was the current mayor, Nick thought this scenario unlikely, but he didn't know American politics. "Or the killer might have been aiming for Mayor Ward. Or the sheriff or maybe even a judge. It's unsettling to know there's a killer in our midst."

Hank rang up the sale on an old-fashioned manual cash register that clanged when it totaled. "Huh. Hadn't thought about that. Might even have been after me or someone else on the council. We was all there. But they'd have to have been a lousy shot."

"Stumbling over a dead man might upset even murderers." Nick pulled out his wallet and sorted through the unfamiliar bills. "Put any man off his shot."

Hank snorted and counted the cash as he put it in the drawer. "Young folk these days want everything right now. Told Albert I couldn't give him credit for that big frame he wanted. Maybe if I'd not been so tough, he'd not have OD'd." He sounded a little sad.

Albert? The dead artist? Uneasily, Nick distracted the store owner from his morbid fantasies. "You sell frames? And supplies?"

Hank yanked back from his morose speculation. "Back right corner. Small town. Got to have a little of ever'thing or customers drive to the big box stores in the city. Once that happens, they never come back, and the whole town dies."

"That would be a shame." Nick put his change in his pocket and hefted the shopping bag. "I'm rather enjoying walking about instead of sitting in traffic."

Hank nodded absently. "Tell Evie I'll frame that picture of Albert's for his family if they bring it in here. Won't charge them nothing but materials. They're good people. They don't deserve what happened."

"Picture of Albert's? Did you see it?" He'd listened in on enough of the discussion to know the artist had been planning a surprise for his family.

"Nah, he just told me about it. Figured it must have been with his stuff somewhere. He was right proud of it."

The square man wearing cowboy boots Nick remembered from yesterday slammed open the front door, causing the old-fashioned bell to jangle. "Hank, we gotta do something about that freak mayor, or I'll have done all this planning for nothing. Can't you talk to the rest of them and fix that zoning so I can at least get started?"

Hank turned his attention to the newcomer and Nick hurried out. Small towns could be just a little too claustrophobic. Everyone knowing everyone else's business. . . And still helpless to prevent an addict from overdosing.

He returned to the carriage house and puttered about setting up lights and a worktable. Deciding he'd wait for daylight to examine the finish, he hunted through bottles of screws for ones that might fit the hinges on the desk. He probably should have bought wood putty.

Gracie appeared with a mug of hot coffee, just as he was about to stop for the night. "You must be freezing out here."

Nick scoffed. "In this humidity? You should try a Yorkshire winter sometime. I'm good, but that coffee is enticing. I was just coming in."

She handed him the mug. "Pris said you liked it black."

Even in his days with a healthy salary and women hanging on his arm, he'd never had anyone waiting on him. Enclosed in darkness, with only an overhead illuminating her pale face and tousled golden hair, the unassuming schoolteacher looked more than a little angelic.

Stupid thought. He sipped the hot brew. "This is good, thanks."

"I just came out to tell you that Craig left a lot of tools in my garage," she offered diffidently. "I don't know if they'll help, but you're free to use them."

He brightened. "That would be brilliant, thank you. I was making mental lists of everything I should have bought."

They entered the warm kitchen where half the household seemed to gather at any given time. His hostess was nuking what appeared to be hot chocolate.

"Evangeline, I have a message for you from Mr. Hank." Nick related what the store owner had said about the frame for the family surprise.

Evie's eyebrows shot up.

Gracie spoke first. "Remember, I told you Bertie was preparing a big Christmas surprise but Sammy never saw it. I don't think the family has whatever he wanted framed."

Evie began texting. "No one mentioned finding artwork in the courthouse attic. Where else would he have kept it? Did he have any other hiding places?"

Gracie shook her head. "You probably ought to go into Charleston and check out the Janus gallery. If he knew this Verity person, maybe she took it there for framing. Just stay out of the courthouse attic, Evie."

Even Nick could tell from Evie's grin that wasn't happening.

Eight

Sunday morning, Evie dug her father's hardhat out of the wooden box Gracie had said she'd look for and hadn't. There were blueprints in there, but she couldn't make heads or tails of them. She left them on the library table to remind herself to ask someone else to take a look.

Then finding a puffy coat in the armoire and pulling on some garden gloves, she biked over to the courthouse. She could hope no would be there, but they wouldn't leave the place empty with gaping windows. She'd simply have to blend in. And yup, there was the work crew already gathering. Oh well, at least court wasn't in session.

Donning the hard hat, she joined a group of construction workers heading inside. One of her father's contracting pals recognized her, of course. Sneaking in might have had its benefits, but she really hadn't wanted to go through that spider-filled shelter.

"What are you up to, Evangeline?" Cal demanded, checking off a worksheet.

"Hired for janitorial service, a little extra Christmas income. I know how to stay out of the way." She saluted and marched away as if she had as much right to be there as he did.

Well, it was a public building, and she was part of the public, right? She went straight to the janitorial closet, grabbed a broom and pail, and trudged up the front stairs so everyone could see that she was working. Cal really didn't know her well.

Knotted yellow tape still clung to the railings. Jax had done a fine job of tying it. It would take scissors or a knife to cut it all off.

The center rotunda wasn't any cleaner after the sheriff's men had gone through it. But the bodies were gone, and what was left behind was mostly plaster. She could handle that. Using a push broom, she shoved the bulk into a neat pile while she glanced around the upper story, hunting for auras.

Damned ghost was hiding. She opened the closet and got hit by a blast of cold air. That might be explained by the open trap door to the unheated attic, but Bertie's gray shadow plainly sat on the pull-down steps.

"You don't have to hide from me, Albert." Huddling inside the puffy coat, she opened an old folding chair someone had left and took a seat.

How'd'ya know it's me? His voice was more in her head than physically audible. He sounded disgruntled.

"Aside from recognizing your creative yellow, who else would it be?" She knew better than to jump right in with her questions. Most spirits had a purpose but tended to be too disorganized or rattled to get straight to the point, as if they'd lost track of their human focus. Of course, in Bertie's case, focus hadn't happened when he was alive.

The shadow shifted uncomfortably. *Place practically dates to the Civil War. It oughtta be haunted, but all I'm seeing is Butcher Block, and he's sulking and hiding.*

Butcher Block, even better than Blockhead. Evie hid her grin and nodded knowingly. "Sorry about your lack of company. That's my fault, I'm afraid. I saw my first ghost here when my dad brought me as a toddler. I think I freaked a little, swallowed it right up without knowing what I was doing. As a kid, I thought it was a fun game and spent a lot of time practicing sending spirit energy on, sort of like Pac-Man, y'know? You're not ready to go yet, though, are you?"

If ghosts could snort, Bertie snorted. *A genu-wine ghostbuster, no wonder people called you a freak.* He didn't answer her question.

"In my world, normal is freakish. I'm good with that. But I was too young when you were in school to feel comfortable telling you that you had a beautiful golden halo." His aura had faded to gray over the years of drug use, but she saw no point in mentioning that. "My sister loves your work. She's been collecting it."

He didn't comment on his *halo*, but a hint of gold shifted through the gray, and a rough outline of a younger-looking Bertie manifested on the stairs. *Yeah, Miss Gracie was always nice to me. Even though she knew I'd probably use the money for drugs, she always bought my stuff.*

"Yeah, my sister is a bit of a sucker. Sammy said you had a Christmas surprise for your mom. Where were you keeping that? Hank said he'd frame it for you." Evie tested to see how much Bertie might remember. Spirits were seldom good at any memory that wasn't related to the reason they lingered. She just hoped the sketch was his reason for his current existence.

Bertie squirmed, glanced at the ceiling, and hesitated. *Up there?*

The sheriff's report hadn't mentioned finding artwork, just a backpack of dirty clothes and some needles.

"Show me," she suggested, dreading going up in the filthy attic. She wasn't a neatnik by any means, but she wasn't dumb. Bird guano caused histoplasmosis.

Bertie blinked out. With an aggravated sigh, she took the steps the old-fashioned way. Once past the trapdoor, she pulled out a small penlight she'd shoved into her coat pocket and flashed it around. The ceiling still had a hole in it, and the canister light was still missing. An electrician would no doubt be up before day's end. She'd have to search now or never.

Bertie's aura hovered uncertainly in a far corner. Avoiding the missing floorboards, Evie picked her way back to the cupola area where the eaves were too low for standing and the floor ended in insulation. A few rags and a plastic grocery bag were buried in the debris but nothing that looked like drawing paper. She dug around but she could see why the sheriff's men had left these here. The grocery bag had a couple of worn out watercolor brushes and bits of what might have been paint color blocks.

"Did the deputies take everything else?" she asked the nervously flitting specter.

A coupla brushes for fingerprints. But all my work's right here, he insisted. *The roof don't leak here. I wrapped it in canvas the gallery person gave me.*

Awkward. Did that mean the sketch was stolen after Bertie died? Or that his memory was faulty? Evie wandered the rest of the enormous attic, but Sheriff Troy wouldn't have left any stones unturned. Gallery person. . . "Verity Janus was selling your work?"

She thought he nodded.

She made me lotsa money. When the mayor's son saw my stuff, even he wanted me to draw for him. I was gonna be famous! The cry was sadder than triumphant.

So, the mayor's son, Toby, and the gallery owner's daughter, Verity, were do-gooding. Evie headed back down the ladder again. "Was that your big surprise, telling your family that you were almost famous?"

Yeah, part, I guess. There was gonna be an article in the paper and everything.

They didn't wanna hang my new stuff until the opening. She said it would be a surprise. But my mom won't go into the city, so I did one for her too. Bertie's aura grew grayer. *But even my paints are gone.*

"What was in the sketch? Maybe I can find it." Evie had an uneasy notion the sketch was long gone, but she couldn't fathom why.

This and that, Bertie said vaguely. *Things I saw. The gallery person said I was imaginative, but I just draw what I see.*

"And this one was bigger than your others?" Knowing ghosts couldn't remember names, Evie understood his vagueness. Bertie drew people. And even buildings usually came with names, if only a street name.

If he nodded, she couldn't tell. He was starting to fade.

Big. He may have stretched his hands, but she couldn't see them.

Bertie had never been a math whiz. Evie held her hands about a foot apart. "This big?"

Bigger, he insisted.

She went for three feet, approximately.

Yeah, like that. For over a mantel, he said in satisfaction. *Can you find it?*

Since that was most likely the reason he was still here, Evie nodded. "I'll try. Was there anyone else besides Miss Janus and Toby who saw your work?"

Maybe, he said vaguely. *Sometimes I don't remember so well.*

"All right, why don't you think about that while I look for Mayor Block. Do you know where he hides when he sulks?"

Little room with flag and a nice couch. I useta sleep on that some nights. He blinked out.

Judge's chambers, Evie surmised, carrying her broom back to the central hall. Did each judge have their own? How many judges' chambers were there? Other than her ghost-busting visits, and her teenage adventures on the roof, she avoided the courthouse.

Downstairs, she scooped the hall debris into a trash bag from the closet, then dug out a vacuum cleaner. She bet there were carpets in rooms with couches. She added a dust rag for good measure and entered the closest courtroom.

The little door at the back of the room was locked. *Dang.* Ghosts might pass through, but she couldn't. How had living Bertie slept in here?

She checked the courtroom across the hall with the same result. If she couldn't get in today, when no official was present, she'd never be allowed in another day. Stupid cowardly Blockheaded ghost.

She texted Roark, their resident lock-picking expert. CAN YOU PICK ANTIQUE LOCKS?

COURTHOUSE? NOT GOING TO JAIL FOR YOU BABE. FIND KEYS

Well, fine. Ariel would probably empty Evie's bank account and Loretta's, too, to get revenge if Roark was locked up. Jax's genius sister did not know normal parameters, and she weirdly liked the anarchic Cajun.

Evie went back downstairs where the construction crew was removing broken windows. They shook their head when she asked if they had keys for upstairs and kept working. *Le sigh.* She was accustomed to being ignored and thought harmless.

Who would have keys? Better, who would have keys who'd let her have them. Answer to that, nobody.

Huffily, she texted Jax and added Mayor Larraine, just in case. They at least knew she wasn't using keys for nefarious purposes. Maybe they could talk to whoever was in charge of a courthouse.

While she waited for replies, she scoured the janitorial closets up and down, hunting for any sign that someone, anyone, might have shoved one of Bertie's sketches out of sight. And she didn't even know why she cared. Finding Bertie's artwork wouldn't produce any rewards.

JAX HAD THE LATE MAYOR ARTHUR BLOCK'S LAPTOP BACKED UP TO A CLOUD drive and was organizing the files when Evie's text came through. He knew better than to ignore her plea for keys.

WHY?

CAUSE BLOCKHEAD IS HIDING

CC'd on the message, Larraine responded with laughing faces and clown hats. Their new mayor wasn't very fond of the old one. Or she could be commenting on the request for keys.

LEAVE IT FOR TOMORROW he typed.

THINK THEY'LL LET ME IN AGAIN?

Jax rubbed his brow. He didn't know how she got in today.

VISIT ART GALLERY.

He knew that was lame. Evie wanted ghosts, not live people or art.

When she didn't reply, he called Roark to put him and Ariel to work on Block's finances. How much trouble could Evie get into on a Sunday?

A lot. Jax headed over to the courthouse.

Construction workers were crawling all over the outside. Wearing business casual—he hadn't adapted to small town ways entirely—he strolled inside like the lawyer he was. No security stopped him. He ought to call the sheriff and warn him of the laxity, but it wasn't his job.

Inside, he nearly ran into Judge Rhodes, who stepped off the front staircase with an armful of files. Without his black robes, Rhodes was nearly invisible—average height, average build, average coloring, no distinctive features. Only his collared shirt and crisp khakis distinguished him from the workmen.

"No security," Rhodes muttered as he grabbed at slipping file folders.

Rhodes was a circuit judge called in to cover excess cases while Satterwhite dealt with the major one of Block's fraud and the various related lawsuits. He wouldn't have keys to the courthouse but presumably had them to the chambers he used.

Jax held one of the file boxes while Rhodes reorganized. "The sheriff only does security when court is in session or offices are open. Did you call the court clerk?"

Rhodes took the box and shook his head. "He's not answering. They could be planting bombs under every chair." He scurried out.

Well, that was just a bit paranoid. It wasn't his job, but he left a message with the sheriff anyway as he ascended the stairs to look for Evie.

Upstairs, he found Theodore Turlock Sr., Block's lawyer, surveying the damage. Although Turlock had been in the courtroom, Jax couldn't remember him being around when Bertie crashed through the ceiling. He'd have to remember to tell Evie, although it was hard to imagine the tailored lawyer crawling into the attic.

Approaching the other man, Jax felt the temperature plunge. It could be because of the hole in the ceiling. . . He looked around for Evie but she wasn't visible. "Sad times," he said to catch Turlock's attention.

With a thick head of silver hair, square brow and jaw, and carved cheekbones, Turlock could have been a star actor portraying an attorney. Jax knew Turlock used his looks to intimidate and woo, depending on his victim. Jax had never been into theatrical performances, which was one of many reasons why he wasn't a courtroom lawyer.

Turlock nodded grimly. "Heard Tobias went to you to argue my bill."

Well, that was blunt and to the point. "As far as I have been able to ascertain, Tobias has no head for numbers and couldn't tell if there's money to pay out. I can't say more than that."

"It's there," Turlock said, returning to staring at the ceiling. "Block owed me a hell of a lot more than that bill. I'll sue."

"Understood. If you have proof. . ." Jax waited, not expecting a reply.

"I'll get it." Turlock strode off.

Right. Bluster or truth? Shoving his hands into his pockets, he waited until the other man was out of sight before easing open the nearest courtroom door with his shoulder. No one inside. He slipped in and skirted the seating to the judge's bench and listened at the door to his chambers. Silence. Using a handkerchief, he tested the knob. Locked. Good.

If that cold spot had been Block. . . Either Evie wasn't here or hadn't found him yet.

He checked the other rooms on this side, including the janitor's closet, then crossed the hall to the visiting judge's courtroom and chambers. The cold spot was no longer hovering under the ceiling hole.

Not finding Evie anywhere on the second floor, Jax started down the back stairs. If there was a bomb shelter, where would the entrance be?

He didn't have to wonder long. Evie was just coming up as he reached the landing. She wore a yellow hardhat covered in what appeared to be filthy cobwebs, and her expression wasn't exactly cheerful. In fact, she glared at him and stalked past, dangling a ring of keys she must have stolen somewhere.

Evie's anger never lasted long. He turned and followed her. "Block was up here. So was Turlock."

"Saw Turlock." Still not sounding chirpy. "He was testing the clerk's door downstairs a while ago."

"Did he get in?" Jax hoped the sheriff found a security detail. With judges and attorneys walking all over the place, helping themselves to anything they wanted, someone ought to be paying attention.

"Turd Sr. did not. It was locked, and I left it that way."

Which meant the bomb shelter exit was probably in the clerk's office and that's how Evie had confiscated the keys.

"I need to figure out which of these keys belongs to the emergency exit to the bomb shelter because that door was unlocked. No wonder Bertie and friends got in and out so easily. They could take the clerk's keys anytime they liked." She stepped under the hole in the ceiling and looked up.

At least she was still speaking to him. "I've told the sheriff. That means anyone who had access to that tunnel could have hidden in the attic."

"Yeah. Our suspect list continues to grow. Bertie is useless. I need to talk to Butcher Block." She swung the keys and glanced from one courtroom to the other.

"I thought we decided to call him Artie. Where did Butcher come from?"

"Bertie. Although maybe it should be Butchered, but that doesn't work so well."

Jax gestured to where they stood. "Can't be certain it was him, but I think I felt our late mayor right here in the hall. The air is about thirty degrees warmer than a few minutes ago. Why is spirit energy so cold?"

"Need a spiritual physicist to explain that. Or maybe a specialist in hell. Heck if I know." She sounded more interested and less disgruntled. "Which chamber would he hide in?"

"There are only two. Block spent a lot of time in Satterwhite's courtroom. Try that first?" Jax couldn't believe he was condoning breaking and entering. Well, they had keys. Trespassing maybe.

"You should go on," she said, as if hearing his thoughts. Or reading his aura. "You need to stay squeaky clean."

"Not until you leave. Clancy's ghost blew transformers. Block might open hell gates." He followed her through the courtroom to the chamber door.

She snorted. "Someone's been reading fantasy."

"When you're living in a hell hole, you want to hear how they work." The base camp library in Afghanistan had been stocked with that kind of fictional delusion. He'd not finished any of it.

She found a key that let her in. Satterwhite liked his chambers cool—or was saving energy. But even Jax could tell the office was ghostless.

Evie locked up and they traipsed across the hall. Below, windows crashed and workmen cursed. Someone played loud music. Anything sounded better than a mob.

"Bertie seems to think he left his surprise sketch in the attic. It's not there. He can't tell me what's on it." She found the key to Rhodes' office and opened it. "Oh yeah, baby."

The room was cold enough to freeze fish.

Nine

THE CHILDREN WERE LAUGHING IN THE KITCHEN AS GRACIE TYPED THE LAST LINE on her second chapter. She'd been up since before dawn. She was entitled to a break. Pris probably was too—especially since she was pretty certain Pris and Dante had finally hit the sack together and probably weren't getting much sleep.

It made her feel a little lonely that she didn't have anyone to cuddle with, but she was done with men. They just complicated her already complicated life.

She saved her work, set the laptop on the library table with the blueprints Evie had scavenged, and again admired the new shelves. The moth-eaten velvet draperies needed to come down. Maybe some gauzy gold curtains, floor-length, the kind with grommets she could just shove the pole through, for an airy look. The walls in here had escaped Evie's penchant for rainbow colors and were ivory. They could use a good scrub, but they shouldn't need painting.

Apparently, deprived of her own home, she was redesigning Evie's.

She traipsed into the kitchen where Pris and Dante vied for the attention of the twins, and Aster painstakingly iced a sugar cookie.

"Tathe teth, Mommy." Evidently imitating her elders, her daughter held out a glitter-bedecked Santa cookie.

"I should probably eat lunch first. Has anyone else eaten?" She opened the refrigerator to a mind-boggling collection of bowls.

"Pris has been feeding us all morning. A few more hours in here, and I probably won't be able to move from this booth." Dante held up an empty plate.

"Captive audience," Gracie's normally scowling cousin said, almost smacking her lips in delight. Sex was apparently good for her. "Try some of the pasta salad in the green bowl."

Maybe she needed sex to get into the Christmas spirit.

"Mr. Dante thez we can watch Dithney on his laptop." Aster added cinnamon buttons to her Santa. Psycat had taken the stool beside her, his tail twitching as he eyed the platter of cookies for anything fishlike.

Guilt crept over Gracie. The house had internet but no TV and no desktop computers. Dante was sacrificing his expensive device and business hours to entertain the children—while she worked on a fantasy.

"Why don't you use my laptop and let Cousin Dante work on his own? You know how to find Disney on it, don't you?"

Dante struggled not to look grateful. "Are you sure you don't need it? I can do my meeting by phone."

"You have kept my kid entertained all morning! We probably ought to sell that old secretaire and see what we can buy with the proceeds." She helped herself to the salad. "Where's Evie?"

"Ghost hunting," Pris said dismissively, stirring some concoction on the stove. "Nick is already fixing up the desk, but I can't imagine it selling for thousands to buy a PC."

"Not to the Antique Barn anyway. Bertie's brother doesn't know squat about antiques. Did Nick have lunch?" She didn't know why she asked. He was a grown man. He could get his own.

"Haven't seen hide nor hair of him since breakfast. Have him test the pasta salad. I'm debating whether it's worth adding to my menu."

"I vote for inclusion." Grace finished her portion, washed her dish, and dug out the bowl again.

She carried a plastic plate of salad and a bottle of water out to the garage while she debated whether she could write by hand or type on Evie's tiny notepad computer.

Nick had left the carriage doors open to the sun. He'd apparently found a light to hang from the loft and created a workbench of sorts with boxes and boards. He had the desk drawers on old newspapers while he worked.

There was a man who worked with his hands! Who knew? She watched as he industriously sanded a door, whistling. Instead of his usual designer duds, he was wearing crisp blue jeans and a navy sweatshirt that revealed the extent of shoulders previously concealed in tweed.

"Lunch," she told him, sitting the plate and bottle on his workbench.

She really ought to return to the house, but she couldn't help studying what he'd done. The raw wood under the pitted, dull finish looked new.

"Bless you, my child, I am fair starved." He glanced up to flash her one of his hormone-inducing grins.

Damn, that grin caused her to flush. Dante and Pris's rampaging lust must be catching.

"The refrigerator is fair game for all. If we don't eat the contents, Pris will have to buy another one. Or return to catering." She started back for the house.

"Wait," he cried through a mouthful of pasta. He signaled to let him finish chewing before he continued. "Shouldn't someone go into Charleston to see if that poor man's sketches might be there? I checked and the gallery is open Sunday afternoons."

She hesitated. "What is the point?"

"If only to chat up the gallery owner. Perhaps they're holding the surprise intended for his family? It's Christmas! It's the least we can do." He shoveled in more pasta, making appreciative noises.

She narrowed her eyes. "And the real reason?"

He shrugged, swigged the water, then gestured at the desk. "In the few spare hours I had to roam the city these past months, I noticed a number of most excellent antique stores. It would be good to find comparable pieces and learn current values. And I have no car."

He'd been borrowing Jax's motorcycle or Evie's Subaru when he had to go in to testify. She winced. The poor Brit really was trapped here.

"Fair enough. I'll admit I'm curious about this gallery that suddenly started taking Bertie's sketches. And if we can make some money off that desk. . ." She eyed the old piece that had sat neglected in a corner for as long as she could remember. "Evie will never allow a TV in the main house, but computers are just as good these days."

"Well, no, the monitors reek, but that's irrelevant to children. I'll clean up. Maybe I can slip in a little Christmas shopping while we're there." He wiped his hands on a rag.

Now she really felt like a selfish rat. The poor man was stuck here in a foreign country with no car, no family, and living in a madhouse of weird people. And he meant to shop for them.

She'd bought boxes of socks for all the men expected for Christmas, not anticipating anything in return. "You'd be better off shopping at Wal-Mart than downtown Charleston, but we'll see what's down by the gallery."

"Antiques," he said unrepentantly. "I Googled."

A few months ago, Nick had been cruising around in a big Mercedes with tinted windows and all the extras.

These days, he was grateful for Gracie's little Kia. Jax's motorbike was bloody cold, and he looked foolish wearing his court suit while buzzing down the highway. He should be more ambitious about applying for another marketing position, but his last experience had burned him badly. He needed time to reevaluate. His goal was still clear—enough money in his bank account for the good things in life. Wine, women, and song were never to be underestimated.

Perhaps he was developing a mature patina. Once upon a time he would have rebelled at the idea of a woman driving him anywhere. At the moment, he didn't mind Gracie driving since she was more familiar with Charleston streets and staying on the right. She was careful, remaining beautifully calm even when more aggressive drivers grabbed the parking spot she'd been positioned to take.

He had to admit, it was almost refreshing not living with his cousins' high drama every second. Without taking a single hit to his already-flattened ego, he navigated, using his phone to direct her down a side lane where they might find more parking.

The area where the gallery was located wasn't in the more fashionable districts but on a quiet side street of mixed historic buildings and modern offices. He loved the charm of pink buildings and palm trees, even if modern vehicles were a blight upon the landscape. Sunday afternoon Christmas shopping had filled the streets. He helped Gracie from the driver's seat, although she insisted on resisting. He liked the human contact, and the schoolteacher looked as if she could use a little coddling.

Janus Gallery was discreetly embossed in script on a bronze plaque attached to white-painted brick beside a lacquered black door.

"Not exactly the kind of place for Bertie's work, is it?" Gracie whispered as he tried the door.

"Ask me about antiques, not art," he murmured as they stepped inside the hushed, open gallery that would fit into any London art scene.

They had time to peruse oils and watercolors of Charleston panoramas before anyone approached them.

Nick gauged the saleswoman to be in her late fifties with artfully colored auburn hair and a discreet Botox treatment or two. Good bones, model frail, pink designer suit with black piping—definitely the owner.

"Mrs. Janus?" he inquired in his best Oxford accent. He'd attended a much smaller university, but he'd been selling himself all his life. "A pleasure to meet you."

She covered her surprise nicely. "To whom do I owe the pleasure of your visit?"

"My friend, Mrs. Jenkins." He gestured at Gracie. "She learned that some of Albert Walker's sketches could be found here. I'm a fan and thought I might find a piece for my collection." He figured Gracie was burning holes in his hide, but pretentious is as pretentious does.

The gallery owner seemed a trifle rattled but recovered well. "Yes, of course, so tragic to learn of the passing of someone with so much potential. You'll understand we had to cancel his opening, under the circumstances."

"Yes, naturally. I assume he hadn't delivered all his pieces. Might I see what he left here or has his family already claimed them?"

"His family?" She seemed flustered. "Verity led me to believe. . . But, of course, there is family. No, no one has claimed them. I will have my assistant bring them out. They're unframed, naturally." She excused herself and fled to the back.

"Weird," Gracie murmured. "Was she planning on selling them and keeping the money?"

"Not planning at all is my suspicion, or they'd be framed by now. There would be a catalog. Or perhaps things are done differently here?" He studied a life-size portrait of some granny's face in a bonnet.

"I wouldn't know. Places like this terrify me."

A nondescript young woman in gray set up several easels, then began sorting drawing papers on them. Definitely not a professional display. Nick produced his high-end camera and discreetly snapped the top images before the gallery owner arrived. He could hear her talking agitatedly in the back.

"Just his usual work," Gracie said, using her phone to snap more images. She shuffled the sheets to take shots of the ones beneath. "A little larger, better paper."

Mrs. Janus finally returned to more professionally display the works. "Was there a piece in particular you were interested in?"

"Places familiar to the inhabitants of Afterthought," Nick said idly, offering no opinion as she switched out the sketches. "We'll be opening a business there and local art is always a draw. I understood he'd been experimenting with watercolors. Do you have any of those perchance?" He rounded his vowels so well they practically rolled off his lying tongue.

She appeared a little flustered. "We'd hoped to display those at the opening, but they were never delivered. Perhaps you could ask his family?"

"No, they've only seen the one," Gracie said quietly, going back to admire an earlier image. "He had promised them one for the mantel, but it hasn't been found. It's a shame these can't be displayed. His family could use the money."

Nick hadn't heard about the mantel sketch, or was she making it up from whole cloth from the antique dealer's mention of a surprise?

"Well, without the artist—" The gallery owner let that thought drift.

"In London, people would be pounding on the door to buy up any available piece by a dead artist. It isn't as if there will be more." Nick stepped back and gestured at Gracie. "Do you see any here that will work with our others?"

She shook her head. "No, but I'll mention them to the owner's of these buildings. A catalog to show would have been nice. We'll have to buy directly from the family, I suppose."

Nick bit back a grin and gave a mental high five. The teacher might be a bit timid upon occasion, but she wasn't stupid.

The proprietor was obviously torn between a bird in the hand and a potential flock. "I would be delighted to discount these for a friend of the family."

Nick pulled out his card case and handed her a card. "We really hoped for the color pieces. If you come across any, give me a call. We appreciate your time."

He practically dragged Gracie out.

"What was that bit about the surprise being mantel size?" he asked as he steered her to the main thoroughfare.

"Evie's been talking to ghosts again," she said stiffly, studying the stores they passed.

Huh, not going there. Instead, he continued, "Did you recognize anyone?"

"Not everyone. The one with children in the schoolyard was nice. I wonder if I could talk the principal or PTA into buying it?" She tried to stop at the corner to look up and down the street, but he dragged her on. "Where are we going?"

"Antique mall. Not as high end as King Street but a good start. So none of those drawings screamed drug dealers to you?"

"Bertie sketched what he knew—Judge Rhodes in his robes talking to the mayor's lawyer outside the courtroom. Tobias watching from the steps as Sheriff Troy takes his father away. I think one was Jax on his Harley, but he had his back turned. The focus was on some female I didn't recognize. There was Mr. Patel who owns the fruit stand near the school. Nothing dramatic."

"I think our gallery proprietor was either planning on stiffing the family or throwing the work out, so we at least did a good deed and made her aware that people were watching." He studied the contents of the antique mall window and grimaced. "Lots of crap. Let's look anyway."

Gracie cast him a considering look. He didn't ask why. He had to work out a business plan and also find a way to recompense his hosts for their kindness. Wondering what pretty schoolteachers were thinking was a concern to someone other than him.

They both aimed unerringly for the booths with the pricier goods. Nick examined the fake early American while Gracie picked through vintage clothing.

"I'm thinking we could set up our own booth," she whispered, holding up a pair of white elbow-length gloves. "There's a whole box of these in the attic."

"Your aunt attended many gala occasions?" He dismissed any of the gewgaws as gifts. Evie and Jax didn't need more old stuff.

"My great aunt is a drama queen. She used to wear hoop skirts and hold balls. Are we done here?"

"Yes, this junk is worthless. There's a more promising venue on the next block. What can your sister use? Perhaps we should stop at a Wal-Mart." He scanned more booths as he weaved a zigzag path in an attempt to price more furniture.

"Buy her something that matches, and see if she'll wear it," she suggested with a touch of sarcasm. "Jax once had it all and probably still does in storage somewhere. Can you buy him a minute's peace?"

Nick chortled. "Look, craft booths, knit hats and gloves. Matching. And I see a few other things. Go away. Meet me here in half an hour."

She actually brightened at the prospect of losing him. So, maybe his ego could be flattened a trifle more.

"There's a children's thrift booth. This was a great idea, thank you!" She rushed off.

All right, not that he was crushed or anything, but buried under a shelf of colorful potboilers he'd spotted a collection of boxed classic books matching Gracie's. Evie's house didn't have a lot of books, and these even included fairy tales.

He found a silver flask for Jax, an Indiana Jones hat for archeologist Dante, a Magic Eight ball for presumably-psychic Pris, and a sequin-bedecked T-shirt for Loretta. He'd have to cash in his plane ticket to London to pay his credit card bill. First-class, it had been issued in the grandiose days of his cousin's fraudulent boutiques.

But judging by the prices he was seeing for junk, he could make some money for his host and hostess.

He was a little worried about one of the sketches they'd just seen at the gallery, however, the one depicting the cowboy-booted man handing what appeared to be a wad of cash to a man who resembled one of the judges he'd seen the day of the mob.

Ten

EVIE HAD REASON TO DISLIKE ARTHUR BLOCK WHEN HE'D BEEN ALIVE. SHE wasn't feeling the love now that he was dead. Unlike poor wraithlike Bertie, Blockhead's substantial aura occupied the judge's chair behind the bench as if he owned it.

Mostly, she saw spirit energy in colors. She recognized the former mayor's selfish hues. But the officious attitude lingered as well. She'd swear he was affronted by their intrusion.

She warned Jax by squeezing his hand. She wanted to see what Block would do if he believed they couldn't see him.

Sure enough, his colors recoiled in an ugly grimace, and he gestured in what she assumed was a middle finger salute. She couldn't actually see his fingers, just the movement and color. Interesting that his face manifested more than his fist. Her last ghost had been much clearer all over.

"Nice, Mayor, very congenial, especially since I'm the only one who can see or communicate with you." Evie settled on one of the courtroom benches, not approaching the flickering energy. She performed a few yoga moves to release the tension in her neck and shoulders. And to warm up. It was shivery cold in here. "I imagine it's a little frustrating being unable to manipulate people anymore."

What new torment is this? With a grumble, the aura rocked back in the judge's cushy chair.

"I believe the Dorothy Parker quote is 'fresh hell,' rather appropriate, don't you agree?" She said this so Jax would have an understanding of the tenor of their conversation.

Jax settled beside her and crossed his arms in intimidation mode. Butcher Block didn't even notice.

"In case you haven't surmised, Mr. Mayor, you're dead and your ghost is the hell in this scene. Your son is foolishly wanting your killer found. You do remember Tobias?"

Useless twit, Block muttered, apparently so accustomed to people speaking to him that he didn't see the difference beyond the grave. *He'll never pull off the zoning deal. He'll lose everything.*

Ah, a glimmer of his purpose here. "Deal?" Beside her, Jax didn't stir, so it didn't mean anything to him either.

Finish what I started, and he can save everything, get me out of this damned mess. Brief confusion colored his aura.

It was very strange seeing the beefy, florid face she knew reduced to a fleshy pallor. She doubted anyone could rescue a ghost, but she wasn't reminding him of that.

"Tell me what Toby needs to know," she suggested.

The spirit snorted. *Lily-livered boy would faint. Tell the bigwig I'll haunt him if he doesn't follow through.* His energy abruptly died and vanished.

"Bigwig?" she asked, hoping he'd hear. "Follow through?"

Nothing. Well, it wasn't as if Artie could say who killed him. And even though he evidently knew who was supposed to score his deal, he couldn't recall their name. Curses. Forget *Artie.* He was still a Blockhead.

She crossed her arms and kicked the bench in front of her.

"Bigwig?" Jax asked, accepting that she talked to thin air and got answers.

"Something about zoning and a bigwig he wants Toby to deal with." She ruminated but couldn't make anything of it.

"Is he talking about Layman, the asshat talking about creating Main Street USA in our not-so-charming town?"

Evie sat back up and kissed his cheek. "Tell me more, Lawyer Man." She slid out of the bench row. "Feed me while you do."

"Why was Block talking about Layman?" Outside the courtroom, Jax hefted the heavy sack of broken plaster she'd swept up and aimed for the stairs.

"He seemed to think some zoning deal would save the hide he no longer has. I can't imagine how. Wasn't the council's zoning law just settled?" Outside, Evie helped him heave the plaster into the dumpster. Then she tucked her hard hat under her arm and shook her hair free. "I need to return these keys, which means locking the clerk's office behind me and retreating through the bomb shelter."

"Bomb shelter should be locked too. Anyone could do what you did." He checked his phone battery, grimaced, and texted a hasty message. He held up the reply. "Deputy around front."

Jax took her hardhat and draped his other arm over her shoulder, steering her toward Main street. They met the deputy on the way up the courthouse steps and handed over the keys without explanation.

Evie figured Sheriff Troy knew where to find her if he had questions, but he was smart. He'd figure out how she'd grabbed the keys on his own. "I hope they searched the tunnel yesterday. It's been used recently, but I'm guessing that would be Bertie."

"If Troy hasn't, he will now. Having the keys to the entire courthouse accessible to anyone who came through that tunnel. . . I'm not even going to contemplate it. This town needs work." Jax shook his head in disapproval.

"Beyond boundary disputes and barking dogs, we never had real crime before. And I doubt most people would have any idea what to do if they did get into files. They might steal computers, I suppose, but the city's are ancient." Evie shrugged. "You were telling me about Asshat."

"I'll tell you what little I know on the way home. Last I heard, Pris is filling the fridge so our grocery bill won't allow eating out."

"Good point. And our phones will need recharging after that encounter. Spill." Enjoying the chilly sunshine with Jax's sturdy arm around her, Evie contemplated the future she'd never have dreamed of this time last year.

She'd found a man who didn't freak when she talked to ghosts and listened when she repeated what she'd learned from beyond the veil. That was more precious than diamonds and grocery bills.

"Layman is cut from the same cloth as Block only on a national scale," Jax told her. "He makes deals. He buys up cheap real estate and builds some destination store, mall, hotel, whatever. When land prices skyrocket around it, he sells everything for an enormous profit and moves on."

"Block never moved on," Evie complained. "He bought and seldom produced."

"Because he didn't have enough money and got caught by a family of witches," Jax said with a chuckle. "Layman was born rich and hasn't been caught. It's all hocus-pocus, borrowing huge sums, using his wealth to stomp over laws, throwing up a shoddy resort without paying his contractors, pocketing the loans, leaving local businessmen holding the bag for his debts. Eventually, the resort flops from lack of support, and the economy collapses with it. It's an artificial balloon that pops."

"And he'll do that here?" she asked in incredulity.

"Main Street USA is being pushed as a tourist draw, although the details are fuzzy," he said. "Since Block was in jail and his assets tied up, I hadn't realized he was involved. Or maybe the governor is interested, and the state is promising casinos or some other gimmick if Layman performs his magic act here. Not sure how you'll investigate that."

"No river for a casino. Liquor laws limit the sale of alcohol, which is where tourist destinations make money. Patel tried to get a license to sell on Sunday, but the churches rose up in arms, and the council turned him down. He doesn't have clout. In his prime, Block might have pushed through changes." Evie glanced down as her phone dinged. She hadn't thought there was enough juice left.

"Gracie." She held up her message. "I need to plug this in."

"Food, phone, and I'll start looking into Layman and zoning after." Jax held the front door for her.

In the parlor, Loretta was showing the twins and Aster how to make paper chains. The smell of glue promised ominous surprises. Not having new carpets or pretty floors had advantages with kids around.

Dante was in the breakfast booth on his laptop. Pris, for a change, wasn't to be seen. Evie plugged in her phone and unloaded food on the counter. She'd missed lunch.

Respecting Dante's meeting, they filled their plates and headed for the library. Evie remembered Gracie's texts and took the phone plug with her. While they scarfed down pasta salad, she flipped through the images her sister had sent.

"These are Bertie's sketches from the gallery. I'm not seeing anyone who looks like a drug dealer. There's one of you ogling some female." She shoved the phone over to Jax.

He flipped through. "Not ogling. I'm parking my bike. An unknown female crossed the street. Why would Bertie sketch her?"

"Is that Verity Janus again? I don't recognize her without the Daisy Duke's." She retrieved her notebook computer from the table drawer and did a web search for images of Bertie's artist friend. "Looks like it." She showed him the photo she'd found from a gallery exhibit. "Where was this sketch done, can you tell?"

"If I'm parking my bike, it's the alley behind the office building. Maybe she's taking a shortcut." He flipped through the images again until he found one of two men. "There's Layman, in the cowboy boots."

"Is that Judge Rhodes? Is Layman handing him *money*?" Evie opened the image wider to see what was in his hands, but Bertie hadn't clarified well. She sent the image to her notebook so she could enlarge more.

They studied the sketch together. Jax shook his head. "Judge Satterwhite was handling Block's case, not Rhodes. And Rhodes ruled in favor of Larraine on zoning, which drove the council crazy, so it can't be a payoff. Maybe Layman is just reimbursing the judge for lunch."

"And that's why Bertie sketched them? Bertie was a flake, but he wasn't dumb. I should go back to talk with him." Except she was pretty well drained for the moment. Like a battery, she needed time to recharge.

Jax leaned over to kiss her. "I have to work on Toby's files. Have Reuben or Roark do a search on Layman. Don't you have presents to wrap?"

She caught his jaw and kissed him more thoroughly. "I can do three things at once, remember? But the guys are better at searches. Find where Block hid his money and make Toby rich again."

"Doubt that's happening." He tugged a curl. "Set a date and decide where you want to honeymoon and let me take you away from all this."

Evie's insides fizzed with happiness, even while her head filled with doubt. *Marriage. Honeymoon. Forever* and ever. Scary.

"Some place where we can easily return to every time we want to kill each other?" she suggested.

Jax laughed and picked up their plates. "I'll just haunt you if you kill me."

Oh, well, there was that.

Later that afternoon, Jax pondered Evie's wariness about setting a date as he settled into his desk chair and flipped on his computer. Understanding human nature was part of his job, but Evie. . . did not operate on normal scales. She liked being seen as fearless and invincible, but he knew she was no such thing. She just hid her fears from herself as well as she did from others.

How did he let her know that he would always be there for her, no matter how weird things got? He was actually starting to enjoy the weirdness. Sitting in on Evie's chat with Block's ghost had been more fun than sitting in on a partners' board meeting, for sure. As long as the ghost wasn't blowing up things, he was good. There had been times that Evie's search for justice was as dangerous as he feared.

He ran a general search on Block's cloud account, hunting for the name Layman. It was unusual enough that he could be confident there would only be one person of that name in there.

Nothing. Not one single mention of a man considering a major franchise within Afterthought's boundaries. Arthur Block wasn't the only Realtor in town, but he was the most influential—or had been before his arrest. It didn't make logical sense that Layman hadn't at least consulted him.

Did that mean Jax didn't have all the mayor's files?

If so, had Block hid others or was Toby hiding them?

Evie was right that a tourist attraction would require a change in liquor laws. He ran another search using the words "liquor" and "alcohol." That brought up reams of references. Crap.

Evie had said Patel once applied to the council for a liquor option. Jax ran his name through the files and came up with a dozen references in city council minutes. That was a starting place, at least. He copied those to a new file and began reading.

On the last page, he found a notation in red with Block's edit attached referencing FL and a number. Jax returned to the main file and ran a search on the two together and came up with nothing. But FL by itself produced a lengthy list. With a whistle at some of the notes, he texted R&R to take a look. If they wanted the reward, they could do the scut work.

It looked a damned sight like Block and this FL owned a lot of local mortgages. What had Block been planning on doing with them?

And now that Block was gone. . .

Jax called Larraine Ward, their new mayor, and left a message.

It was at that point he heard sirens screaming down Main Street. In a small town, that always induced a racing pulse. He knew too many people. . .

He called Evie. She was already on the phone.

He got up and looked out the window. Gray smoke billowed from the direction of the school.

He was out the door before he even gave it a thought.

Eleven

Once they returned to the house, Gracie printed out the photos she'd taken of Bertie's gallery art. She'd like to show them to a few people, see if they might be interested in purchasing the sketches to help out his family. There were a couple she wouldn't mind owning, but her finances could barely pay the mortgage on a house she couldn't even live in.

She settled in her bedroom with wrapping paper and the loot from the antique store. She had a kaleidoscope and a stereoscope with cards of animals in national parks for the twins. Sometimes, old-fashioned toys could be as much fun as computerized. And she added a vintage Maid Marian costume to Aster's gift collection, one complete with bow and rubber arrows. Who needed Disney princesses?

It was almost dinner time when she was done, so she jogged downstairs to see who needed help with what.

Instead of setting out food, Dante, Pris, and Evie were gathered around the kitchen island watching a notebook computer. The kids were in the breakfast nook, scribbling on coloring books and ignoring the adults.

Aster waved her artwork at Gracie, so she went there first. "That looks like Honey! Is she wearing a Christmas collar?" Honey was her mother's golden lab. Gracie shot a surreptitious glance to the counter, but she couldn't see what everyone was watching.

Loretta was serenely coloring bubbles into the midsections of various

Disney princesses and didn't require attention, but the twins had to show her their creations.

It was a few minutes before Gracie could peer over Evie's shoulder to the computer screen. All she could see was smoke and fire engines and people running around. "What's happening?"

"Jax is filming the fire at Patel's fruit stand. I'm not entirely certain why." Evie stepped back so Gracie could see.

"Where are Roark and Reuben? I trust they're not involved?" Gracie asked. It wasn't actually as strange a question as it seemed. R&R had occasionally explosive habits.

"Reuben's there, reporting to Larraine and keeping Patel from running inside. I think the firemen have it under control, so Roark is apparently not needed."

"Do I need to start dinner?" she asked tentatively.

Pris stepped away from the video. "I have pizza ready to pop in. There's a salad in the fridge. Nick's still in the garage. Warn him we'll be ready in half an hour. Jax will just have to eat leftovers."

Assuming she'd hear the story later, Gracie ran her hand through her hair to straighten the layers and checked that she didn't have wrapping paper bits stuck to her sweater—then mentally slapped herself. Nick wouldn't notice, and she didn't care if he did.

Winter dark was settling in. She switched on the ancient porch light, but it didn't add much illumination. A square of light lit the driveway, so Nick must have the door open.

She heard voices as she approached. She didn't want to wait in the cold and eavesdrop until the visitor left, so she continued through the shadows until she reached the open door.

Covered in sawdust, Nick was swishing paint brushes in turpentine and talking to a man whose back was turned to her. Slouching shoulders in a tailored jacket, brownish-blond hair shaved on the sides—Gracie recognized him before he turned at Nick's greeting.

"Grania, good timing. Do you know Mr. Turlock?" Nick beamed. "He's interested in Bertie's work."

Grania? He was using her real name for why? As a warning? Or did she just go into fear mode because she seriously disliked Teddy Jr.?

"Hello, Ted," she said with a curt nod, before turning to Nick. "Pris says dinner is almost ready. Do you need any help cleaning up?"

"Grace." Teddy acknowledged her with a nod, before turning back to the sketches she'd bought at the Barn. "How much do you want for these?"

"They're not for sale." Rudely, she removed them from his hands. "Bertie was a friend. These are all I'll ever have left of him."

She tucked them under her arm and glared at Nick. "Why are they out here?"

"They need better frames. Now you've ruined your Christmas surprise." Nick turned back to Teddy. "Sorry. They're not for sale, as I said. But the Antique Barn had quite a few. Didn't Sammy show them to you?"

"Haven't been there yet. Just heard you were collecting. I'll try Sam, thanks. Consider that offer. You'll not get a better one." Turlock tipped an imaginary hat and strolled off.

Gracie wrinkled her nose in distaste. "What offer?"

Nick wrinkled his forehead in thought. "Some company wants a local marketing coordinator for a land project. I'm not sure why the owner of a sporting goods store is involved."

"Huh, that's a little weird. And he hated Bertie. Why on earth would he want his work?"

She didn't think Nick had any interest in remaining in Afterthought any longer than it took for the court case to end, so the job offer was just weird and possibly an excuse for asking about the sketches. She examined them in the dim light. Only one contained an image of Teddy. Perhaps he hadn't wanted to specify that one? Not out of modesty, for certain. Teddy considered himself a rock star. There was something surreptitious about all this.

She gave that a second thought. "*How* did he know we have the sketches?"

"Mrs. Janus maybe? I never question potential customers, only think how I can squeeze their wallets. She worked quickly, if so. If there really is interest, I think I'll run down to the Barn tomorrow and acquire a few more of those. Your family has quite a few good frames sitting around. I can probably make fifty to seventy-five dollars on the small frames. Add the sketches —maybe a hundred fifty?"

That number drove Teddy straight out of her head. "I only paid twenty for the sketches already framed!"

"As you say, Sammy is not a natural salesman. He picked those shoddy frames up at a garage sale by the box for a few dollars. Probably gave his brother a tenner for each sketch. If he came off with ten profit, he'd be happy."

"If he can't sell them for twenty, how are you—"

Nick grinned, caught her by the waist, and steered her out the door, flipping off the light as he went. "He's not me."

"This isn't like stolen auto parts, is it?" she asked in suspicion as he locked up, avoiding any reaction to his manhandling.

They'd never locked the garage before. But Nick was seeing money where no one else had. She hadn't even known there was a lock.

"Not stolen," he reminded her. "I'll pay fair price. I add a little magic to the frames, spend a little more on good mats. . . I won't make a fortune but a few dollars for groceries helps."

She was so rattled she forgot his too-familiar arm around her until they reached the porch. Then she stiffened and walked ahead. "Maybe you should buy all of Bertie's sketches. I don't think he would want Teddy Jr. anywhere near them."

She marched inside, leaving him to follow, whistling. The Brit took everything with insouciance. What was *wrong* with him?

Inside, the kitchen filled with the aroma of pizza, and the kids were carrying plastic plates to the dining room table. Gracie was utterly amazed at how domestic weird Pris had become.

"Is Jax done filming disaster?" Gracie asked as she dug out napkins and utensils.

"He's helping Mr. Patel take a few of his family's heirloom fruit carts back to his house. That poor man has suffered so much. It doesn't seem fair he should have to start all over." Evie was in the booth, texting rapidly. "Mom and I are contacting a few contractors."

"If his insurance is as slow as mine, they'll have no income for months. I think he has a dozen kids to feed. He's been bringing in a lot of his younger siblings." Grace grimaced. "Do they celebrate Christmas?"

"Don't know, but if we do, then we should be the Magi and bring gifts to them." Dante jotted notes on his phone. "Food, first. Rent?"

"Let's wait for Jax. He'll have a better idea about what kind of insurance they have." Evie scooted out of the booth.

Nick washed the wood stain and turpentine off and dried his hands on a towel Pris handed him. "It took Jax to bring the insurance company in with a reasonable offer after the fire that left me unemployed. Mr. Patel will need an inventory of everything in the store. In the meantime, is there any place else he can set up?"

"Being out there at the end of town, he had a lot of parking space. I don't think there's any place with enough room for his carts in town," Gracie called from the dining room where she helped the kids set the table.

"What about the Antique Barn? Maybe Sammy could rent him some space?" Nick asked. "It's just down the road. I could make signs."

The others leaped on Nick's idea and ran with it.

Stunned at how easily the suave Englishman had inserted himself into her family, Gracie remained silent.

What if Nicholas Gladwell decided to stay in Afterthought? Set up the antique shop he obviously knew how to operate? Or accepted Teddy's weird offer of a marketing job? What if the too-sexy Brit was right here in her face every day from here on out? Her cautious nature clenched in panic.

Jax's motorcycle roared up, diverting her distressing train of thought.

He came in smelling of smoke and casting off his motorcycle jacket, trailing Reuben in a leather blazer. Still wearing his kinky hair in a man bun, the engineer inhaled the pizza aroma and produced a six-pack of beer. "Got salad?"

Gracie handed him the bowl. Reuben looked weary but content, which was more than he had when he'd arrived last spring. Wearing a stylus instead of a bone in his hair, lacking all his former metal except one earring, he blended into the family chaos.

Finding people to care about had helped him heal.

Did Nick need that too?

Watching the Brit plot and plan with the others, she didn't think so. Nick was a confident man of the world, like Dante, sure of himself and his place.

Once Pris set the first two pizzas on the table and had the second set cooking, they all settled down at the table. That's when Jax dropped the bombshell.

"Patel thinks the fire is arson. He's been receiving hate threats. He swears he turned off the space heater and unplugged it before he closed up. The place is little more than a cement block shack. There was nothing else flammable."

"The electric box?" Dante asked. "In these old places—"

Jax shook his head. "New wiring, inside and out. He wanted to expand. Larraine's staff was helping him fill out permits."

"Hate crime," Evie agreed flatly.

Nick looked from one to the other and shook his head. "Hate to talk conspiracy, but a murder, a riot, and arson all in a few days? Are you sure?"

Twelve

～✦～

MONDAY MORNING, EVIE HANDED THE KEYS OF THE SUBARU TO NICK SO HE could drive down to the Antique Barn and haggle with Sammy Walker over the sketches. At her request, he let her out at the top of the hill in front of the smoky remains of Patel's produce stand.

The Barn and the school were only a short walk downhill, and traffic was slow once school rush hour ended. She didn't need the car.

The produce stand had once been an old service station between the school and town, an ideal location. Patel had painted it in tropical colors, set his old wooden handcarts out front filled with fruit, stored his carts and inventory in the service bay at night, and done a nice business. Since he was in walking distance of the school, he'd added lighting and shelves in the interior for school supplies and snacks and a few freezers for ice cream—a family friendly destination. It was all gone.

She didn't even know why she was here except she was procrastinating. She hated to risk the courthouse again to talk to Block's ghost about Layman. Would it even be open?

"Keep seeing you at crime scenes and I'll start suspectin' you one of them crazies who return to the scene of your crimes."

"Philomena Marquette." Evie acknowledged the skinny cop and her former schoolmate without turning around. "I'm just looking for ghosts. So it really was arson?"

"Possible arson but ain't no bones. If whoever did this wanted to off a raghead, then he shoulda done it when the place was open." Philomena shoved her hands in her back trouser pockets and surveyed the destruction. "Can't blame the arsonists all that much. These furriners take food from the mouths of our kids."

Evie snorted. "Good one. For starters, you don't have kids and Patel does. Main menu—this service station sat empty for as long as either of us can remember and not one single person stepped up to do what he did. If I didn't know you graduated top of your class, I'd say you were the raghead."

She shrugged. "I got *ambitions*. I plan to blend in and get ahead. Patel here's been harassed by our finest citizenry. I gotta keep my Black ass on the right side of public opinion."

"A hundred years ago, public opinion supported the Klan. Would you wear a sheet on your head? You're smarter than that. And if this hick show is your Columbo act, give me some credit too."

"I mean to make detective someday," she said ominously. "Think your little Solutions Agency ever gonna solve a crime?"

Ah, the snot was seeing Evie as competition. Given their history, she should have seen that coming. "I do *ghosts*, Philomena. We can't solve crime without the help of the law. But if the law wants my help, you have to give up the attitude. This isn't the schoolyard. Trash talk gets us nowhere."

Talking to Philomena was always entertaining but seldom informative. Evie had been a bad student. Philomena had worked hard for straight A's and resented Evie's irresponsibility. That didn't mean either of them knew more than the other.

She should probably ask Gracie which of the school's delinquents had harassed Patel. Philomena wouldn't tell her. But would a school kid set a fire?

The cop shrugged off her suggestion. "I can't give you ghosts, but you might want to ask yourself why the Shepherd boys are trying to buy old Mrs. Satterwhite's farm when they can't afford the land they already own." She dropped the drawl but might as well have said *them white trash Shepherd boys*. Without further explanation, Philomena walked off, back toward town.

The Shepherd farm was on the west side of Afterthought. The family had been landowners since forever but not very good farmers. They were down to a few acres of barren fields, a little weed, and hogs these days and most likely had mortgaged the lot.

Judge Satterwhite's ancestors once farmed an entire plantation on this side of town. It had all come down to his father, who'd been dead for a decade. The judge's mother now owned what had become the Antique Barn, plus all the fallow fields around the school. She rented out the land and whatever else she could. Everyone figured the property would go to the judge when his mother died.

If his mother sold to the Shepherds, capital gains would eat half her profit. Mrs. Satterwhite wasn't stupid and had no need of the money. If she left the property to the judge, he could sell without taxes after she died and retire early. Lots of people did that. Evie hadn't worked for a CPA without learning a few things.

The Shepherds might be stupid enough not to understand that, but where would they even find the cash to make an offer? Was their little patch of marijuana selling that well? They needed a better investment plan, if so. That rumor was probably just Philomena blowing smoke.

Time to face the ghosts. Seeing nothing she could salvage for the Patels, Evie turned toward town. Long-legged Philomena was already out of sight.

Once in town, Evie ran into Mayor Larraine emerging from Jax's office building. Her normal welcoming smile took a moment to warm up until she was certain Evie was alone. "Pumpkin, you need a warmer jacket! Where are your gloves?" She was wearing a fur stole and gorgeous tanned leather gloves.

"Sun is out. I don't need gloves. Are the reporters still bothering you?" Evie fell in step with her, figuring the mayor was heading for city hall on the far side of the courthouse. Having a mayor she could actually talk to almost felt like she was a respectable citizen—instead of one step above homeless Bertie.

"At least that Lawless Jane blogger has hushed up since she tried to burn down the town. I checked, and they've got her in a mental cell block." Larraine returned to her normal swagger and waved at people on the street.

"I was wondering about that. Jane hated enough people that she was my suspect number one for Patel's arson. Do you think one of her fellow bigots set a copycat fire?"

Larraine sighed. "You don't think that mob scene was sufficient? If I'd known I'd stir up all those old hatreds, I might not have let you talk me into running."

"What, you want the cockroaches to stay hidden and breeding in the dark? Does that help anything? This way, you know your enemies. Besides, look at everything you've accomplished in a few short months! The library has their funding. You kept the old goats from throwing out every business they don't like. . ."

Larraine nodded, looking a little more reassured. "And I wouldn't have met Reuben. I'm just having a bad day. I was trying to help Mr. Patel get what he needed to open that convenience store, and now he has nothing to put it in."

"Insurance?" Evie stopped at the courthouse steps.

"Estimator is a prick. Says old places like that aren't worth a thing, he should sell for the value of the land."

The land next to the Satterwhite farm? Oh, that could not be good. "The land? Why do I have the feeling someone's been bribed?"

Not giving Larraine time to question, Evie ran up the courthouse steps. Looked like the place was back in business. She'd have to hope her ghosts hung out in public. She had a lot of questions—starting with who would want useless land in Afterthought? Blockhead had been a Realtor. His ghost should know if anyone did.

"WHATCHA GONNA DO WITH ALL THIS OLD CRAP OF BERTIE'S?" SAMMY ASKED, helping Nick pry the sketches out of the cheap discount store frames.

If Teddy Jr. was after these sketches, then Nick had beat him to them. He shouldn't feel triumphant about ruining his credit card, but he didn't want the lawyer's son Gracie didn't like to have Bertie's artwork.

Although that offer of a real job was mighty tempting. He probably ought to call the number on the business card he'd been given. It would mean staying here instead of returning home to the big city lights. . . He should at least make inquiries.

The workshop off the back of the Antique Barn smelled of old manure and damp wood. An ancient gas furnace rattled and clanged and wasted good heat on the uninsulated shed. Sammy's workbench seemed to be held together by crooked nails and string. But he had hammers and screwdrivers, and that's all they needed.

"Thought I might scan them into a computer, use them for graphics, things like that," Nick said vaguely, figuring Sammy would have no idea what he was talking about.

The dealer probably had kids who knew Nick was full of blarney, but he nodded as if he understood. "Bertie would like that, I guess. He shoulda thought of it himself."

"I suppose the world is full of graphic artists. I'm just not one of them." Nick popped a sketch out, checked the back, saw nothing of interest, and changed the subject. "The Malcolm ladies were wondering if you had space you might rent to Mr. Patel while he rebuilds. It seems he needs a parking lot."

Sammy shrugged. "Don't know how much longer I can keep this place going." He brightened a little. "But if Patel can help with the rent. . ."

Excellent, they'd planted a little seed. A community that worked together, stayed together. Good motto. Maybe he could sell it.

"Is that your door ringer?" Nick asked at a clanging in front.

"Monday, right." Sammy set down his screwdriver and hurried to greet his customer.

A regular Monday visitor, perhaps?

The inept Sammy had agreed to sell the sketches for fifteen apiece without the frame. Nick didn't feel too sorry for a man who'd probably paid his starving brother a mere tenner for hours of work. If Nick's strategy worked, and he actually made a profit, he'd have to donate ten percent to Bertie's mother.

None of the sketches Sammy had produced had been mantel size. If even Bertie's ghost didn't know where the surprise drawing was, then it was long gone. Damned shame. Curiosity was killing him.

He pried the last sketch out of its cheap frame and added it to his designer leather briefcase. Maybe he could sell the briefcase for half the fortune it had cost in his glory days. He really wasn't eager to cash in that first class ticket just yet. But if he took a job. . . Cashing that ticket would put him in a place of his own.

Wiping the frames down so Sammy could put them back in stock, he considered leaving by the back door so he didn't disturb any customers. He'd already paid with his nearly maxed credit card. He'd better sell these fast.

The furnace popped loud enough to startle. Worrying the thing would explode, Nick hurried to set the workbench to rights.

The front door rang again. New customer or the other one leaving? He waited for Sammy to return. When he didn't, Nick carried his briefcase out the back and to the little red car he'd parked there.

In London, he hadn't needed transportation of his own. He'd had public transit and a company car when needed. If he stayed here, he'd have to earn enough to buy a vehicle. Why was he even considering it? No way could he afford so much as a bicycle.

And he needed to contribute to Evie's generous family. Trading was all he knew—unless her Solutions Agency needed a marketing campaign. He could organize one, but he didn't think they could afford the ad space.

The real danger of staying in a rent-free room was coming to enjoy family life a little too much. If he returned to the UK. . . Maybe he should move back to York, start a little shop there, rebuild his life. . .

He was out of his blooming mind. Too much Christmas cheer, obviously.

He parked Evie's car in its usual space beside the house, unlocked the carriage doors, and brought out the old heavy canvas he'd found buried in a corner of junk. He'd added some weights and magnets with a glue gun so he could cover the Subaru with it. The makeshift cover wouldn't last, but it might keep the Subaru's windows frost free through the winter months. The winter here was certainly more pleasant than in York. Or London.

Wearing sweaters against the morning chill, the children raced around the backyard playing a game. He could remember he and his siblings running down alleys, daring each other to steal apples from vendors, but they'd never really played games. He couldn't recall any, anyway.

The kids came running as he covered the car.

"Are you making a tent?" Gracie's girl inquired politely.

Alex and Nan, Dante's pair, peered under the edges as if he were concealing a magic trick.

"Just putting a blanket on the car to keep it warm. Would you like a tent?" In the garage junk piles, he'd seen what might have been one once.

All three heads bobbed eagerly. Oh well, it wasn't as if his time was heavily scheduled.

Gracie came over to the gate to see what they were up to. She looked rosy-cheeked and more approachable somehow. Maybe it was that sweater she filled out better than any skinny model. The surge of lust was purely natural after months of abstinence, he told himself.

"Did you buy all the sketches?" she asked.

"I did. They're in my briefcase. Want to flip through and tell me which I should frame first while I go tent hunting?" He led the procession into the carriage house.

"We have tents?" She glanced around the dim interior while he opened the briefcase.

"Maybe. I didn't look closely." He pointed at a pile of yard games and lawn ornaments in a corner. "You need shelves or storage boxes to organize this mess."

"Or throw it all out since no one uses it anymore."

"You have children in the house these days," he reminded her.

After casting the toys a dubious glance, she spread the sketches across his workbench while Nick dug into the junk pile for the vinyl dome tent he'd seen.

"Bertie drew his family home," she exclaimed.

Not being from around here, Nick hadn't recognized any of the places or people. He'd just liked the simplicity with which they'd been drawn. "Is that significant?"

"The Walkers rent the old Satterwhite farmhouse. This looks like Sammy's kids playing outside. Why wouldn't Sammy keep it?" She set that sketch aside.

"Maybe he has others? Or he hates being reminded of his brother's failures? Who knows what makes people tick?" He triumphantly retrieved a bent aluminum pole and hunted for the other.

"I thought marketing people knew what makes people tick," she said in obvious amusement.

"Selling is different. The person is right there in front of you. Talk, figure out what they want, tell them they'll be rich, famous, glamorous, whatever. Although heck if I know *why* anyone would want fame and fortune. They're a bloody nuisance."

"Said someone who's never been poor and unattractive." She came over to examine the damaged poles he'd extricated and to lift Alex off of a teetering stack of boxes.

"I was skinny and spotty as the next kid when I was young. My da was an alcoholic, and we lived on the dole as often as we didn't. I've seen both ends of the spectrum. Worrying about food on the table is a whole lot healthier than having the press clamoring at your door every time you spit in public." Uncomfortable with expressing his opinion, he carried a bent pole over to his worktable.

"Interesting perspective. I wouldn't mind experiencing wealth for a while. I'd like to know how it felt not to worry about how to make the mortgage or put Aster through college."

"Not the same as filthy rich and famous, surrounded by sycophants, not knowing who to trust, and worried your financial advisor is robbing you blind," he argued.

Huh, where had that come from? He was all about money, which came with a certain degree of recognition.

"OK, I'd rather be comfortable than wealthy." She held up the second badly bent aluminum pole. "I don't think these are salvageable. We need to rent a dumpster and clean house."

"I make a living out of spinning straw into gold. I'll see what I can do with these before giving up." He turned to the kids. "What if I just hang the tent over a bush right now so you can crawl under it?"

They cheered, too young to disdain makeshift toys. Nice that he could feel like a hero for little kids.

The schoolteacher stayed behind to study the sketches. He wasn't trying to impress her anyway, was he?

As they pushed through the gate, Pris leaned out the back door waving a phone. "Have you seen Evie? Sheriff wants to talk to her."

"Left her heading for the courthouse. Does he want to question ghosts?" Lawmen always worried him, but he played blasé well. He chose a couple of branches that might support the vinyl and began arranging it.

Pris relayed the message and started to retreat. Her phone beeped again. Nick's did the same. Gracie emerged carrying hers, looking worried.

"It's Jax," she said. "Sammy Walker has apparently been robbed and murdered, and Evie's car was the only one seen over there."

The schoolteacher didn't even look at him accusingly, even though she knew Nick had just been there, not Evie.

Thirteen

EVIE SAT ON THE FREEZING ATTIC STAIRS AND TRIED TO REASON WITH A SPIRIT who hadn't been too rational while alive. "You sketched Layman and Judge Rhodes on the courthouse steps. Why? Did you hear what they were saying?"

Bertie's colors rotated in and out of faint. He was a challenge to read.

Nah, man, I don' know nothin', he insisted. *I was just followin' the turds and their buddies around, y'know, and they looked. . . I don' know. Shifty? So I drew them.*

The turds. The Turlocks had earned that epithet over the years. Did that mean Block's lawyer or his son had been nearby when the money exchange happened? How could she figure out who their *buddies* were? How many questions would Bertie answer? She tried not to press too much.

"One of your sketches shows Mr. Patel outside his fruit stand. Did he look shifty?" She'd already ascertained that Toby and Verity had been sketched because they were helping Bertie. And he liked Corvettes. He'd not said anything about Teddy Jr. being present though. He seemed to leave him out of most of the drawings.

Peaches man. Bertie brightened. *He gave me peaches. I helped him paint a sign. Nice guy.*

This wasn't getting anywhere. Evie called up another sketch on her phone. "Is this your mother in her vegetable garden?"

He appeared to nod. *I help weed and eat the tomatoes. She's sad.*

Evie studied the brief lines creating the woman's face. She could see the wrinkles and worried frown. "Is she sad about you? Or something else?"

She has to move. I wanted to help so she wouldn't have to. Bertie's colors dimmed to gray. *Gallery said they'd help.*

"Gallery" probably meant Verity or her mother. "So you gave all your work to the gallery to sell?"

Not all, he said defensively. *I sketch a lot.*

She was lousy at interrogation. In frustration, she asked, "How do you choose your subjects?"

His colors brightened a little. *People I like, mostly. Places I like.* He dimmed, as if a gray thought passed through his limited brain. *Gallery Girl wanted sketches of places the creep went, but he doesn't go anywhere. She said follow his minions.*

Gallery Girl. Probably Verity. *Creep?* Did anyone say *creep* anymore? *Minions?* She imagined little yellow animated bullets running around town. Focus, Evie.

It would be a waste of time attempting to pry names out of a ghost, and she never knew how much time she had. How did she get where she wanted to go? "So where did his minions go?"

Like I said, I followed the turds. They talk to the creep, and they make my mom sad. So I got them good. He sounded as satisfied as his aura looked.

"How did you—" The closet door opened and Bertie vanished.

Jax leaned against the door frame, shivered, and glanced around. "Your phone is dead again."

She pulled it out and checked. Yup. Bertie had drained it. "Hazard of the trade. Did you need me for anything urgent?"

"Not to be scary or anything, but the sheriff is looking for you, and none of us could reach you, so. . ." He didn't look too concerned but straightened when she stood and dusted herself off.

"Troy wants to see me? That's a new one. He usually runs the other way when he sees me coming." She was wearing a down vest, but she welcomed Jax's heat as he put his arm around her.

"The reason isn't good. A customer found Sammy Walker in a pool of blood this morning, and yours was the only car seen in his lot." He led her toward the back stairs.

Thinking of Sammy's poor wife and kids, Evie filtered a load of bad language before she finally spoke. "That makes utterly no sense. Sammy Walker never hurt anyone. He'd hand what little cash he had to a thief rather than fight. He wasn't the smartest man on the block, maybe not even the most honest, but he wasn't a fighter, and he certainly didn't own anything worth killing over."

"Whoever did it emptied the cash drawer, so the sheriff figures robbery. Maybe one of Bertie's druggie friends? I imagine Troy just wants you to tell him if you noticed anyone around."

"A morning robbery? When there were no sales yet? Even drug addicts should have more sense." Evie frowned and nearly tripped on the stairs. "Besides, I wasn't there. Nick was."

Jax stiffened. "Nick?"

She shrugged as he reached for his phone. "He wanted to buy Bertie's sketches, and I gave him the car keys. He dropped me off at Patel's so I could take a look around, and he went on down the road. Is he back yet?"

"Don't know, but I'd better have him come in with you. Sheriff doesn't know Nick except as a relation to a family of killers. And Nick has a juvie record, so it looks bad."

"Nick's aura is clear," she protested. "He has self-esteem issues, but he's not his family by a long shot. I don't think he even knew his family reprobates until they hunted him down when they needed a cheap hire for their marketing department."

"Troy won't buy auras." Jax left a message telling someone he'd found Evie and would be over shortly. Then he hit his contact list again. "Nick? Tell the family I've found Evie. You'd better meet us over at the courthouse. We can go over to the sheriff's office together."

"I don't like this. Who reported my car? I don't see how anyone noticed the Subaru and not whoever arrived after." She dragged her feet as they stepped outside. The back stairs faced the county's tiny police station. The sheriff's car was parked out front.

"Reuben and Roark will dig into police reports once they're filed, but right now, Troy is just starting the legwork. So play nice and maybe he'll tell you what we need to know."

Evie snorted. "Don't pacify me, Jackson Ives. I know Troy a lot better than you do."

He gave her the smashing grin he reserved only for her. "I like it when you call me names."

She elbowed him but reduced her anger to simmer. Jax hadn't known his real name until recently. They waited for Nick, who arrived on her bicycle, apparently unwilling to borrow her car again without permission. "Honest," she told Jax.

"Broke," he told her. "Not a farthing to his name, as they say in the books."

"Smart," she retorted. "Too smart to kill for morning cash."

He nodded agreement as Nick locked the bike to the rack and ran up to meet them. "I didn't hear a thing! I swear. I paid for my sketches and went out the back and never saw anyone except Sammy!"

"Sheriff just needs to ask questions," Jax assured him. "He needs all his i's dotted and t's crossed."

Given that the sheriff was now sitting on three deaths and an arson, Evie suspected Troy might be inclined to grab any suspect he could just to have someone behind bars. Maybe it might even be safer there, because she was starting to feel like Afterthought had a giant target painted on it.

"You're both telling me you were right there in the vicinity when a man was shot and robbed and saw nothing?" the sheriff asked in incredulity.

Jax bit his tongue hard and let Nick and Evie speak for themselves. He hadn't been there but even he could see the gaping hole in this accusation. Troy was pushing.

"It's a state highway on a weekday morning!" Evie was the first to kick the hole shut. Nick wasn't familiar with local traffic. "Everyone and their siblings was on their way to work. Which busybody even noticed my car *behind* the building much less recognized it? And why don't you ask them why they didn't see the *killer's* car, which had to be out front since Nick didn't see it either?"

Jax hid his grin. Evie had no need of his help. It was Nick he worried about. The pretty Brit was looking grim.

The sheriff grimaced. "Philomena told me your car was at the Barn, and you were on the hill. She left before seeing anyone else."

"Then Philomena is as much a suspect as I am and can bear witness that I was at Patel's when we talked, not at the shop. She knows that! Did she tell you what time it was?"

"I'm asking the questions here, Evangeline," Troy retorted sternly.

"I wanted to be at the Barn when it opened." Nick interrupted Evie's no doubt tart reply. "I dropped Evie off right about nine. I probably spent an hour working with Sammy on the frames, until he had a customer and went to the front. Evie would have been long gone by then and wouldn't have noticed anyone pulling in. I didn't see anyone in front or back when I pulled out."

"We could see the barn from the top of the hill. Philomena probably saw you park. But anyone coming in from the road wouldn't notice the Subaru in back." Evie crossed her arms angrily.

Evie was almost never angry. Jax wouldn't want to be Philomena, whoever she was. Before she could hex anyone, he stepped in. "Which probably means whoever did this didn't know Nick was there, or he did it after Nick left." He knew better than to ask when Sammy was killed. It had to be after Sammy left Nick around ten and before the sheriff started hunting Evie less than half an hour ago. Very short time frame.

Nick didn't relax. Neither did Evie. They both appeared ready to commit murder. Only Jax knew their target was whoever had killed the harmless father of two.

The sheriff nodded wearily. "Let's go over this again. You were there from nine until approximately ten? When Sammy went out front. Did you hear anything?"

Warily, Nick thought about it. "I finished up the last frame and cleaned up while I waited for him to be done with his customer. The only thing I heard was the bell over the door and the furnace making popping noises. When he didn't return, I packed up and went out the back." He looked unhappy. "If the second door ring wasn't a second customer, then it may have been the first one departing. Since Sammy didn't return, he may have been dead when I left. Had I gone out that way, I might have saved him."

Evie reached over to squeeze his arm.

The sheriff shook his head. "He died instantly. You left when?"

Nick shrugged. "I didn't look at the time, but you can verify my return to the house with Gracie. She helped me unpack the sketches."

"Was there anything interesting in the sketches?" Evie asked, having overcome her snit. "Bertie said he was following the *turds*. I think he meant the Turlocks."

Jax almost sympathized as the sheriff rubbed his wrinkled brow. Only Evie would talk about a dead man as if he were alive and turn a murder investigation to ghostly artwork.

"The people and buildings in Bertie's work are meaningless to me. I really didn't have time to study them after I returned. I was building a tent for the kids." Nick sat up eagerly. "Teddy Jr. said he meant to talk to Sammy today about the sketches. Do you think the thief was after the *sketches*? They might be more valuable than we thought."

"What the *hell* are we jabbering about?" Troy lost his patience.

"Ghosts," Jax said succinctly, warning the officer. "Evie believes Bertie Walker may have sketched the mayor's killer or at least knows who it is."

"And if Bertie was following Teddy Jr. until someone gave him drugs. . ." Evie jumped in. "You need to talk to Junior Turd. Why does he want Bertie's art? Maybe whoever gave Bertie drugs needed to get into the attic to figure out how to shoot the mayor and Bertie sketched him. Maybe he saw something when he was following Teddy. Maybe both of the Walker brothers were killed for the sketches! We need to study those pictures."

The law officer looked to Jax in frustration. "I don't know how you do it. You're a lawyer. Tell them everyone knows ghosts can't talk and their sketches aren't evidence or a reason to kill."

Jax shrugged. "They know."

"We don't care." Evie stood up as if she'd been dismissed. "We want justice. If the courts won't give it—"

"Don't finish that sentence, Evangeline. We won't have vigilante justice in this town." The sheriff stood up with her. To Jax, he added, "Get them out of here and may God have mercy on your sanity."

That didn't sound like the sheriff meant to question the Turlocks. If Evie was chasing a potential killer. . .

Jax gave Nick's shoulder a shove to get him moving and practically dragged Evie until they were back on the street. "What the hell was that about the ghost and the Turlocks? You know Toby is refusing to pay his father's bill to senior Turlock, claiming he's being defrauded?"

"You interrupted before I could find out more." Instead of being grouchy, Evie wound herself around Jax and kissed his cheek. "You're practically glowing with the need for answers."

"That's not a thing." So, he was the grumpy one. He didn't like his fiancée accused of murder. "I read about auras. No one mentions glowing for answers."

She looked pleased. Nick looked thoroughly confused.

Instead of arguing, Evie turned to their befuddled guest. "I read auras. I do not read them the way they do in books. I can't explain better than that. I mean, yes, I can read ordinary aura things like if someone is unhealthy or worried or whatever. That's amateur stuff."

"Why don't you stop right there before you drive Nick screaming into the streets, if he isn't ready to already?" Jax suggested. "Let's look at sketches. Troy will eventually admit he needs to see them."

Nick grabbed Evie's bike and fell in step. "I don't much like the law," he admitted. "They lack imagination and empathy. I don't believe in ghosts or auras, but at least they're creative."

"Cops aren't paid to make up things or feel them. I don't think scientists would accept auras or ghosts either." Jax understood how Nick felt. He'd had his run-ins with officialdom. And Evie's family. . . still ran circles around laws.

"You believe people wear rainbows?" Nick asked him incredulously. "You're a lawyer!"

Evie patted Nick on the shoulder. "You don't have to believe. You just need to *listen*. Let me tell you that the sheriff is in over his head. Accept that he doesn't have the force capable of solving all these crimes. You don't have to know how I know. Or why I believe the sketches are our best clue. Just apply your creative brain to help solving the puzzle."

Jax absorbed the wonder that was Evie as they strolled home in harmony. He didn't understand what she did any more than she understood the law. All they had to do was accept each other's expertise and go from there.

Except one of the Turlocks could be a murderer, and sooner or later, Evie would go after him. Jax inwardly shuddered. How did he keep Evie safe while she was bent on catching cold-blooded killers?

"If the killer was at the Barn when I was, what are the chances he'll come after me next?" Nick asked gloomily.

Which neatly nailed Jax's fear and shattered any sense of peace.

Fourteen

By the time Jax, Evie, and Nick returned to the house, Gracie had all the sketches laid out in the library. She'd even made prints of the photos from the gallery, although they lacked dates.

She was trying to keep busy and not fret at the news of Sammy's death or the sheriff's demand to see Nick and Evie. She was obsessing about so many things right now that she'd soon be considering moving to another town to avoid crime. Occupying her mind helped.

"What are we doing?" Evie asked, entering with a platter of Pris's experimental air-fried chicken wings. Where Pris had acquired an air fryer was anyone's conjecture, but the house was redolent of frying chicken.

"You said Bertie was following the Turlocks, so I wanted to see how Bertie spent his last days. I doubt these are all his recent sketches. We know we're missing the mantel-size one at least. But the ones we have do seem to fit a pattern." She hadn't heard about the Turlock part until Evie texted her, but it might fit in with what she was seeing.

Gracie waited anxiously to tell if anyone else could see it too. Nick and Dante couldn't, of course. They didn't know the area. Jax wasn't as familiar as Evie. If Evie saw it—then they could call Mavis to verify. Their mother knew everything and everyone.

"Where's the starting date?" Evie set down the platter for the men following on her heels.

Gracie pointed at the image of Bertie's mother looking sad. "Last spring, before the mayor went to jail."

Jax pointed at the one of Rhodes and Layman exchanging cash at the other end of the table. "This?"

"Midsummer, *after* Block went to jail." Gracie turned it over to show there was no date. "This is only a photo, so I'm guessing based on short sleeves and the geranium in the foreground. The flowers turn scraggly by September."

Studying an image of a group of men in a booth with beer mugs on the table, Evie looked troubled. She flipped it over for the date. "I can't tell for certain, but this appears to be Teddy Sr. and half the city council—before the mayor's trial starts? Who is the guy in the cowboy boots?"

Jax glanced over. "That's Layman, the big developer." He sounded worried.

Nick looked over his shoulder. "He was at the courthouse when the mayor died and came out along with the judges on the fire engine."

Gracie nodded and waited. Dante and Nick studied the rest of the images, but they were clueless, although Nick pointed out one of the last ones. "That's Mayor Larraine, right? Is she talking with your mother?"

"Yes. That was before the special election, not long before the Halloween party where your cousin was killed."

Nick frowned. "None of my family is in these. He didn't draw the boutique that opened around that time?"

"If Bertie was following someone, that someone wasn't involved in the boutique." Or property on that street, but Gracie didn't want to give that clue away.

"So, if this is the Turlocks he's following. . ." Evie trailed off and went back to the beginning. "The Satterwhite Farm and Bertie's family last spring. The courthouse. A meeting at the Shepherd's farm with Toby and friends. . ."

"That one seems out of place," Gracie admitted.

"So that may just be Verity's posterior and not relevant, although Teddy Jr. was obviously there, and he's not in the others." Evie continued down the table while the men munched wings and watched. "Bertie got around. Jax's office building. Half of Main Street in this image of Rhodes, Turlock Sr., and Layman walking together. Guns and Hoses, the barroom by the courthouse. Patel and his fruit stand—I wonder if he'd buy that sketch? A pumpkin patch—that's in the empty lot past the fruit stand in the fall."

"The students set that up. Mrs. Satterwhite owns the property and allows them to raise funds there." Gracie started doubting her theory.

"This is down past the Walker farmhouse." Evie tapped a sketch of horses with a couple of kids saddling up. "A bunch of moms want to start a riding school there, but the town's new zoning doesn't include agriculture, so they're having a debate."

"And that's when we come to Larraine and your mother talking on the street—with a Turlock off screen watching maybe, if we stick to that theory? The zoning law was still being written. The council insisted on the no-agriculture rule, and Larraine gave in to fight for more important ones for established businesses." Jax studied the back of the final sketches and frowned. "You'd better call Reuben."

Gracie blinked. Her theory had nothing to do with the mayor's new boyfriend.

She studied the sketch Jax saw—a man who might be Layman talking to Turlock Sr. and a couple of councilmen in a . . . barbershop? They were all looking out the window at. . . Larraine?

According to the date on the sketch, a week later, the mob stormed the courthouse, and Block and Bertie were dead.

Evie walked around the table again. "If Bertie was following the Turds. . . then the ex-mayor's lawyer and son visited a lot of useless property on the east side of town, including the area around the courthouse, and consulted with an out-of-town developer, a judge, and the town council outside of office hours. Reporting their findings maybe? Bertie said his mother was sad because she had to move." She tapped one of the first prints. "Why does she have to move?"

Gracie knitted her fingers into fists, waiting. Her neighborhood wasn't far from Jax's office or the courthouse—or the bar and tavern, for all that mattered. Afterthought was a small town. The school was across the street from the Satterwhite farm, but Bertie hadn't sketched it or her neighborhood —because he died?

Evie continued her narration of her path around the table while Jax texted Reuben. "Mrs. Walker is being told to move. Patel is burned out. A judge takes a bribe. Zoning laws go in place. And angry white men eye the new mayor who might stand in their way. Of what?"

Gracie almost melted in relief. "I wasn't seeing it in political context, just property. Except for the Corvette image, these are all properties on the east end of town, even the one of the men strolling Main Street. I suppose the group images might have nothing to do with property, but these others. . . If the Turlocks were at every one of these places, even if they're not in the sketch, why was the mayor's lawyer scouting the east side?"

Pris entered bearing more food. "Are we turning the library into a buffet? The kids are missing you."

Nick took the tray. Dante circled Pris's waist and pressed a kiss to her forehead—to Pris's head, grumpy, witchy, spiky Pris. Gracie squashed a surge of envy.

"Who's watching the kids?" Evie munched a cheese cracker Jax handed her and continued examining the sketches.

Gracie gave up. She wasn't needed here. "I'll keep an eye on them. You solve the mystery."

Nick picked up an empty plate and followed her. "I'm useless. I'll go back to tent building. I gather I won't be framing those prints any time soon."

"Mavis is with the kids," Pris called. "Dark clouds and all that. You might want to hang more Christmas lights."

"Right," Gracie muttered. "Let the teacher deal with the children. I'm sooo good with them."

"Well, you are," Nick agreed. "That doesn't mean you're any less important. You were the one who looked for the sketches and saw the pattern. But I gather Evie doesn't have any other job but snooping, so let her snoop."

She didn't want to feel grateful for that sop to her ego, but she did. "Fine, then. We'll take photos of the sketches, front and back, and then you can frame the originals and do your salesman thing."

Her mother was in the kitchen, ignoring the children in the breakfast booth, leaving Loretta to mop up spills, while Mavis perused a dusty tome from the kitchen shelf.

"No eye of newts here, Mom. Who's minding the store?"

Mavis glanced up. "Not Evie. I had to close up for lunch. Tell Jax he's sitting on a time bomb and Toby should probably leave town." She slid off the stool, tucking the tome under her arm.

Unfazed by this dire prediction, Nick asked, "May I help with anything?"

Mavis raised her eyebrows. Short, stout, wearing her graying hair in a frazzled bun, and cloaked in a red-and-green Christmas caftan, she studied him, then waved her hand regally. "Frame the sketch of me and Larraine. I'll hang it over my counter with your card in it."

She sauntered out without farewells. Gracie had to pry her mouth shut. That was Mavis giving her blessing—to Nick? Why? What had her mother seen in her crystal ball?

"I'll have to have cards made," Nick muttered. "Should have thought of that. Can't use the boutique cards anymore."

"A man's just been murdered, and you're worried about business cards?" She was trying to convince herself he was just as bad as the next man.

He looked her straight in the eyes. His were a gorgeous golden brown. "If you will donate your family frames, I can donate my time. What happens if we hold a public auction of Bertie's works, giving the proceeds to his brother's family? We could even put it online."

Gracie felt that look straight to her soul, striking every impossibility she'd ever envisioned. She didn't want to like him. She had to remember men were dangerous to her safety. "A public display of all those evil people presumably doing evil?"

"Precisely." That wasn't his genial salesman smile.

MONDAY EVENING, AFTER DINNER, NICK JOINED JAX AND THE SOLUTIONS CREW in the cellar man cave. The women had objected to his auction proposal as too dangerous. The men had other plans.

Nick was having his own second thoughts. He'd never been a Santa Claus sort of fellow. He needed cash. He didn't know why he'd made that offer—except a grieving widow and children and a mother who had already lost one son should know others cared. Someone was killing people for a reason. He could hope maybe Bertie's sketches would draw the cockroaches into plain sight.

He'd developed a dislike of manipulative cockroaches and a burning desire to stomp them all. His cousins would be first in line, but they were already in jail.

"What have you found on Layman?" Jax asked, slapping a photo of the cowboy-booted man on the cellar wall.

Above it were images of Bertie the artist, his brother Sammy, the late Mayor Arthur Block, and Patel's burned out fruit stand—all recent victims of violent crime. Well, in Bertie's case, maybe not violent.

"It would take a squad of Secret Service, FBI, IRS, and forensic accountants to penetrate the thicket of bribery, theft, mysterious mishaps, and blackmail related to Layman." Roark, the muscled Cajun wearing a tank top in midwinter, sipped a beer and leaned back on a gaming chair. "So far, he's remained untouched by the law. Ariel is picking apart local finances, but he's not laid down much money that can be traced. He's flying under the radar."

Jax turned to the scarred, professorial Black man working his way through computer files. "Reuben?"

"Layman and Block go way back. Not old school. Block graduated USC and Layman is Yale. Well, barely. Rumors say daddy bought him the degree. Layman inherited money. Block inherited overworked cotton fields he's been selling off piece by piece in his effort to build a rural empire. When you yanked the Witch Hill deal from under our ex-mayor, his empire started collapsing. He owed a lot of people. Looks like Layman is one of them." He printed out an image of the elusive businessman.

Nick frowned and hit a cue ball. He knew about back scratching. If the late mayor had something Layman wanted. . .

"There's nothing Block owns that isn't mortgaged to the hilt," Roark argued. "He has nothing to offer."

"He had power until we took it away." Jax taped up an image of Layman and the city council.

Reuben scrolled through more documents. "Someone did a damned good job trying to put Block back into power. Larraine's opponent tried to over-turn the election. A mob of out of towners tried to influence the judge into releasing Block—and maybe into overturning the recount? Both the governor and the council detest Larraine. Before he died, Block was the only one with the influence to control this town. Larraine's hands are tied unless she gives the council what they want in return for what she wants. No one's approached her about backscratching. Seems like the powerbrokers would want Block alive."

"But if it became evident that Mr. Block *wouldn't* regain control, did he become a potential liability because he knew too much?" Nick asked, because it seemed obvious.

"Possibly." Jax added the image of Judge Rhodes and Turlock Sr. next to Layman's. "Someone may still be pursuing whatever the goal is without Block."

"Layman's habit is to make grandiose promises of investment potential," Roark reported. "Since he drains his properties of cash, they inevitably end up bankrupt. That leaves the banks selling his assets, usually for half what's owed, and the contractors with empty pockets. Only someone really stupid or desperate for influence would actually give him money."

"Influence," Nick repeated, getting into this brainstorming. "He trades for influence—a council that does his bidding receives a piece of the action, a judge who upholds needed legislation is rewarded with a share, a landowner with nearby property who stands to make a killing. . ."

"You think like a crook, Brit boy." Reuben nodded approvingly.

"Takes one to know one," Nick muttered. He'd known his cousins weren't on the up and up. He'd ignored the signs because he'd loved the money. And the women. The line between him and the felonious Arthur Block was thin.

He had no clue how to survive without making deals. What the bloody hell did he do with his life now?

Roark hit up his computer. "We went through Block's files searching on that FL you found. It's looking like this FL was a client hunting real estate. Because of Block's arrest, the computer doesn't have anything more recent than last spring. But FL could stand for Franklin Layman. They may have been working together since last spring. The properties they looked at were all over. If he bought anything, it's not under FL, but we did find something interesting."

Everyone waited as Roark printed out a list.

"The files are thick, but here's a list of what appear to be parcel numbers." Roark handed it to Jax, who glanced down and shook his head.

Reuben took the list and began typing into a website. "First parcel is owned by Patel and mortgaged to *FLAB*? Flab? Are you kidding me? What kind of mortgage company calls itself fat? As in fat cats?"

"If Ariel's file is correct, FLAB is a mortgage company holding the deeds to half the property in Afterthought. It was created last year when Arthur Block was putting together his development plans for Witch Hill." Roark opened the folder on his computer. "FLAB, as in Franklin Layman Arthur Block LLC. All the mortgages were transferred from Block's name to this corporation."

"Crap." Jax looked over Roark's shoulder. "Block needed funds and offered up all the property he holds a mortgage on? Why the hell didn't these people go through a real bank?"

"How many people have the cash to make down payments on houses and office buildings?" Reuben asked, still working through the parcels as far as Nick could tell.

Nick was here to attest that only people who had money could borrow money, but that seemed obvious as well.

"So Block literally owns half of Afterthought?" Jax asked in incredulity. "I thought Loretta's parents did."

"Which may be why Arthur thought he owned Witch Hill—he owns everything else." Reuben sat back and glared at his computer. "Loretta's parents might even have been trying to prevent him from acquiring more. Not everyone's land is mortgaged. If I'm reading the parcel map correctly, this house is free and clear, as is the Psychic Solutions shop. But your accountant friend's office building isn't, Jax. A lot of those buildings on Main Street are mortgaged through FLAB. No wonder Block had influence. He owned these guys."

Nick studied the image of the parcel map on Reuben's computer. "Bertie's scenes were mostly on the east side of town, Gracie said. That's where most of those highlighted parcels are."

Jax slapped an image of a fancy resort with palm trees on the wall. "Mayor Block's goal was always to make Afterthought a destination for rich city dwellers, with the hopes they'd drive up the value of his cotton fields."

"But his mortgages were already underwater when he transferred them to the LLC." Roark sipped his beer.

"And his property is mostly downtown or on the north side, away from the interstate, unlike the Satterwhite farm." Reuben started tapping fast on his keyboard. "Which isn't mortgaged at all."

Jax glared at his suspect wall. "I won't go into tax laws, but it's possible, if she was convinced it was for the good of the community, Mrs. S might trade her prime eastside land for the LLC's ragtag collection and some other bits that might become valuable. . ."

Nick interrupted Jax. "First, they'd have to frighten off everyone using Mrs. Satterwhite's property so she didn't feel as if she were putting people out of their homes and businesses."

"Bingo," Reuben whispered. "Get rid of the Antique Barn, the Walkers—what else is there? Then she's receiving no rent. The devil stops by and whispers in her ear. Why not trade—if it's good for the community and it's not taxable."

"We need to talk to Mrs. S," Nick said flatly.

"Mavis," the others cried in unison.

Fifteen

"You do not want to get our mother involved if Mrs. S is at risk," Evie warned when the men reported their findings Tuesday morning. She noticed Jax hadn't been foolish enough to mention this to her last night, after the men left their basement cave.

"Mavis will call in our aunts and the witches union and even Val from Atlanta if she deems the problem serious enough." Gracie buttered toast at the counter.

"And this is a bad thing how?" Assembly-line fashion, Dante cut up the buttered toast for the kids.

Pris had dressed the twins in flannel Santa Claus pajamas. Combined with their dark curls, they were a holiday card in the making. Evie suffered a pang of envy. Instant children had a certain appeal, although she was still none too certain about her parental skills. Poor Loretta was her test run.

"You have seen our mothers in action," Pris reminded him. "Logic is not their strength, unless you see beard burning as a sensible response. There is a reason our family was thrown out of Salem or whatever." She stopped and thought about it. "Although given that back then, no one listened to women, I really can't blame our ancestors for flinging hexes and burning brooms."

Evie rolled her eyes at Pris's insight and brought the discussion back to today. "If there is any chance that Mrs. Satterwhite is being used, or the town's future is jeopardized, a plague of locusts would be mild in comparison to our mothers' reaction. *Not logical* does not even begin to cover the circus they'll create."

She wished they were discussing holiday pageants. Murder at Christmas was just not right.

"Judge S used to be sweet on Mavis," Gracie said thoughtfully. "Whatever our mothers did, he'd probably let them get away with it."

Evie flung a toast crust at her. That was not the direction she wanted to go.

"Is that how they avoid prosecution for burning brooms?" Nick caught the crust before it hit Gracie.

Evie forced her wandering thoughts back to the conversation. "Yup. Satterwhite concluded the brooms were an illusion and harmful to no one. The judge has a few blind spots. I'd still rather have them replacing the town Christmas tree."

She really wanted to go down to the Barn and look for Sammy's ghost, but maybe that wasn't such a great idea given the sheriff's suspicions. It took a while for spirit energy to coalesce anyway. "Gracie and I can take some of Pris's cookies next door to the judge's mother and have a neighborly discussion. Give us a list of concerns so we cover everything."

"I have some fresh banana bread. Let me wrap that up." Pris gestured at the loaves on the counter.

"Can I go?" Loretta asked. "We don't have practice until this afternoon."

"You won't learn much," Evie warned. "Mrs. S is nearing ninety. Sweet as can be but that's intense magnolia sweet. She's made of tough stuff. She'll interrogate you."

Loretta shrugged. "I'll be your distraction."

Evie knuckled her ward's head. "You're too old for eleven. Invite her and the judge to Christmas dinner. If we haven't solved anything by then, we'll let Mavis at her."

Which was how Evie ended up leading a holiday parade of Gracie and Loretta and platters of goodies across the lawn to Mrs. Satterwhite's elegant home.

Unlike Evie's neglected but colorful Victorian, the Satterwhite's gingerbread lady was always freshly painted in white. The judge hired a host of maintenance workers to clean and spruce it up. Their elegant porch had a pristine blue ceiling, polished wooden floors with colorful outdoor carpets, a small Christmas tree in a pot, railings wrapped in real evergreen boughs, and cushioned wicker chairs. It had probably been photographed for every garden, interior design, and architecture magazine in existence.

Evie preferred her cluttered porch of birds' nests, frost-bitten geraniums, and messy porch swings where the kids could roll around toy trucks without harm.

"Not good for reading," Loretta whispered as they rang the bell.

"Good for the backs of old ladies," Evie whispered back, tickled that her ward understood the differences in their living spaces.

A housekeeper in lumpy dark woolen skirt and sweater answered.

"Mrs. Brown." Evie lifted her plate of cookies. "We've come bearing gifts. Does Mrs. S have time for a chat?"

The housekeeper opened the door. "She'll be glad to see y'all. She needs to sit down and rest for a bit anyway. She's been trying to do too much. I'll bring tea. C'mon in."

The waxed halls smelled of evergreen and scented candles. The stair rail was dressed in pine and sparkly silver ribbons. Mrs. S hired decorators.

"Wow, is this what Val's house is supposed to look like?" Gracie whispered.

Considering the scarred floors, orange flocked wallpaper, and stacks of boxes and furniture their aunt had left behind, Evie tried not to laugh. "Not unless she wants to send us fortunes to hire help. It's not as if we invite the garden club over for tea." Evie followed Mrs. Brown to the sunny parlor at the back.

To Evie's shock, boxes filled the parlor—not Christmas presents but moving cartons.

"What a lovely surprise! Come in, come in, sit down." Holding a cane for balance, Mrs. Satterwhite strolled into the room as if she were still young and hosting a lavish party. "And you brought Loretta! How are they treating you, child? I knew your grandmother in her day."

While everyone settled into flowered, overstuffed couches and chairs, Evie opened her extra sense to study her hostess. Sadness surrounded her elderly neighbor. There was the usual fog in her fourth chakra, the heart, possibly a little darker than usual. At ninety, a bad ticker was to be expected. But it was the unusual bleakness of her overall aura that worried Evie.

"What's with the boxes?" she asked at the first opportunity.

Mrs. S waited until the housekeeper had poured tea and left before answering. "Hugh convinced me it's time to move into one of those residence homes where people come running if I fall down."

"One of those medic alert buttons would bring the paramedics right over," Gracie protested. "You have your room set up down here, don't you?

And if you carry your phone, we're right next door and can be here instantly."

"That's sweet of you, dear. You've been the most entertaining neighbors. . ." Her cup rattled a little in her frail hand. "Your great-aunt was a hoot in her day. But. . . well, I. . ."

Evie saw the gray flicker in her aura and frowned. "You're worried about more than your health."

Once tall and straight-backed, Mrs. S had shrunk with age. Her narrow shoulders slumped. "It's my mind, dear. I fear it's going. I hate that. I refuse to be a burden on my son."

Loretta shook her head just as Evie did. Interested in what her Indigo child was seeing, Evie let her speak first.

"Your bubble is big and glittery. I don't see any shadows on it. Some people, when they're not quite right, have shadows." She shut up abruptly, as if she'd revealed more than she ought.

That was the first Evie had heard about shadows, but she wouldn't question now.

She handed Loretta a cookie in approval. "Loretta's right. There's nothing wrong with your noggin. What makes you think you're losing it?"

Mrs. S smiled faintly. "You have a quaint way of expressing yourself. But I've taken to seeing and hearing things that aren't there. I've called Hugh so many times in the middle of the night that he had my doctor going over my medications to make certain I'm not being overdosed."

Gracie nodded in understanding. "I have a neighbor who swore she had squirrels in her living room, and they talked to her. Once they adjusted her meds, she was fine."

Mrs. S smiled in relief. "So you understand. I'm seeing and hearing my dear Kenneth, who passed on a decade ago. I think it means my time is near."

Evie shook her head again. "It's comforting to know he's here to lead you to the next plane, but if your meds have been checked, then it's not in your head. He's either really here. . . or someone wants you to believe he's here."

This was not the subject they'd come to talk about, but it was equally worrisome.

Their hostess frowned. "I'm not certain I understand."

"Evie sees ghosts," Loretta piped up. "Who is Kenneth?"

"I attract ghosts, at least," Evie corrected. "Kenneth is Mrs. S's husband, the judge's father. Would it be all right if I poked around a little? Is there any specific room where you're seeing him?"

"Oh, I don't think. . ." Her wrinkled face sagged, then brightened just a little. "You really think he may have come to warn me?"

"Is that what he's doing?" Gracie asked, doing a better job of hiding her eager interest than Evie. "What is he warning you about?"

"I'm not sure, dear." Her wrinkles settled into a thoughtful frown. "I'm usually asleep. I sort of feel him, and I'm not sure I'm really awake. He tries to tell me something, but. . . It's not clear. I sense worry and love, and in the morning, I find a feather on my floor. Marjorie wants to replace my pillows."

Without asking permission, Evie went in search of Marjorie Brown, the housekeeper and cook. Middle-aged, plump, and efficient, Marjorie had evidently been listening. She met Evie in the hall and gestured to follow her down the hall.

"Miz Charlotte is as sharp as a tack," Marjorie whispered as they traversed the thick carpet. "These spells didn't start happening until she started getting them offers."

"What offers?" Evie stopped when the maid did, in the doorway of an ornate bedroom. Fat roses and peonies in shades of pink adorned plump pillows and comforters and splattered the walls. A neutral gray carpet covered the floor. A florist bouquet of pink roses filled a crystal vase on the mahogany dresser.

"For Mr. Kenneth's farm. Started last spring. She threw the letters out. Then they started calling. She gave them the judge's number. He's handling it, but she's been having nightmares for months. There ain't nothing wrong with her head. She's just plain worried."

"All right, that's good to know. Will it be okay to leave me here alone for a little bit? Mr. Kenneth has been gone a long time. I don't know if he'll recognize me." That was one way of putting it. Evie didn't really know why ghosts materialized for her.

"Your mama is a good woman. She raised good daughters. You do what you have to do. Miz Charlotte don't belong in no home." Marjorie walked away.

The housekeeper would lose her job and the roof over her head if Mrs. S moved. Evie got that. She didn't know what she could do about it, exactly, but one thing at a time.

Warily, she stepped into a room heavily scented with roses and the powdery cologne her hostess wore. Her short legs would require a ladder to climb onto that fancy tester bed. She chose a low ladies' boudoir chair decorated in a collage of gray and rose flowers.

"Mr. Satterwhite?" she whispered, opening her third eye. "If you're here, could you make yourself known? We're awfully worried about Mrs. S."

Was that a thread of gray near the floor-length floral drapery? Clenching her hands, Evie pulled together her usually scattered thoughts and focused all her considerable energy on that thread of gray. "What are you trying to tell your wife?"

It could be wishful thinking, but the gray appeared to widen. The room became chillier. Evie left her third eye open so she could hold her focus.

"Don't sell." The words resonated in her head more than her ears. "Protect her. Danger."

The wisp of gray dissipated like smoke, leaving Evie to wonder if she had imagined it all. Really, dog walking was so much simpler.

Now what did she do? *Protect Mrs. S?* How?

From whom?

Someone had shot Arthur Black, killed Sammy Walker in broad daylight, and possibly drugged Bertie. They'd burned a man's livelihood.

Was Mrs. Satterwhite next? Sammy had died on her land. Evie tried not to choke on fear.

Sixteen

~~

WITH A CLIENT SITTING ACROSS HIS DESK, JAX HELD HIS PHONE CLOSE TO HIS EAR as Reuben on the other end read off information hacked from the sheriff's computer. Jax had given up telling Evie's team that hacking was illegal. The computer whizzes had probably been born with processor umbilical cords and had backdoor portals into so many servers they could access the Kremlin.

He supposed it was a blessing that Evie offered R&R opportunities to use their expertise for justice instead of going rogue.

"No one saw any cars at the Barn except Evie's," Reuben reported. "Didn't mean there wasn't one, just that no one looked, and the victim had no security cameras. Time of death is based on Nick's report and that of the customer who came in before noon and found the body. The coroner confirmed a slightly wider range, but we know ten to twelve is the widest time frame. Bullet is for a .38, same as used on Block, but that's a common weapon and meaningless. Can't even tell if it's the same gun until they find it. The Barn hasn't been cleaned in months. Fingerprints everywhere. They have zero leads. Motive is our only hope."

"And we have none except for wild speculation," Jax concluded gloomily.

"And Evie's ghosts, exactly. And I can't see a gazillionaire like Layman crawling around in attics and doing his own dirty work. One more thing. . ."

It sounded as if he were reading from a different page. "Prelim tox report on Bertie shows opioids and fentanyl. He died of an overdose several days before his corpse flattened Block. Weird part—no paraphernalia or traces found elsewhere with the body." Without further speculation, he hung up.

Damn, what had Evie got herself mixed up in this time? If there were no needles or traces of drugs in the attic. . . *Triple damn hell.*

Jax clicked his pen in irritation before regarding his privileged client on the other side of the desk. "Evie says you're in danger and may need to relocate for the time being. Is that feasible?"

"Evie said that?" Tobias Block asked in amusement, obviously unaware that death could touch him as it had his father and Bertie. "She's worried about my worthless hide?"

"Not particularly." Jax's irritation escalated for no good reason, except Evie had dated the former mayor's golden boy in high school. "She's just passing on information from her mother. What do you know about the Satterwhite property?"

Toby straightened and became wary. Finally. "Why?"

Just for fun, Jax gave him a mixture of truth and speculation. "Because Kenneth Satterwhite's ghost is concerned for his wife, who is receiving offers on that land that she wants to refuse."

Tobias shook his long blond ponytail, in confusion or rejection, it was hard to say. "And you buy that ghost crap?"

Well, no one had said Tobias was more than book smart. But Jax needed all the information he could gather before he confronted Judge Satterwhite about those *offers*. Could he sound Toby out about drugs? But Evie would have told him if Toby did drugs, so he stayed focused on the property.

"Then let me lay it out in terms you might understand," Jax suggested. "Your father's computers show that early this spring he was showing a client called FL properties on the east side of town. Do you know anything about that?"

Toby shrugged. "Dad's a Realtor. That's his job."

Jax didn't see his space cadet client as a killer, but he trod carefully. "After your dad went to jail, did he have his lawyer showing the properties?"

Toby looked puzzled. "Dad's office has been essentially closed since last spring. I suppose Mr. Turlock could have done him a favor in hopes of getting paid."

That's what Jax suspected anyway. Carefully, he led his client down the garden path. "It appears Bertie Walker may have been following the Turlocks around to the various properties this FL looked at."

Toby's reaction remained neutral. "Unless Bertie uncovered gold to pay the bills, how does this concern me?"

The airhead was holding back. Jax tapped his pen impatiently. "Your father made deals. They weren't always cash deals and won't necessarily show up in his records. If Turlock was handling real estate deals, he expects a commission. Your father's death put a wrench in that hope. Unless you have other computers or notebooks or information, there may not be much we can do. So far, my accountants have found nothing in his normal financial records."

His accountants—his financial genius sister Ariel and her mad consort, Roark, neither of whom were actually CPAs. But if they couldn't find the money, no one could. Toby still hadn't mentioned the LLC they'd found.

Toby slumped. "I've been hunting all over the house and his office and can't find the binder he kept his confidential information in. I'd hoped he kept copies in his computer."

Jax raised his eyebrows. "Interesting. We've only been going over the normal information. Your father's attorney insisted that your father had funds, but we're not finding more than the usual. But if he had hidden accounts or holdings. . . We can start by tracing websites he visited. That's a time-consuming effort and likely to be costly. Should we proceed?"

His client squirmed in obvious discomfort. "Look, I know my dad had some shady dealings with some unsavory characters. The prosecutor practically crucified him on everything that went down last spring on the Witch Hill development. That's all public record. They set the bail so high he didn't have enough unmortgaged property to pay it, so he couldn't do much. He may have used attorney-client privilege to put Turlock up to something. I just don't know what. I admit that I was suspicious and paid Bertie to follow both Turlocks around, but Bertie was never a talker, and I didn't find anything useful in the sketches he showed me."

Slowly he turns, step by step. . . Jax had an appreciation of what it must have been like working with the Three Stooges.

"Did you keep any of the sketches?" Jax asked, hoping his client would come clean.

Toby shook his head. "Just the ones we left with the gallery."

Hard to tell if that was a lie, but if Toby was suspicious. . . it was looking more and more like the death of Bertie might be related to Block after all. Evie was damned good, even when she didn't know what she was doing.

"All right, let me make some more inquiries. I have one more lead, but after that, it's the computer forensics team who has to step up." R&R would dig in anyway, but Jax didn't have to tell him that.

"You didn't find a single property that I can sell to pay the bills?" Toby slumped in the chair and shoved his hands into his pockets.

"All mortgaged. Bankruptcy looks like your best alternative. Unless you have a real estate license, you'd have to pay commission to sell them. I don't know land prices, but your father did. I suspect all the land is mortgaged well beyond what you'll receive for it."

Toby nodded gloomily. "That was my assumption. I don't know how Turlock thinks I can pay him more."

"How did you plan to pay the reward you offered?" Jax asked out of curiosity and for the sake of Evie and her team.

"GoFundMe. Dad had a lot of connections, and they're all paying in. Even the city council donated. We're not there yet, but we will be. I can't use that for anything but the reward though."

"Do you know a Franklin Layman by any chance?" Jax threw that out there to see his client's reaction.

"A real sleazebag, I hear, but ten kinds of rich. Layman is dating the mother of a friend of mine. She doesn't like him, so we looked him up."

Inch by inch. . . The mayor's son had learned from a true gambler to play cards close to his chest.

Jax returned to opening and shutting his ballpoint. "Would the friend to whom you refer be the daughter of the gallery owner who offered to show Bertie's sketches?"

Toby looked surprised again. "You know about Verity?"

"Evie talks to Bertie's ghost," Jax reminded him. "Never underestimate what she knows."

"Evie and her whole family are snoops, but they're good at it, I'll grant." Toby looked thoughtful.

Interesting perspective. Evie and her family could have gone around town looking for information on all the parties involved, but that would take time. She had no particularly good reason to convince people she obtained her information from ghosts. She simply did and let people think as they would—as did the rest of the family.

Toby continued. "Verity said Bertie's sketches were quality work, but she really didn't expect her mother to show them. They're not exactly representative of what the gallery does. We were surprised when she accepted them."

Jax set his pen aside so he wouldn't destroy it. "Do you happen to know if Bertie had a stash of artwork anywhere besides the Antique Barn?"

Toby sat up straighter. "Where Sammy Walker worked? *Sammy* had sketches?"

Interesting. Jax watched his client's face as he told him, "Sammy had several but apparently not all."

Without revealing anything, Toby pushed himself up. "Damn. If Bertie left stashes elsewhere. . ." Apparently realizing he was repeating Jax's question, he shut up.

"That's the question, isn't it?" Jax asked. "Was Sammy killed for those sketches?" In which case, Nick and everyone in Evie's house was in danger. "Was your father killed for them? What did Bertie see?"

"Buildings and people, that's all Bertie ever saw." Toby headed for the door.

"That's the business your father dealt in," Jax called after him. But he figured Toby already knew that.

What did Bertie know might be the key to the whole case—unless they could find Block's little black book.

❧

Carrying boxes of paper ornaments pasted and colored by the kids, Evie met Jax and Gracie at the courthouse. Their mother's senior citizen gang had bought another tree for the lawn and was stringing it with lights. The material damage left by the mob had been hauled away, but the spiritual wounds needed healing. The courthouse's sparkly new windows had bars on them—bad juju. Cheerful lights and evergreens were needed.

"You talked to Toby?" Evie asked Jax, setting down her box so she could hug and kiss him because he looked decidedly sour. "He's keeping his father's funeral private?"

"And in another county. Your old boyfriend isn't a total airhead, and I'm not sure he's telling me everything." Jax hugged her back.

"Hang this star on top, will you, Jax?" Mavis called from her stepladder. Her short arms couldn't reach the treetop from her perch.

Evie pecked his cheek. "That's her way of showing her approval," she whispered.

"Not setting my hair on fire works as well." He climbed up and set the star straight, then plugged it into the string of lights.

The day was gloomy enough for the lights to look festive when someone plugged them into the outdoor outlet. Everyone cheered and Gracie hung the first aluminum foil star from a branch. Evie's veterinarian cousin Iddy hung popcorn-and-cranberry roping for the birds.

Judge Satterwhite stepped outside wearing an overcoat and not his robes. Mavis waved at him. He straightened and brushed his white hair back, but spotting Jax and Evie, he hurried down to meet them as planned.

"His aura isn't as clear as usual," Evie whispered. "I'd better go with you. It's either that, or I go down to the Barn and look for Sammy's ghost."

Jax didn't exactly look happy about either, but he was just her team's lawyer. If she meant to run a business, she had to be boss. Somehow. Maybe. Sorta.

She was still taking baby steps away from her dog-walking persona. Observation was her superpower, and she had to broaden her spectrum.

The Oldies' Café was the closest thing Afterthought had to a coffee shop. It stayed busy—which was why Bertie had sketched the town council members meeting in a barbershop and bar, where they weren't quite as visible to the entire town. Pris really needed to open a café in the empty boutique just down the street, but if Dante returned to Italy. . . *Focus, Evie.*

At this hour, the diner wasn't as busy as it would be later. They found a booth by a window.

"What's this about?" the judge asked after he'd ordered a coffee and donuts.

Evie sipped her tea and let Jax open his phone to show the judge images of Bertie's sketches. She kept her eye on the older man's aura. It didn't seem to flicker with any particular recognition.

"We have reason to believe Block's lawyer was showing east side property to a developer. Bertie Walker followed him all summer and into the fall. We don't have all the sketches, but we've taken pictures of those we've seen."

Nice safety net, Jax, don't let anyone know about their trove of artwork.

Artwork the gallery owner had tried to hide? For why?

"Do you recognize them?" Jax handed over the phone so the judge could flip through.

Another good move, Evie decided, totally tickled with her brilliant fiancé. See if the judge opened up without questioning. His aura. . . she couldn't quite translate what was happening there. The judge was an honest man, but all men his age had shadows of some sort, if only a lifetime of doubts. If she had any proof, she'd say his revealed anger. . . and maybe *fear?*

"Are you sure that's what Turlock was doing?" The judge handed the phone back. "Or Bertie, for all that matters. The boy wasn't quite right in the head."

"Just like I'm not quite right in the head," Evie said cheerfully. "But thinking outside the box does not mean we don't know what's going on around us. We can tell from Bertie's sketches that he was on those properties. If I recognize them, you do. We do not have pictures of Turlock, or his son, but Toby said he asked Bertie to keep an eye on both of them. Bertie was trying to earn money with these sketches to help his mother—who said she had to move from the house she rents from you. Do you know anything about that?"

The judge looked genuinely shocked, *good*. Evie hadn't wanted to believe he'd put that poor woman and her family out of a home. Half her groceries and part of her income probably came from her garden.

Satterwhite wrapped his gnarled hands around his coffee cup as if to warm them. "Louise Walker is having difficulty making the rent. Sammy and his kids moved in with her, ostensibly to help take care of things, but feeding them can't be helping a lot. She's been catching up gradually with his contribution, but she's still raising her late daughter's two teenage grandkids, and feeding Sammy's family. She sells produce at the farmer's market, but that doesn't pay in the winter. The teens get some SSI, and she has social security, but kids aren't cheap. I'm not sure how she's paying what she does."

"That's why Bertie wanted to sell his sketches." Evie frowned and studied her tea. "But if Sammy was already helping his mother, paying Bertie for sketches so his brother could take the money to her doesn't make a great deal of sense."

Jax tapped her hand, reminding her to focus. She scrolled back through the phone images. "Except for Patel, all this farmland Turlock was purportedly looking at belongs to your mother, doesn't it?"

Satterwhite nodded and the lines in his face deepened. "A development corporation has been pestering her to sell. She won't, of course. The taxes would be too steep. I talked to them, and they offered a tax-free land exchange."

He sighed and looked out the window at people passing by, carrying bags and boxes destined for holiday gifts.

Evie elbowed Jax. This was where lawyer talk was needed. Or maybe just man talk.

"But the exchange involved Block's already mortgaged properties and people living on them." Jax completed the judge's thoughts. "So you couldn't move the Walkers or whoever to new homes."

"If I thought the developer meant to build an asset to the community. . . I might have worked it out somehow," the judge admitted. "But he has a bad reputation. And while the trial was going on, I didn't think it ethical to deal with Block's properties, even if they were inside a corporation. The whole thing seemed suspect to me. But now. . ." He shook his head in sorrow.

Had the pressure to sell gone up?

Evie politely didn't say Arthur Block was no loss to the community. He was a loss, in his own way, and he'd been Toby's dad. It still made no sense to kill the man who could make the deal happen—except *now that Block's death ended the trial, there were no ethical barriers to the sale.*

"I hate to say this. . ." She hesitated, knowing the judge was open-minded but probably not open-minded enough to believe his father was talking to her from beyond. "But if people in the way of this land deal are being driven off. . . Your mother may be in some danger."

Surprisingly, Satterwhite nodded agreement. "That's why I want her removed to a retirement home in the city, where she'd be surrounded by security. My kids live in Charleston. They'll look in on her."

"And yourself?" Jax asked.

The judge opened his jacket. "I'm carrying a gun these days."

Seventeen

With Christmas music blaring, baking aromas filling the air, and the children bouncing like crickets, Gracie gave up on writing. Joining in the holiday spirit, she helped Loretta swathe the staircase with fake evergreen boughs they found in the attic. Aster and the twins "helped" by pulling off old tinsel and relocating it to the Christmas tree.

"Is this the lead kind of tinsel?" Loretta whispered as shiny shreds fell on the stairs and the hall below.

"Lead? There's lead in tinsel?" Alarmed, Gracie studied the mess they were making. "Is that why they quit making it?"

Loretta nodded solemnly. "This is really old garland."

"Like everything else in here." With a sigh, she began scooping up the threads and pulling them off before the kids could make any more depredations. "Our parents survived lead tinsel. . . Although maybe they'd have been a lot smarter if they hadn't inhaled the dust."

Pris appeared in the hallway below. "Soup's on. Someone want to take some out to that poor idiot freezing in the garage?"

Nick had been out there framing sketches all morning. Gracie didn't know what to make of the man, but he'd already carried the requested picture down to her mother's Psychic Solutions shop. She thought Reuben had printed business cards for him so he could install one in the frame. She wasn't certain why he'd do that.

For now, she assumed he was avoiding the high octane excitement building in the house as presents grew under the tree, and the kids shrieked and bounced off walls.

"I'll do it," she offered, not out of generosity, but because she wanted something. That made it all right, didn't it? She wasn't interested in him or anything, except as a partner in crime. He seemed to understand her need to help.

She untangled Alex, Nan, and Aster from the tree, helped them clean up, and led them into the kitchen where Loretta was already presiding over the breakfast nook. Pris had Dante pounding out his frustration on bread dough. The archeologist was almost healed and stewing in frustration at his inability to start the dig on the twins' newly inherited farm. Apparently permits and grants and legal whatnot were needed before he could proceed.

Leaving the children in their hands, Gracie carried a giant soup cup and fresh bread out the back and over to the garage.

The Brit had hooked up an electric heater near his workbench, where several old frames leaned in various stages of renovation. Cheap gilding had been stripped off the more ornate ones. Several deep-set frames had been sanded and repainted, and he already had a print matted in one of them.

"You work fast." She set the tray down on the bench. "Wouldn't you rather come in and warm up?"

"Not cold." He was wearing only an open flannel shirt over a turtleneck, with a wool scarf dangling down his. . . nicely sculpted. . . chest. He stepped back to admire his work. "What do you think?"

"They look like real art instead of Bertie's scribbling," she admitted, admiring the result. "And those frames are worth something now that they're prettied up?"

"These aren't shoddy, stapled plywood from China." He hefted a dry, newly stained one and showed it to her. "If you went to a frame shop, this would set you back a pretty penny. Solid wood, mitered construction, your family bought good stuff."

"That would be Val. She tended to marry rich men. The rest of us, not so much. I don't know where you'll find customers willing to pay more than Wal-Mart prices." She held up the sketch of the children in the schoolyard. "Won't they need glass?"

"To protect the work, sure, but the kind is up to the customer. If they want glass, I can arrange it, but it will cost extra. And we're not selling these to discount store customers. I'm working out a website on Reuben's computer. I understand why your family doesn't want an auction, so I'm keeping the location of these secret by selling direct from the website. Reuben's set up a mailbox address in the city so it looks legit."

"No one can trace the mailbox address? That's like, one of those storefronts that give you a street address and hold your mail?" She fretted over the deceit and who might see through it.

"Yup. Website requires a street address. We're good. Quit worrying. I know we're not talking fortunes, but if nothing else, Bertie will receive some well-deserved recognition. Once the website is ready, I'll send press releases to local media."

"Press releases? Wow." Publicity. Her family avoided publicity. Until Evie decided to go public with her Solutions business, they'd kept their gifts quiet. But this was what Nick did for a living, and for Bertie. . .

The Brit set down the frame and inhaled the aroma of soup in his cup. "This smells delicious."

"I don't know what happens once Pris and Dante return to Italy. We'll all starve. So enjoy while you can." He'd probably move on then. She'd be back at work. This needed to be done now. If she meant to write mysteries, she had to learn how to investigate them.

She crouched down to examine another frame, mentally flailing over what she wanted to ask.

"I'd like to poke around that gallery a little more," he said out of the blue, sipping at minestrone broth. "Jax said something about the Layman person dating the gallery owner. And we have the sketch with her daughter and Toby and the others, so the daughter might know something. I called there this morning, and Verity works afternoons."

Gracie thought her jaw dropped. She hastily bit her tongue and glanced up at him. Had he taken up the family habit of reading minds?

He was inhaling soup and bread and watching her as if she were the last woman on earth. She hastily adjusted her sweater and stood up. That didn't help. His gaze followed, and she could feel the heat of it clear to the bone. The sweater must be too small. Maybe it had shrunk. She should have put on a jacket.

She swallowed. She had to be brave like Evie. "I was thinking the same thing. We could ask this Verity person if she's seen more of Bertie's sketches and if they'd like to contribute to the website for his family."

He beamed. "Most excellent. This afternoon?"

It wasn't as if she was doing much of anything else. She nodded. "Should we take the color sketch with the Corvette? Use that as our excuse for returning?"

"Good thought. If it's not part of the pattern, it should be harmless. And maybe she'd like to buy it. Let me finish up here. Say, in about an hour? Do we need to do more Christmas shopping?"

"I'll ask if anyone needs anything. There's always something. But be warned, Pris will want spices from some fancy store downtown. This could take a while." She'd be in his company all afternoon. Flashing warning lights and alarms screamed in her head.

Recklessly, she refused to heed the warnings. She liked being a school-teacher, but she wanted. . . something more. She had to overcome her cautious nature and decide what she wanted.

She ate lunch and hastily tried on several tops, but everything she owned showed her boobs. She was too big in all the wrong places. She needed to look more like Pris. Maybe she could borrow from Evie's closet. . . Except her sister wore t-shirts with ridiculous sayings and didn't own anything decent.

Maybe ridiculous sayings kept people reading words instead of studying boobs. Evie might be onto something there.

She found a blouse that tied with a big bow at her neck. The bow had long, wide ties that blew about in the wind and distracted to some degree. Then she pulled on a cardigan and considered borrowing one of her mother's shawls. Oh well, too late for that. She debated skirt or pants and decided on pants. They seemed safer.

Evie was back scraping walls in the guest room—which probably meant she was plotting. Pris and Dante had the kids studying. Gracie kissed Aster, collected shopping lists, and was outside with the Kia keys by the time Nick emerged, showered and dressed like an announcer on BBC. He picked up his briefcase with the sketch.

"It's a shame you have to hide behind a website," she said tartly, climbing into the driver's seat. "You could have every female on the planet drooling over your social media posts."

He looked vaguely startled. "Me? Why? And would it sell art?"

She sighed and bit her tongue. If he didn't know his photo would have women swarming to the site, she wasn't telling him. "Forget it. Gallery first?"

"Yes, after we question Verity, if we can, then we'll be free to have fun." He settled back in the seat with a smile.

Gracie didn't want to know what his idea of fun was. She hoped it meant thrift stores. "You think Verity might know where to find Bertie's surprise sketch?"

"One can hope. If not, maybe she'll drop a tidbit that might lead us to

Bertie's drug dealer or Layman's plans. I don't suppose she'd actually tell us why she and Toby had Bertie following the Turlocks."

"You probably don't suppose right, but it's a good goal."

Once in the city, they found a parking space down the street from the gallery and walked under the ancient oaks to the renovated townhouse with its elegant molding and shiny black door. The bell rang as they entered. As before, no one was present.

"Terrible way to do business," Gracie murmured.

"Only one person on the premises to keep costs down." He scouted the walls, presumably looking for Bertie's sketches. "They haven't hung any, much less any mantel-size one."

Gracie went directly to the small desk in a back corner and delicately rang the bell. No one appeared. Nick joined her, frowning.

The telephone on the desk rang. No one answered.

With all the confidence she didn't possess, Nick strode toward the door that said "private" and pushed it open, then shouted, "Call the police, Grania!"

He dived inside while Gracie's trembling fingers hit 911.

Eighteen

Nick flung the first object he touched—an empty metal frame—at the balaclava-masked intruder rushing out the rear exit. The frame connected with a puffy coat shoulder, producing a grunt, but only a minor stumble.

Ignoring the bound and gagged gallery owner at the desk, Nick dashed across the crowded workroom and tackled the escaping thief, grabbing fistfuls of coat for his effort.

Encumbered by an armful of small frames, the thief tried to tug himself loose rather than fight. Nick flung his weight into bringing the other man down, but his grip on the slippery fabric threw him off.

Grace shrieked like a banshee, and the intruder struggled harder.

In the heat of the fray, logic wasn't uppermost, but the frame the thief jabbed into his thigh brought clarity. Nick released the coat and grabbed the thief's haul instead, tugging hard.

Unexpectedly, and to his utter amazement, the heavy load of framed artwork jerked free. Nick staggered backward, arms full of slipping wood and metal, and hit the floor on his rump. Startled, the thief scarpered down an alley.

Dumping the artwork, Nick took off in pursuit. At the end of the alley, a man in a puffy down coat hopped on a small black motorcycle and sped off. Cursing, remembering the two terrified women he'd left in possible jeopardy, Nick gave up. If the bike had a license, he didn't see it.

As he turned back, a nondescript white vehicle pulled from a driveway and sped away. For half a second, Nick hoped some Good Samaritan chased the thief. He quickly rid himself of that idiocy and realized artwork couldn't be carried on a bike. That had been the getaway car.

Cursing himself for three kinds of fool, he limped back to the gallery. Metal frames *hurt*.

Back in the office, Gracie was weeping while attempting to disconnect the plastic zip ties binding the gallery owner. She'd removed Mrs. Janus's gag, although that had obviously been a mistake. The sheer volume of the woman's ranting should have encouraged Gracie to stuff it back in.

Because he needed reassurance as much as he figured she did, Nick wrapped his arms around Gracie's waist and kissed her ear. "Let me do it, luv. I hear sirens. Go signal them?"

Shakily, she nodded. She seemed to be staggering as if unbalanced, but she made it to the showroom door without falling.

Nick turned back to the cursing gallery owner. "Knife? Scissors?"

She blessedly shut up and nodded at her desk. "Third drawer down."

He cut the main tie and left her freeing her wrists with the scissors while he returned to the work the thief had dropped. Stacking them upright, they seemed unharmed. Several had glass and thick frames, which was why the load was so heavy. Maybe the thief grabbed more than he could carry.

Only then did he realize what he was holding.

The cops eased in, guns out, and he nearly dropped to the floor and held his hands up. But Mrs. Janus returned to her hysterical shouting, and Gracie joined him in picking up the fallen pieces. He took her silence as shock, so he played the part of gallant hero and didn't descend into a gibbering prat.

One of the cops ran into the alley in pursuit of nothing. The other holstered his gun, regarded Nick dubiously, then turned to quieting the gallery owner.

"They stole everything!" She wept. "Everything! I'll have to close and start over." She reached for her phone.

"Methinks the art world is even more crooked than the antique," Nick whispered.

Gracie nodded agreement.

"Ma'am, if we could have a description. . ." The young cop tried to get a word in edgewise.

When Mrs. Janus hysterically hit her phone contact buttons rather than reply, Nick reluctantly offered, "One intruder."

Mrs. Janus ignored him and spoke to what was apparently her insurance agent.

The cop held up his notebook and waited.

Grimacing, Nick continued in his thickest Oxford accent. "The thief was about my height, Officer, wearing a silver, down coat, making it difficult to guess weight. Black balaclava. Escaped on a black motorcycle. A small white sedan followed. I'm unfamiliar with vehicle models and didn't catch the plate. They were too far away to see inside."

The other cop returned to hear this. "And you are?"

Bollocks. Here they'd go. Maybe he should change his name. He drew on the officiousness he'd learned to bully his way into offices where he wasn't wanted. Pulling out his new business card, he handed it over without a word, an old trick learned at his pappy's knee. Say nothing and there was nothing to question.

"And you, ma'am?" The officer turned to Gracie, who amazingly hadn't retreated from Nick's protective hold.

"Grace Jenkins," she answered in a weak voice. "We were just checking on a friend's sketches, when. . ." She gestured helplessly.

Cops liked helpless. They probably also liked white and female with a good bosom. One offered her a seat. The other found bottled water to hand her.

Nick had a strong suspicion she was playing the part of wilting magnolia. The Grania he knew never wilted.

While Mrs. Janus continued in a rant about the city not providing enough protection against drug gangs ruining lives of innocent business owners, Gracie studiously ignored the artwork he'd rescued.

So, she had seen it too.

With every fiber of his body he wanted out of there, away from officialdom and authority.

But those were Albert Walker sketches in those frames—and the one the thief had stabbed him with was *mantel size.*

While Nick debated how they might smuggle out those works under the nose of the police, a burst of energy blew in through the connecting door to the gallery.

"Mother! Are you all right? Why are all the police cars outside?"

Verity . . . was as curvaceous as Bertie's sketch had shown. Today, she wore a shrink-wrapped yellow print dress that cut across her thighs. Her long auburn hair tumbled in luxurious waves over her shoulders. She was just the kind of high-maintenance woman Nick loved. . .

Once upon a time. Women who dressed to be noticed had more ulterior motives than he cared to invest in these days. They had been meaningless fun back in the day, but he was done with game-playing. Now that he'd seen how a proper family operated. . . He'd probably never have one, but at least he now knew arm candy like Verity Janus was not family material.

Since when had he wanted family?

While the two statuesque gallery owners threw themselves into each other's arms and talked over one another, Gracie stood up. The cops barely noticed.

"Let's get out of here," Gracie whispered, taking his arm.

He glanced questioningly at the sketches, but she shook her head.

Right-o. Never going to escape with those.

Wielding his Oxford accent and a condescending smile, he passed out more cards, ordered the officers to call him if needed, empathized with the sniveling gallery owner, then took Gracie's arm and escaped.

They could interview Verity Janus at a better time.

"Evie would have read auras and looked for ghosts and interrogated everyone in the room," Gracie complained as they escaped. "I make a terrible detective."

"You are a mother with responsibilities. Taking risks is not what you do," he reminded her. "And I, for one, am grateful. I am still none too comfortable around the law. I was a hair's breadth from sitting behind bars with my cousins."

She absent-mindedly patted his coat sleeve. "Evie would have saved you. That's what she does. Everyone can see you were duped."

"Yeah, that's what I am, a stupid dupe. Just what a bloke likes to hear. But this stupid dupe is beginning to think there's a reason someone is after Bertie's sketches. Who even knew about them?" As they hurried to the car, he started mental lists.

"Teddy Turlock, Tobias, Verity, her mother, Sammy, us. . ." She obediently listed the obvious.

"And quite possibly whoever killed your mayor," he reminded her. "If Bertie had sketches up there, the murderer stole them."

"Or the drug dealer did, unless they're one and the same. I should text Evie. She needs to talk to Bertie more." She pulled her phone out of her pocket and began typing as they reached the car.

Nick was shaken enough to not even respond to the idea of calling for help from a dead drug addict. His mind traveled to more sensible grounds. "They need to be looking into the backgrounds of the Turlocks. I'll wager they both carry guns and the younger one probably knows where to find drugs."

He didn't like Teddy Jr.'s type—all flash and no cash in his experience. The privileged class activated the resentments of his childhood.

Nick assisted Gracie into the driver's seat while his mind grappled with theft. He should probably hide the sketches he'd bought from Sammy, except he didn't think anyone knew he had them other than Evie's family. Unless Sammy had told the killer. . . *Dang.*

Mental alarms rang. He'd never worried about himself before, but there was an entire family of innocents. . .

"Teddy Jr. won some marksman award." Gracie returned to her list of suspects as he took his seat. "And I'm sure he was like every teen in town and climbed into that attic a time or two. Like Bertie, he knew it was there. Out of towners like Verity wouldn't."

"What about Toby?" Nick glanced down at their shopping list, but Gracie seemed to know where she was going.

"The mayor's golden boy went to a private school up until the last few years, so he was an outsider. Although he dated Evie, so there's that. Bertie was at least ten years older than those people in the Corvette sketch. How did they get together?"

Nick rubbed the bridge of his nose. "Because he drew something they liked and tried to sell it to them, I'd wager."

"We really need to talk with Verity," she concluded. "Those sketches weren't framed the last time we were here. At least the large one is new. Where did she or her mother get them? And we can't forget that the mayor's death might be totally unrelated to Sammy's. A lot of people hated Block for a lot of very good reasons, even Mayor Larraine. And over half the town and any contractor who ever worked on that courthouse knew how to climb into that attic."

"But the sketches seem key here. Why would the mayor's killer care about Bertie's artwork? Do we assume the drug dealer stole the sketches, or that he might have told someone about them? It doesn't make sense that a drug dealer would kill Block though. Or that Block's killer would be after the sketches."

She grimaced. "So, how does one go about finding a drug dealer?"

"Sheriff's records, courthouse records, local pub. . ." Nick texted Jax. "Or your local lawyer."

~

Jax glanced at Nick's text and nearly walked into Mayor Larraine in front of the café. She sidestepped and tapped his shoulder with one of her long, glossy nails. "Love note?"

He snorted and returned the phone to his pocket. "Evie's idea of a love note would be along the line of *don't forget the meatballs, turkey.* And I'd have to figure out whether she wants turkey meatballs or if I'd annoyed her somehow."

Larraine laughed. "I'd go with buying meatballs *and* turkey. One can always eat both. And I'd rather have her hunting killers. The town is developing a bad rep for our crime rate."

"We can compare ourselves to Charleston, then." He'd already heard about the gallery robbery. Evie was frothing at the bit. "Did you happen to know Bertie in school?"

The mayor looked taken aback but recovered quickly. "He was in special ed. I was just *special.* So, not the same circles, no."

"We're trying to find people who knew him. Block and Turlock the Elder were too old to be in the same class."

Larraine's eyes narrowed. "Why do you want to know?"

Jax shrugged. "Making connections. I didn't live here. Evie is too young to know a lot, other than that Bertie was bullied, because she relates to that. Why the sudden interest in his work after all these years?"

"Huh." She frowned in thought, remembered it caused wrinkles, and tapped her lacquered nail to her cheek instead. "I can send you our yearbook. But if I'm remembering rightly, most of our class moved on, married, found jobs elsewhere, except for people like the Shepherds who farm here. It wasn't a large class, just mean-spirited. I'm not sure why."

"Around twenty-five years ago? The economy? It's hard to say. It was just a passing thought. How much do you know about this Layman who wants to buy up the east side?"

"For that, we need a bar and alcohol, and it's too early in the day. I'll have my secretary send you the public file. We passed those zoning laws just in time, although I'm starting to believe they'll turn into a nightmare." She waved at someone across the street. "Have to go."

Before she walked away, she swiveled on her high heel. "*Rhodes* was in the same year as Bertie's class. He was one of the bullies."

Jax whistled. Now *that* was interesting, a bully who went on to become a judge.

When he reached the old Victorian, Evie met him at the door. She flung a scratchy artificial greenery wreath around his neck like a lei and hugged him. "*Bertie*, now, before the courthouse closes."

"Maybe we should wait until Rhodes is cycled off the circuit. Now that the Block trial is at a standstill, Satterwhite shouldn't need his help." Removing the wreath, Jax attempted reason, even knowing it could take weeks to be rid of Rhodes. But he needed time to think.

Thinking wasn't easy with ripe Evie entwined around him. He wanted to carry her straight upstairs.

But Loretta was hollering for him to admire her decorating skills, the twins were jabbering about the Christmas tree, or maybe the presents under it, and Dante was looking like an Italian thundercloud as he popped out of the library. Afternoon delight wasn't happening.

"Going *now*. Nick and Gracie left R&R an entire list of topics to pursue. And we probably need to hide Bertie's sketches. See you in a bit." She kissed the corner of his lip, slipped from his embrace, and all but skipped down the porch steps.

Jax couldn't exactly blame her. She'd probably been stuck in this madhouse all day. Recalling what the mayor had said about Rhodes, he swung to warn her, but she was already off on her bicycle.

Shouting *Rhodes is a bully* in front of the entire neighborhood probably wasn't a wise idea.

Nineteen

EVIE DEBATED VARIOUS ENTRIES INTO THE COURTHOUSE, BUT AFTER MEETING WITH Judge Satterwhite today, she chose to be blatant. She didn't want to catch any man carrying a gun by surprise. She wondered if that had been a .38. She was clueless.

If she thought there were any chance a stout old man like the judge could climb into the attic, she'd suspect Satterwhite of killing Block. He had every reason in the world. Judge S was presiding over Block's trial and knew how many people the former mayor had harmed. Block's cronies were presumably pressuring the judge's sainted mother. Means, motive, opportunity. . .

It simply didn't fit right in her head. Or with his aura. Six of one and all that. . .

In her search for Bertie, she met Judge Rhodes in the upper hall. Now there was a man she'd like to consider a suspect. His aura was as dismal as his clothes—but she really needed to learn this evidence thing. *Facts, Evangeline.*

Bertie had sketched Rhodes taking what looked like cash from Layman. But even if anyone had seen the sketch, they wouldn't think anything of it. Bertie "wasn't quite right in the head" always prevailed.

And there was no other connection except age and her dislike. She didn't think Rhodes even lived in Afterthought. As a circuit judge, he could live anywhere. She supposed he had the same opportunity as Judge S to kill Block, but why? Did he even own a gun?

Wearing a suit and not his robes, probably on his way home, Rhodes walked right past her as if she were invisible. Oh well, do or die and all that.

Given the opportunity, Evie turned and stood in his path. "Have you noticed your chambers feeling colder than usual, your honor?"

"And you are?" he asked. His eyes were flat and gray, and Evie wondered if any woman had been stupid enough to marry him. She didn't dare open her extra sense, but what she could see of his aura wasn't exactly charming.

"Evangeline Malcolm." She smiled broadly while dropping her father's name in favor of her mother's infamy.

The supercilious idiot stared at her blankly. Oh well.

Coldly, he asked, "Are you with the company working on the heating system? I told the clerk to call them hours ago."

Oh, nice opening. . . "We think some of the ducts may have been damaged in the riot. We didn't like disturbing you in your chambers. . ."

He juggled the files he was carrying to reach in his pocket. "I keep the door locked. Return the keys to the clerk when you're done. I don't think the heat vent is working at all back there."

Heat was fine. Block was his problem. Not explaining that.

She accepted the keys with a smile. "I appreciate that, your honor, and I'll get right on it."

He stalked off without any pleasantry, a busy man with so much on his mind he hadn't even asked for her credentials. Stupid.

Did she really look like a furnace inspector? She tapped the knit hat hiding her hair and glanced down at the puffy coat she'd worn anticipating ghostly cold and shrugged. Everyone looked alike in winter. She should wear sexy sweaters like Gracie, although her lurid t-shirts worked as well. But apparently, she'd unconsciously decided to blend in today.

Figuring she'd never be given permission again, she skipped Bertie and hurried into the empty courtroom. Not too cold there. Block would avail himself of the familiar, which meant the cushiest corner—the judge's private chamber. Wondering how far Block could wander, she unlocked Rhodes' hideaway.

Shiver. It would be warmer if a hole was knocked in the wall to let the outside air in.

"Mayor Arthur," she called cheerfully, spotting the aura in the judge's desk chair. She settled on the leather couch. "Have you figured out why anyone would kill you yet?"

Opening her third eye, Evie could see the former mayor's spirit swirling like the aurora borealis. With no way of controlling events, he was lost and starting to panic.

Nobody he muttered, probably unaware she could hear him in her head even if he didn't speak loudly.

"It's always a possibility that it could have been an accident," she agreed. "Your son is trying to do what you wanted, but he can't find your binder. Do you know where it is?"

Binder. Block's colors swirled a little more cohesively. *Lawyer. Turd has it all. Wants it all.*

Interesting. Block couldn't remember his lawyer's name, but apparently epithets were emotional and lingered. She assumed he meant Turd the Senior, his lawyer. "Mr. Turlock thinks you owe him money."

All bluster, no muscle. All that hair, rots the brain.

Block had worn a topper to conceal his balding head. Evie tried not to snort.

The aura steadied a little more and Evie had the feeling he'd finally focused on her. *You hear me?*

"Yeah, imagine that," she said dryly. "Your only connection to your son is the Gypsy's daughter. Irony, huh?" Block hadn't the imagination to call Mavis a witch. Apparently *Gypsy* had been his euphemism for *trash.*

Want to talk to him. He almost sounded like his cranky old self.

"Toby can't hear or see you. Only I can. He's asking about your binder. If Turlock has it, how can Toby get it back?"

His aura grew muddier. Evie waited.

Contains will and deeds, he finally said. *Belongs to family. Theft.*

Evie tried to follow that train of thought. "The binder contains your personal property and if Turlock doesn't return it to your heir, it's theft?"

Thief he muttered in apparent agreement.

Evie stood up before she turned into a popsicle. "All right, we'll try to get it back. In the meantime, do us both a favor and stay out of these chambers while the judge is in them. Otherwise, he'll have me banned from the court-house, and you won't have any way of passing messages to Toby."

Shivering, she left the rotten old goat to study on that. She'd never been able to talk to the man in real life. She should feel triumph that she was all he had now. She didn't. It was all very sad. He'd run out of time to learn the error of his ways and would never become a better man and father.

She checked her phone—almost drained. Having learned from Jax, she attached a backup battery and went in search of Bertie. She really needed to check on Sammy's ghost, but the Antique Barn was locked, and she didn't want to be arrested. Troy really hadn't liked her Subaru being parked there around the time of a murder.

She found the artist's spirit contemplating an ancient oil painting of some dead judge on the upper story rotunda wall. Evie had a feeling he'd been spying on her and Block, but she couldn't blame him there.

Midafternoon, the area was empty. Court wasn't in session. She pretended to talk into her phone as she leaned against the wall. "Hey, Bertie. Whatcha doin'?"

Didn't kill myself he said defensively, following his own train of thought.

"Didn't think you did. But I'd like to find out who gave you the drugs." Evie knew he couldn't give her names, but she didn't know how to ask otherwise.

Party, he said wistfully. *I never got to party.*

Huh. Special Ed kids were seldom invited to parties, she guessed. As an adult. . . well, homeless druggies weren't exactly popular. "Someone invited you to a party? But you didn't go?"

She thought he nodded. His aura was almost totally gray, so it was like watching wisps of smoke. He was fading fast. "I saw one of your sketches with Teddy Jr. in a Corvette and Toby and Verity and the Shepherds, so you must have been there. Was that a party?"

He brightened a little. *No, later. I gave them my sketches. They said they'd have my surprise framed. They were going to take me home.*

How long ago had he asked Hank at the hardware to frame his "surprise"? She doubted Bertie would remember, but she needed a timeline. If Toby had announced Bertie was doing sketches around town at this Corvette not-a-party, what had Bertie uncovered after that? "Toby and Teddy and the Shepherds framed your sketch?"

Toby and the girl, to thank me. He brightened a little more.

Apparently he remembered names if she fed them to him. "Can you remember when?"

Uncertainty slipped through the gray. *He came to get me. But then. . . I woke up here.*

The effort to work it out was apparently too much for him. He vanished.

All—or some of—those pretty young people were taking dirty, homeless old Bertie to a party? Why? Not because of the sketches she'd seen so far, right?

She'd have to interview real people instead of ghosts. Ouch.

Which was worse, interrogating real people or risk arrest looking for Sammy's ghost?

What had Toby and Verity wanted Bertie to sketch? She texted Jax. Tobias was his close-mouthed client.

～

SHE'D USED HER TELEKINESIS AGAIN.

Restlessly, Gracie tried to block out that unwelcome thought while she waited on Nick. Currently, he was providing credentials to obtain his international driver's license. He'd promised her thrift stores next.

She'd helped Nick save Bertie's sketches. The adrenalin rush of using her telekinesis had almost knocked her out. It had been a significant physical strain, but *she'd done it.* She hadn't been certain she could. Fortunately, Nick hadn't realized exactly how much extra. . . pull. . . she'd added.

She had a superpower.

She'd yanked framed artwork out of the hands of thieves!

And now she wanted to go back and look at that artwork before it disappeared again. But she had no superpower for that.

And to make her head even dizzier—that handsome Brit at the counter with clerks swooning at his beck and call had *kissed* her. Mousy little schoolteacher *her.* He'd held her and called her *luv.* It was undoubtedly an unconscious habit, she told herself.

She wasn't Evie—she couldn't think two mind-altering things at once. So she mentally erased the comfort he'd offered. Nope, no way, not going there. Superpower was what she wanted.

If she wanted to see those sketches, she needed Evie. Or even Pris. While Nick chatted, she hastily sent a family text. There was time before dinner. Maybe someone could break away?

Evie answered instantly, ON MY WAY.

Even the way her sister drove, it would take her nearly an hour to reach the city. Gracie hoped she brought Jax. Evie could tell when people were lying, but she wasn't good at persuading them to do things. Nick might be, but Mrs. Janus knew them. Verity probably didn't. Her thoughts were bouncing like her sister's.

When Nick was finished and sauntered toward the exit as if he hadn't a worry in the world, Gracie showed him her messages.

His dark eyebrows shot up, and he studied her for half a minute, making the heat rise to her cheeks. But they needed to do this.

"You're right. We need to stake out the gallery while we wait," he said, surprisingly. "Make sure those sketches don't disappear before Evie arrives."

"You think they'd come back to steal them again?" Horrified, she hurried to the car.

"The sketches do seem to have someone's attention, don't they? Maybe we ought to have someone following Mr. Turlock Jr. the way Bertie did." He clipped on his seatbelt. "So far, he's the only one we've seen asking after them."

"Evie doesn't have a *real* detective agency. I think that requires working with the police or lawyers a bunch of years. She doesn't know how to follow people." She drove back towards the gallery wondering how one did a stakeout. She'd read a million mysteries but fiction wasn't the same as reality.

"Bertie wasn't exactly a real detective but he followed Teddy," he said in amusement. "Let's stop at the little sushi place we passed and stock up. Pity detectives can't drink wine on duty."

"It's the middle of the afternoon! I'd fall asleep. Coffee will work better. Although their pastries won't be as good as Pris's." She pulled into a coffee shop where she knew they had decent restrooms. She remembered that much about stakeouts, and she wasn't urinating in any bottles.

He grinned. "I don't know if that's the mother or teacher speaking, but I like it. I stand corrected." He pried his long legs out of her small car and took her arm as they went inside.

She'd just *told* him what to do. When was the last time she'd told a grown man what to do? And he'd listened? Her ex never had. She wasn't part of Evie's agency, so she had never bossed around R&R. Her domain was little kids and other teachers, none of whom were male at the elementary level.

Maybe using her superpower was going to her head, in which case, she was probably in deep trouble. Timid Gracie had no business telling people what to do.

They carried their coffee and snacks to the car and returned to the gallery neighborhood, where Nick directed her to a driveway.

"The thieves parked there. It gives a good view of the alley and the street, so we can keep watch." He sipped his coffee without concern for private property.

Nervously, Gracie backed into the drive, certain a silver-haired owner would run out with a shotgun and blast them into the next world, leaving Aster with only a criminal for a parent.

Twenty

"THERE THEY ARE," THE DELIGHTFULLY NERVOUS SCHOOLTEACHER MURMURED AS a black SUV circled the block looking for a parking place.

Nick had thought Gracie might crawl under the car rather than spend this last pleasant hour with him, but he'd finally teased her into talking about her daughter, which had led to her tentative attempts at writing. He'd been having a fine old time.

But he studied the unfamiliar SUV with puzzlement. "I thought you texted Evie." Nick tried to see inside the dark windows as the big vehicle circled. Was that a dog in the back seat?

"For reasons we'll probably never understand, my sister seems to have enlisted our cousin Iddy. How do we want to do this? Can I park somewhere else now?" Gracie reached for the keys in her ignition.

He'd have to remember that he made her nervous by asking her to do anything improper. *He* was the callous bastard who trod all over meaningless regulations. She did things by the book. Not seeing an advantage in staying in this spot now, he nodded at a car pulling out on the street. "Grab that spot and let's give your family a minute to go in and engage whoever is handling the gallery. Who is Iddy?"

"You met her at Thanksgiving, Idonea, tall veterinarian looks like a spooky witch? She takes after her father." She skillfully parallel parked the Kia in the opening.

"Ah, the one with the raven, right. Is her father a warlock?" Nick had no

138

idea how weird this family could get but he was ever curious.

Gracie laughed as the SUV's driver stepped out with a raven on her shoulder. "He claims to be Cherokee. Maybe there was a medicine man in his ancestry. We'll never know. I think he's in Hollywood these days, giving sensitivity lessons to writers or producers or some such."

Evie climbed out with a golden retriever—Honey, their mother's dog, if he remembered correctly.

"Why on earth are they taking the animals into an art gallery?" Gracie shook her head in disbelief.

Her cousin's long black hair and brown skin looked more Cherokee than witchlike, in Nick's estimation. The raven was a dramatic touch. "Nice distraction. Whoever is manning the desk will be so rattled that we can do anything we like when we go in. Are you ready for this?" They'd discussed what they'd intended to do but Nick knew Gracie wasn't fully on board with his plan to examine the sketches.

"I expect them to be flung out on their ears before we even reach the door," she muttered, climbing out. "I can't believe Iddy fell for one of Evie's stunts. I thought she had more sense than that."

"Maybe she wanted to go Christmas shopping." Nick hummed a little tune and took Gracie's hand. He'd more than enjoyed that hug earlier. It had given him ideas he shouldn't have. His imagination had ever been his downfall. Maybe he should try the slow, rural method of courting, holding hands and the like.

Was he really interested in *courting*? He was out of his frigging mind even thinking in such dated terms. It was just, around Gracie, he was out of his shallow depths. He needed to do a lot of mental adjusting.

She didn't draw away, so he figured she was frightened. She had good reason to be, he supposed. Last time they'd entered this building, a thief was running loose.

Which might be why Evie had brought animal reinforcements—to scare off intruders. His admiration for the orange-haired mischief-maker rose another notch, although not in the same way he admired quiet, respectable Gracie. Gracie was far out of her comfort zone but willing to do what it took to find justice. That took guts.

The dog and raven both looked up when they entered but lost interest quickly. Iddy and Evie had engaged Mrs. Janus in discussion over a watercolor of the harbor. He saw no sign of Bertie's sketches in front, but if they'd been framed since their previous visit. . . Were they planning an exhibit?

He eased Gracie to the other side of a folding partition. The bell over the door should have notified anyone in the back of their arrival. He was hoping Verity Janus was still here.

Sure enough, the towering auburn-haired bombshell strode from the back a moment later, blinked at the sight of the dog and raven, then hurried toward Nick and Gracie. He didn't see recognition in her eyes. Yet. Gracie's hand gripped his tighter.

"Good afternoon, Miss Janus." He offered his best oozing charm and posh accent out of habit.

She merely raised her carefully-sculpted eyebrows in surprise. "Have we met?"

"This afternoon, I fear. I do hope your mother has recovered?" He gestured toward the other side of the gallery where Evie and Iddy had moved out of sight.

Registering wariness, she nodded. "Frightening when thieves attack in broad daylight. One would think art galleries would be the last target for thieves. I'm so sorry we were unprepared for you. Was there something we can help you with?"

Gracie took a breath and performed her sweet schoolteacher role. "We visited a few days ago and asked about Albert Walker sketches. We have a watercolor of his and hoped to acquire more for our. . . café."

They'd spent part of the last hour decorating this imaginary café to amuse themselves.

"And we couldn't help noticing when we were here earlier. . . that his works are the ones the thief tried to steal." Nick added an appropriate frown. "Considering what has happened in our small town, this is causing us some trepidation."

"And we wondered if perhaps we should sell the piece we own." Gracie offered an anxious smile that probably wasn't acting. "Now that we've met you, I believe it may be you and some of your friends in the image. It's quite unusual for Bertie's work."

"You knew Mr. Walker?" Verity kept her voice low and glanced anxiously toward the desk in back, but her mother was still distracted by dog and bird and questions.

"Oh, yes, of course, and his family. Afterthought *is* a small town after all, and that was the reason we were hoping to display local artists." Gracie looked wistful.

Nick knew she wasn't acting there either. They'd created quite a lovely imaginary café for her cooking cousin.

The act apparently worked. Verity Janus nodded and gestured toward the rear. "Let me show you what we have."

Triumph! That's the most Nick could hope for. They couldn't afford to buy anything, but if they could at least see the mantel sketch, maybe grab some more photos. . .

Gracie's phone binged with a text message. She glanced at it, nodded at her sister as they passed the desk, and continued onward, clinging to his hand.

As Verity unlocked a closet door, Gracie showed him her phone.

MOM AURA FUNKY. VERITY SCARED

What the hell did that mean? He glanced questioningly at Gracie, but she just shook her head and smiled her delight as Verity brought out the sketches.

And there it was, the framed mantel-sized watercolor piece. Gracie dropped down in a crouch to study it and surreptitiously snap photos while Verity opened an easel to place the others on.

Nick all but growled his disappointment. It was a nice piece, in the same style as the others they'd seen. Nothing dynamic, just buildings and people, more than usual and with dashes of color. Maybe Gracie saw more in it.

He nodded knowledgeably over the work Verity displayed, as if he had a clue. Shoving one hand in his trouser pocket, he studied Verity instead of the work. Scared? She didn't look it, but he supposed she had some right to be.

"I've been asked to start an online auction site for Mr. Walker's work." They had dropped this original part of their plan, but if Miss Janus was *scared*. . . He could work with that. "Some of the work will be donated, and the funds will go directly to his family, who have been deprived of much needed income with his death. I wonder if you might be interested in listing your pieces and donating a percentage of your profits?"

Gracie stood up, brushing off her skirt. "I love this color piece. It's a shame we can't display it the way Bertie would have wanted. It's a loving tribute to the town."

Verity looked startled but also warily relieved. Had she thought the sketch revealed secrets? That's what Nick had hoped, although he had doubts now.

"We might be interested," the dealer said tentatively. "I framed these last night for an exhibit. It's just. . ." She glanced at the easel. "As you said earlier, I'm concerned about the circumstances of Mr. Walker's death and this afternoon's attempted theft. It's almost as if. . ."

"There is something in his work that someone wants concealed?" Gracie asked with such honest openness that no one could take it for anything except concern. "Yes, that was our fear as well. His brother was selling these, and he was murdered the other day. Which is why we're thinking online might be better until the matter is settled."

Matter. As if murder was just a nuisance to be cleared up. Southern manners were almost as stuffy as aristocratic discretion.

Verity nodded, checked the front room where the dog had started barking, and whispered. "That's my thought too. I'm thinking an exhibit is not the wisest choice right now. If you have a safe place. . . Consignment might be the best option."

Nick did his best to prevent his eyebrows from skyrocketing. Even in his wildest dreams he hadn't thought she'd make that offer. She really was frightened. How had Evie known?

Pulling his shocked thoughts together, he nodded thoughtfully. "Yes, we've told the family we'll store what we have in a climate-controlled vault. I'll photograph them there. We'd need to draw up a consignment contract specifying bottom line prices and so forth. . ."

He lied through his pretty white teeth, but that's what he did for a living. Marketing and sales were all abracadabra, making people believe what they wanted to believe. Gracie shot him a look he couldn't interpret, but Verity was already hurrying to the computer. They probably kept blank consignment contracts on file.

In front, the retriever was growling dangerously. The raven flapped through the open connecting door to land on Gracie's head. She didn't shriek, although Verity did. Both their phones beeped.

Nick glanced at a text message from Evie.

LAYMAN JUST WALKED IN

～

ONLY THE SIMMERING SCENT OF GARLIC AND ONION IN THE KITCHEN, PLUS EVIE'S information about Block's binder, had kept Jax from fleeing a chaos escalating to asylum proportions. The Victorian was about to burst apart at the seams. But he'd promised Evie to do his guardian gig and look after the household. The sketches in the barn worried them all.

Apparently having been informed—half a century after the fact—that tinsel was dangerous, Mavis and her sisters had descended and were systematically working their way through all the holiday decorations, using him as their pack mule to carry boxes from the attic.

The kids were in seventh heaven, pouncing on rocking teddy bears and wooden nutcracker soldiers and ungodly tinkling ornaments and strings of sleigh bells. It was like every Macy's Christmas display from the past fifty years.

With all the boxes delivered, he was hunkered down in the library when Turlock Sr. finally returned his call. Evie's revelation that Block's lawyer had the binder Toby had been seeking had shot his hopes sky high. Maybe they could resolve a few of their problems.

"Have you called to tell me the payment is in the mail?" the lawyer asked dryly.

"No, I've called to ask for my client's property back. Arthur had a black binder containing his will and deeds. We appreciate that you took care of it while he was incarcerated, but the binder belongs to Tobias now." Jax's experience was in business fraud, but sometimes the line between family law and corporate was thin.

"I know nothing about it. I believe we have some boxes that he sent over last spring. I'll have my secretary locate them, if Toby wants to pick them up. Is that all? I'm pretty certain there are no maps to pirate treasure in there." Turlock's scorn was thick.

So, maybe the old guy didn't know anything. It happened. Or maybe he was just stupid. "I'll give him a call. When should he stop by?"

They made the arrangements and Jax had just shut off the call when Loretta ran in holding a package.

"For you! Do you think it's a present? Should we put it under the tree?" Her pansy blue eyes sparkled like the tree lights, and her shoulder-length brown hair bounced with her colt-like stride.

She'd be a teenager in a blink. Jax was not looking forward to that. He took the manila envelope with Larraine's stamp on it and shook his head. "Hate to break the fantasy, but this is business. Do you have all your presents wrapped?"

She nodded happily. "Evie helped me. This will be the best Christmas I've ever had!"

"Me, too, sweetheart. It's more fun to give than receive, don't you think? And when there are so many people to give to. . ."

She grinned. "Well, it helps if you have the money to buy. Evie said I could have more than my allowance. Did she tell you that?"

"She did. She's spoiling you, but she said it's for a good cause. How soon to supper?"

Loretta headed for the door. "Not until everyone returns. They're still in

Charleston. Evie says to tell you that Mr. Layman is more rotten than Blockhead."

She skipped out, leaving Jax in a state of alarm. Evie was with Franklin Layman? *Why? Where? How?*

He tore open Larraine's package in frustration—a stack of magazine-size high school yearbooks from different decades. He flipped open the newest one from fifteen years ago. Why had Larraine chosen that one? The images were all black and white. With only about a hundred students in all four classes, the books were paperbound. He flipped through, looking for familiar names since the faces of pimply, long-haired teenagers rang no bells.

Teddy Turlock Jr. was in the senior class fifteen years ago. Unlike the floppy curtain of hair or spiked and bleached styles so many of his male classmates sported, he wore a traditional barbered cut, parted to one side. He was one of the very few wearing a tie and jacket. Obviously, the lawyer's son intended to follow in his daddy's footsteps. What had happened? As far as Jax was aware, Teddy Jr. ran a sporting goods store these days.

Right beside him were two identical Shepherds, Matthew and Mark. Jax didn't know the names of the brothers living out on the farm, but he assumed this was them. They had all the earmarks of jocks, shaved hair, big shoulders, wearing what appeared to be football jerseys. Did Afterthought even have sports teams?

He flipped to the back for group photos. There was the. . . very small. . . football team. They'd been on a losing streak that year it appeared. And there were the Shepherds, front and center. Looked like Teddy Jr. played baseball, but that was a losing team as well.

Whoever once owned this yearbook hadn't had anyone sign the photos or pages in back. Maybe it came from the school library.

He flipped to the front again, looking for more familiar names. He didn't find any until the freshman year. There was Tobias Block, the former mayor's son. He'd worn his light hair floppy with styled highlights. He wore a coat but no tie, halfway between his former preppy self and his new high school persona, Jax assumed, remembering Evie had said he'd attended a private school originally. He must have made the football team the next year because he recalled Toby had been a football hero at some point.

His gaze fell on one of the cheerleaders. . . buxom, long wavy hair that didn't look blond or black. . . He scanned the caption for a familiar name —*Verity Janus*. Huh. Evie hadn't mentioned the gallery owner or her daughter living in Afterthought. He flipped back to the front and found her in the same year as Toby. That would have made them both about fifteen.

Evie would only have been eleven, her sister thirteen and in middle school, so they might not have known Verity if she left after that year.

Out of excess curiosity, he left the yearbook open and braved the front parlor where Evie's mother and aunts were repacking boxes. "Does Evie have a high school yearbook?"

They all sat back, wrinkled their noses in almost an identical manner, and gave his question some thought. As if they'd been mentally consulting, the aunts went back to work and left Mavis to reply.

"The girls were all about the same age, so we bought one yearbook for all of them. There were plenty of blank pages in back. They each had a page for their friends to write on. Evie graduated last, so she had her senior yearbook to herself. It should be around somewhere." She waved vaguely.

Which meant it was probably packed in one of the many boxes Evie had removed from their bedroom and stored who-knows-where. Oh well, it had been a thought.

He texted Evie with a question about Verity Janus and went on a hunt for Albert Walker.

Bertie showed up in a yearbook from twenty-five years ago. He'd been a sophomore. Kids that age were all unprepossessing but Bertie even more so: lank hair that looked as if it hadn't been washed in weeks, a dark T-shirt with probably the name of a band on it, a ring in one ear, and what appeared to be a hand-inked tattoo of a shooting star on his cheekbone. It wasn't easy to tell from the old black-and-white photo, but the tattoo might have been right below the remains of a real shiner.

He flipped to the group photos. The only place he found Bertie's name was as set designer for the school play. But the name *Larry Ward* caught his eye in the same photo as one of the actors. All he had to do was look for the tallest kid in the photo and there was their current mayor, dreadlocks and all. Jax wasn't familiar with the play and had no idea what character Larry was playing. Had transgender kids used the designation "they" back then? Probably not. Larry preferred "she" these days, but they hadn't transitioned in high school.

Checking the front pages, there Larry was in the senior photos—still presenting as male, wearing what appeared to be a tailored jacket to fit their skinny shoulders, an open-collared shirt of indeterminate color—probably pink, knowing the mayor—and a braided necklace that probably matched the beads in their dreads. They made a very pretty boy, but the expression was sullen.

And here's what he'd been looking for, although Jax hadn't been overtly conscious until he saw the photo—*Ralph Rhodes,* the high school bully. The judge looked like any average kid, nondescript features, hair slicked back, wearing shirt and tie but no jacket. Jax went to the group photos but couldn't find Rhodes in any of them. Afterthought didn't have a debate or chess club or any of those things he'd associate with the judge. Ah, but the *gun club.* . . There he was, top point scorer on his team. The judge could shoot.

Sammy was in that photo too. Would he have had a gun at the Barn? Had the thief taken it?

He returned to Teddy Jr.'s yearbook of the younger group, but by then, the gun club had apparently gone off the grid in favor of football and baseball.

Larraine had said hers was a mean-spirited class. Besides the mayor, Rhodes, Bertie, and Sammy, Jax didn't recognize any other names in this group. They'd all be in their forties now. . . Two were dead. What had happened to the others?

He forgot idle speculation when Toby showed up at the door with the box of his father's effects.

Twenty-One

EVIE HID BEHIND TALL IDDY AS FRANKLIN LAYMAN TALKED TO MRS. JANUS. THE man radiated bad vibes without her even turning on her extra sense. Tall, his paunch almost concealed by a tailored gray suit, his bulk making two of the skinny gallery owner, he leaned intimidatingly over the small corner desk.

Evie wanted out, now, but this opportunity might never happen again. Clasping Iddy's arm, she let herself go space-eyed.

Mrs. Janus's root chakra was a strong red survival color. Evie assumed that meant she'd conquered hard times and would do whatever was necessary to survive. Likelihood was high that she was short-tempered and a bit of a bully, or at the least, pushy. Normally, artistic types might have bright pink, but there was no sign of it beneath the shimmering red.

Blue in her fifth chakra probably reflected her ability to communicate, which made her a good salesperson, but the muddy shade meant she wasn't communicating truth, for whatever reason. Evie would have to know her better to understand if she hid a fear of rejection—possibly from Layman— or if she was lying to her potential clients or her boyfriend. Interesting.

Evie dug her fingers into Iddy's arm and reluctantly turned to Layman. His aura had been dark even before she'd turned on her sensitivity. She winced at all the muddy shades sifting through an extremely strong rainbow of color. He definitely had a dull sheen to his red, signaling an irritable nature and suppressed fury. His life energy was an equally harsh yellow— dishonesty, a tendency to gamble, a cold, sarcastic nature. Ugh.

And yeah, there was the ugly dense blue in his fifth chakra reflecting an opinionated, intolerant nature. Mayor Block had that streak. It hadn't been pretty.

But Evie's ability couldn't show blood dripping from Layman's hands or any other sign that he was a killer. He was just a cold, ambitious man. They already knew that.

When she returned to the real world, Evie was surprised to see Nick talking to Mrs. Janus. She'd known he was here, but she'd hoped he was in back taking photos of Bertie's sketches. He'd left Gracie alone?

That made her unreasonably nervous. What if Verity was one of the bad guys?

Evie left Iddy to talk art with the gallery owner while she wandered off, trying to keep an eye on the door to the office. Nick, weirdly, struck up a conversation with Layman. To give Gracie time to take photos?

Nick was discussing marketing and exchanging business cards with the billionaire, like the good networking consultant he was. She'd be suspicious, except his aura was crystal clear. That didn't mean he wasn't doing something dangerous—just that he enjoyed doing it.

Iddy thanked the gallery owner and made farewell noises. On the verge of panic, Evie glanced at the back room but heard nothing. She texted Gracie, who didn't reply.

OK, then, fine, she'd go around the back way. Tailing Iddy out, grumbling, Evie studied the street, trying to decide the easiest way of reaching the back of the building.

Holding onto the retriever's leash, Iddy grabbed Evie's elbow and dragged her away. The raven flew ahead. "They're loading the sketches into Gracie's little car. They might be better off in my van. C'mon."

"Gracie is stealing the sketches?" Evie asked in horror, running after her long-legged cousin.

She didn't have to ask how Iddy knew. The raven would have shown her.

"No idea." Iddy's long strides carried her down the street faster than Evie could walk. "But if Mr. Gladwell is covering for her, we need to get moving."

Gracie wasn't the world's swiftest person. She dithered a lot. Evie ran down the street hoping her cousin knew where she was going.

They met Gracie and Verity Janus at the alley, shaking hands. Evie almost expired of relief. Verity had a few suspicious shadows in her aura, but on the whole, she seemed to be the same kind of intense do-gooder personality as Toby Block. She hoped. Because Gracie dragged Evie away before she could look deeper.

"I have to go back in and let Nick know we're done. Keep an eye on my car?" Gracie started to walk away.

"Wait, give us your keys. If you just stole those sketches, we should move them to Iddy's van, redirect suspicions." Evie didn't know how. She simply didn't want stolen art going home with Gracie.

"We need a vault to hide them in." Gracie tossed the keys and hurried back up the alley.

"Right, vault, sure." Evie took Gracie's Kia and drove it deeper into the alley far enough that Iddy could back in her SUV, and they could shift the covered artwork unseen.

"Musical chariots," Iddy muttered as they transferred the art and the cars, and Evie handed the keys back to Gracie when she reappeared with Nick.

They all jumped into their respective vehicles and peeled off before anyone could chase after them.

"Where does one find vaults?" Evie asked from the passenger seat of the Tahoe. She typed the same question to Jax.

Jax, understandably, exploded all over the screen in reply.

"I didn't know these emoticons existed." Evie showed Iddy the screen while they stopped at a light.

Iddy laughed. "Your lawyer is highly articulate in hieroglyphics."

Evie sent hearts and flowers and smiles back and waited. Sure enough. The phone rang.

"My landlord has a vault for his accounting files. He'll rent us space. But do you really want him to see stolen art?" Jax sounded resigned.

"Do you really want it in the garage?" she countered. "I have no idea what Gracie and Nick have done."

"Why not just a storage facility for now? There's a small one over by the city utility lot. I can rent one and meet you there. Pris is threatening to throw out the lasagna unless we're at the table soon."

"Remind Pris of the existence of microwaves. Just stay out of pot-swinging range when you do. And thank you. I love you more than orange dreamsicles."

He laughed and clicked off.

"I want a man like yours someday," Iddy said. "How did you ever convince a supremely useful lawyer that you're not a candidate for an asylum?"

"Jax has his own devils. You want to explain what a hunk like Dante sees in grumpy Pris?"

"Huh. Maybe I've not been looking in the right places. I've been thinking I have to settle for local yokels when I should be checking in at Yale and Harvard?"

"Go for it, wealth *and* intelligence! Like Great Aunt Val. Except she's gone through multiple husbands. All I want right now is dinner and to look at those sketches."

Jax called back when they were almost home. "I'm going through Block's black book. Do you know anything about your sister's mortgage?"

"I thought you were renting a storage unit!"

"Multi-tasking. I've stored your other sketches and now I have to do something while I'm waiting. I figured Gracie was driving and didn't want to call her."

"I know nothing of mortgages. She and Craig bought that house together. I assume she acquired the mortgage with the house after the divorce. Why?"

"Do you really want to hear this right now?" He seemed to be flipping pages.

Evie anxiously watched mileage signs. She needed to be home. Gracie's house was everything to her sister. But Evie had a feeling that getting there faster would not solve whatever problem Jax had uncovered. "Is there a better time?"

"Probably not. This way, I can turn off the phone while you scream." Pages rustled. "Judging from what I found in Block's files, your former mayor not only sold real estate, but he often provided the mortgage loan so people with limited means like your sister could buy what he sold. A traditional bank requires big down payments, excellent credit, and proof that the buyer can make payments. When a client couldn't provide all that, Block did an end run around the requirements by borrowing the money himself and loaning it to his buyers, at a higher rate, of course, because of the risk. He had access to private lenders like Layman."

"So he was like one of those extortionate pawnbrokers or paycheck loan companies except he dealt in real estate? I'm not ready to scream, but we're inching closer. He charged rates poor people couldn't afford, then took their houses when they couldn't pay?" Evie wondered if she could punch a ghost.

"It gets better, or worse, depending on perspective. I'll have to confirm with R&R, but in my casual understanding of the contracts they found, Block and Layman formed a mortgage company together. Block owed Layman a fortune on the loans, so he transferred his mortgaged real estate and the mortgages into this LLC."

"Motive for murder?" Evie sat upright. "Layman gets everything Block owned?"

"We've assumed that all along. If this is all his property, and we haven't found more, Block owed more on the properties than they're worth—individually. Afterthought real estate prices are stagnant. No one wants land in a cotton field, which is why Block has been pushing development. He was hoping to drive up the value of the properties he held liens on."

"I'm not liking the sound of that *individually*. Grouped together his holdings are worth more? How?" Evie checked the road signs. Almost there. She didn't understand the path of this conversation but she still felt ready to explode. She needed to be doing *something*.

"Blocks of land are worth more, yes. And what I'm looking at is a list of mortgages this LLC holds. My landlord's office building and surrounding property, your sister's house and half her neighbors. . ."

"Not screaming yet," Evie said cautiously. "Gracie pays her bills. I'm sure your landlord does too. Mortgages are just loans, right?"

"The screaming part comes in when you understand that the way these contracts were written, the mortgage owner has the power *to demand payment in full at any time*. If Layman calls in all these contracts, how many of the current owners could go to the bank and borrow enough to pay them off? If they can't, he will own half the town and can turn it into a three-ring circus."

He clicked off when the screaming started.

Twenty-Two

WEDNESDAY MORNING, WAITING OUTSIDE THE STORAGE UNIT IN THE CHILLY AIR, Nick clicked off his cell phone and shoved it into his pocket with satisfaction.

He had a job, a real actual job paying enough money to have some sort of life again.

So why was he feeling as if he dangled on a precipice?

Because Gracie's family didn't like the man who had recommended the company who had just hired him? A man like Franklin Layman knew people all over the world. Just because Turlock Jr. had told him about the marketing gig, and Layman had recommended the company, didn't mean anything bad. Nick had sent in his resume earlier out of curiosity. Apparently after a call from Layman, the Charleston import business had taken a look at Nick's international experience. It sounded like an ideal fit.

Evie and Jax would probably be glad to see the back of him. He'd have to move into the city since he still didn't have a car, and it would be a while before he could afford one. Instead of paying off his credit card, he'd have to cash in his plane ticket to put a deposit on his own place.

Having a job grounded him so he could smile with his old confidence when Gracie pulled up in her Kia. He'd bicycled over while she delivered Aster and Loretta to some Christmas activity. He'd unlocked the padlock Jax had provided and had the protective wrapping off the frames.

"I'm thinking we should have done this last night, in the dark." Gracie climbed out wearing neat wool slacks and another of those lush sweaters, this one in a blue to match her eyes. "I'm not sure what we're doing should be seen in the light of day."

"We were hungry and lasagna called. And you've been reading too many mysteries. You saw the sketches yesterday. They're nothing ground breaking." He gestured toward the unit's open door. Even in daylight, the interior was dim.

"But this is all the evidence we have!" she all but wailed. "Jax said this awful man could demand that I pay off my mortgage! I can't do it, not on my salary. Block was the only way I could get that loan after Craig bailed. We *have* to find out what Layman is doing."

The niggling discomfort in Nick's midsection increased. "I'm not sure these sketches will help. Maybe we're making mountains out of molehills?"

He wouldn't actually be working for the monster, he reminded himself. And maybe Layman wasn't the monster they were painting. He'd been generous enough with his information.

"That's not the way my life works. I'll just have to make sure I make all my payments early and pray a lot." With an air of gloom that did not sit well on her normally serene features, Gracie yanked a dusty plastic lantern out of the back seat. "Will you be able to take photos? Evie found a battery-operated lantern, but I can't imagine the light will be good."

"It will be useful for propping up the frames. The outside light and my flash should be sufficient otherwise." Relieved to have the uncomfortable discussion diverted, he dragged out the longest sketch, the mantel piece Bertie had wanted for his family.

Gracie crouched down to study it. "It's almost a collage. Maybe of places he liked? There's the courthouse, and the fruit stand, and the Barn, and his mother's house. He's colored in Toby and Verity by the courthouse, Mr. Patel at his stand, his brother and a few of Sammy's kids at the Barn, and his mother and more of the family at home. It's just a nice mantel piece of people and places he liked."

All places to which Block held the mortgage? Nick couldn't help thinking, causing his insides to grind more. Anyway, half these places belonged to the Satterwhites—

Who were being threatened. *Gag.*

"We can't take this to Mrs. Walker if there's any chance these pieces were the reason her sons were killed," he warned. Nick used his good camera to take the full-length image.

"We don't *know* he was killed. He overdosed on bad drugs. That's not murder."

Nick wanted to trust that, but his cynical side had taken over this morning. "Someone gave him drugs. And if we're listening to Evie's ghost tales, he thought he was attending a party, so why would he break his abstinence at a happy time?"

Not having an answer, Gracie set the first piece aside and picked up the next. "This is my street!"

"These are lovely old homes. Is that you and Aster outside your cottage?" Hiding his discomfort, he snapped the photo.

"It is! This is recent, just after she had her hair cut with bangs." She studied it in surprise. "This must be one of the sketches he did while following the Turlocks."

Nick didn't like the sound of that. He reached in and helped himself to another he'd seen earlier. "Your street is a block or two back from Jax's office? And is this the street in between?"

"He's sketching every street from the courthouse back to my house? Why on earth?"

He snapped phone photos of all the sketches and forwarded them to Jax and Evie. "I don't know, but I don't like it." He *really* didn't like it. Could his first paycheck take Gracie and her daughter out of town, to somewhere safe?

With a taut expression, she sat down on the hard concrete pad and began dismantling the mantel-sized piece. "Take photos of the backs too. Maybe he dated them."

"The art would look a lot better in the frames I was working on than these cheap ones, but if we're selling online, I suppose these are easier. Be careful with that backing. I don't want to have to buy more." Preferring to focus on making money, Nick shoved his phone back in his pocket and helped her.

"There's something else under here. . ." Gracie lifted off the layers of cardboard and removed *two* sketches.

They both stared at the hidden drawing of a street of fancy shops with *Main Street USA* on an arched banner above. In the upper corner, barely noticeable, was the historic courthouse. Nothing else on the street looked familiar. Even the town's old-fashioned lantern light poles normally decorated in festive flower baskets had been replaced with modern stylistic arc lamps.

Behind the shops, where Jax's office and Gracie's house should be, was a giant parking lot and what appeared to be an enormous, upscale restaurant with outside seating.

"Did Sammy copy this or steal it?" Nick asked in shock.

Gracie turned it over to show a stamp from some architectural design firm and the title *Layman Main Street USA complex, Afterthought, SC.*

"Someone stole it. Verity framed it." Gracie looked terrified. "And now three people are dead. She may have reason to be afraid."

WEARING A BRIGHT GREEN SWEATER OVER HER DENIM OVERALLS AND HER distinctive hair tucked into a knit cap decorated with reindeers, Evie paced up and down in front of the courthouse. The image of the architectural drawing Nick and Gracie had sent burned in her brain. She didn't have the right words to ask the meaning of this horror. "I don't know what to say!" she shouted at nothing and no one.

The massive Cajun accompanying her didn't bother pacing but stood there, arms crossed, waiting for her to work out her tantrum. "Sounds to me like the ghosts do the talkin', bébé. Just go in and pick a topic. If what Jax and those pictures are saying is right, then you ain't got nothing to lose."

"If he's right, we could lose the *whole town*!" she cried. "We could lose the entire town as we know it! How can I halt that travesty by talking to cold air?"

Jax had insisted that Roark accompany her if she meant to go into the courthouse again. She still didn't see how Judge Rhodes could be a murder suspect just because he knew guns and was present when Block died. He had utterly no motive. He didn't care about Afterthought.

And Turlock Sr., the lawyer, might be a turd, but that didn't mean he'd shoot Block, his own client, even if he knew about the Layman connection. The Shepherd twins and Teddy Jr. had probably been in the riot, plus the entire town council, but no one she knew made good suspects.

Layman was the only one who had motive and opportunity. He'd been listening to Block's last speech, and given the cowboy-boot theme, he probably owned a gun. He wasn't anywhere in town today as far as anyone could determine. She should be fine. She just didn't know what to *say*. Or do.

"We prove the crooked cowboy committed murder to get his hands on Block's property, and he won't be allowed to profit from his crime," Roark pointed out, reasonably enough.

"Crooked cowboy," she scoffed. "Just because he wears boots doesn't mean Layman can even ride a horse, much less use a gun. All right, going in."

Unable to focus on questions, Evie observed the people entering with her: everyday, ordinary people going about their lives, paying fines, sitting on juries. . . her *neighbors*. What would happen to them if Layman had a chance to plop a huge shopping mall on top of their homes and businesses?

Cotton fields would start looking attractive.

Aware of the towering Cajun trailing a distance behind her, Evie took the stairs to the second floor where she usually found the spirits of Bertie and Block. Jax had told her that Rhodes had no session at this hour. That didn't mean the judge wasn't around.

The courtroom floor was relatively quiet with no juries in session. She opened the janitor's closet hoping to find Bertie first, even if she had no idea what to ask him. "We found your sketches," she whispered, hoping he'd appear. "Gracie says the mantel one is lovely."

"Jeez," Roark muttered from the rotunda. "Dat's one hella draft."

Evie backed out of the closet. Roark of the thick skin hadn't worn a coat or even long sleeves, all the better to show off his bronzed biceps and tats, she figured. He had his hands shoved in his jeans pockets now.

For good reason. *Both* Block and Bertie were glaring at each other in the area where they'd essentially both died. Interesting. Apparently just her presence acted as magnet.

Evie pulled out her cell phone so she could fake talking into it as she approached the freezing energy. "Good morning, gentlemen. Disagreement?"

Roark backed off, standing guard over the main stairs as she took a bench near the railing in the rotunda.

It's all his fault! Bertie cried. *Everyone says so.*

Who is everyone? Block countered in obvious boredom. *I don't have to listen to this moron.*

"Wait, wait," Evie cried, keeping her voice low and exerting her mental one. She didn't want to play the blame game, for whatever blame they were flinging. "Don't go yet. Is Rhodes in his chamber? Then we have to talk here. Bertie found a drawing of Main Street USA. Do you know anything about that?"

Bertie's rainbow beamed with pride. He knew what he'd done.

Block's aura swirled erratically. *Big plans. Put us on the map.* He swirled into a gray outline of himself facing Bertie's rainbow. *You stole that drawing!*

He told me to. Bertie developed a nice bright orange streak. *Land needs protecting.*

That pretty much sounded like something Toby, the mayor's son, would say—worried about his danged frogs and not the people being trampled. Translating ghost-speak took a clairvoyant, which Evie wasn't. "What land, Bertie?"

Toby had protected Witch Hill against his father's depredations because of some stray frog or toad, and his father had gone to jail in consequence. Surely Layman wasn't after her family's frog-infested land? Why would Toby be involved otherwise?

Swamp. He says swamps are important, but I like houses.

Moron, Block repeated. *Swamps should be drained and then you'd have houses! A trailer park would go there! Your mama would like her own trailer, wouldn't she?*

"Wait a minute, wait a minute!" Evie's head spun. "What swamp? What trailer park?" Even her leapfrogging brain couldn't put all these pieces together at once.

"Evie? Who are you talking to? What is this about swamps?"

The ghosts vaporized, and Evie was looking up at Judge Satterwhite. Well, if she was a ghost magnet, the judge was an anti-magnet.

Roark had mysteriously disappeared into the woodwork. He wasn't good with authority.

She pretended to click off her phone. With two spirits draining the battery, it was dead already. "Hi, Your Honor. Is Toby protecting another swamp?"

The judge looked a little grayer than usual. "Wetlands out behind the farmhouse and where the fruit stand used to be. We used to go fishing out there, but the creek dried up. It's just a watershed in rainy season now, like your family's pond. Toby has another bee in his bonnet is all."

"But someone wants to build a trailer park on it?" Evie could just imagine the mosquitoes. But it *did* sound like something Blockhead would do. After he'd torn down the perfectly good mobile home park in town for a city parking lot, he'd probably got it in his head to put another on a swamp, believing people would be *grateful*. Typical.

The judge nodded uncomfortably. "It was mentioned in the discussion of selling my land. I don't know how Toby knew about it. Was that in his father's papers?"

"Probably, and you know how Toby is about the environment and his frogs. But Bertie knew about it too. Given what you've said about threats. . ."

On the other side of the rotunda, Judge Rhodes exited his courtroom, and Satterwhite shut up. Instead of heading down the stairs, the younger judge stalked over to join them. "The heat still isn't working right. We need to tear down this piece of crap and build a modern courthouse with insulation and real heat."

Evie wasn't certain this was addressed to her, but the idea of ripping out the historic courthouse didn't sit well. She yanked off her knit cap so her hair spilled out, just to make certain he didn't think she was a plumber. She was starting to wonder about his eyesight. "Global warming, Your Honor. You'll welcome the cold in years to come. Or you could give the ghosts what they want, they'll leave, and it will warm up instantly."

Rhodes stared as if she'd blinked into a magic genie. Or witch. But her orange hair was more clown than witchy. Evie offered her best smile.

"Ghosts?" he asked warily, perhaps sizing her up for a straitjacket.

"Spirit energy is cold. Until the late Mayor Block figures out why he's still here, he's not leaving. I'm not sure about Bertie, though. He may just want his mama's Christmas present back." Being polite hadn't helped, so she might as well take stabs in the dark and pray no one heaved her over the railing.

The Cajun wasn't as overprotective as Jax. He stayed hidden and let her do her thing.

Satterwhite was the one who stepped in. "Evie is a Malcolm, Rhodes. I don't suppose you had any of her family in your classes when you lived here? Extraordinary women."

Rhodes rolled his eyes. "Unless our late esteemed mayor can return from the dead to fix the mess he left behind, I don't believe I'm interested."

He started toward the stairs. Unable to resist, Evie called after him, "Bertie's ghost says you're a bully, Your Honor. Maybe if you make it up to him by helping his mama, he'll go away. That's a whole lot cheaper than building a new courthouse!"

Rhodes didn't even turn around.

"Oh well." Evie sighed and turned back to Judge Satterwhite. "Maybe I should look for *Sammy's* ghost. Will you tell the sheriff it's okay for me to go in the Barn? Mr. Patel might be able to use some part of it for his fruit stand. And Nick might be able to sell off the antiques, if that would help."

The judge patted her on the shoulder. "Stay home and bake cookies, Evangeline. You don't want to be mixed up in what you don't understand. Whoever is behind these deaths won't care who or what you are, and you have a daughter now."

She ground her teeth on the *baking cookies* bit, because he was probably right about the rest. She had no illusions about killers, and she wasn't a real detective. But Loretta had Jax and money. A lot of people who had nothing were counting on her for a lot of reasons. If she wanted respect, she had to fulfill her responsibilities.

Or die trying, if that's what it took.

Gulping, she headed for her next stop—access to the Barn.

Twenty-Three

GRACIE LOOKED UP FROM HER LAPTOP AT NICK. AFTER THEIR EXPEDITION TO THE storage unit, he had changed from his jeans to dress-up clothes. Appearing very British sophisticated, he wore a silky black turtleneck under a tailored gray suit coat he wore open, displaying his awe-inspiring physique. "You're going into the city?"

Without her, went unsaid, because it was too pathetic.

"Jax said I might borrow his motorbike. I've taken a position, and I need to look for a place to stay. I can't live off your family's good will forever." He smiled confidently, as if this were his dream come true.

Taken a position? What did that mean? A job? He had a *job*?

Stunned, she mouthed platitudes. "You know you're welcome here. Evie said she was getting keys to the Barn from Mrs. Walker. We thought you might be interested. I hadn't realized you were job hunting." That came out all wrong. She should be expressing her excitement for him, not whining about what *she* wanted to do.

He shrugged one broad shoulder. "It would take years to make antiques pay off. This position is practically designed for me. But there's travel involved, so there won't be time for hobbies."

She offered a weak smile. "You'll enjoy that. Will you at least stay for Christmas?"

"If your family will have me, I'd like that. I don't want this to be farewell.

Perhaps I can take a look at Sammy's inventory and advise the family a tad on what to do with them. I've done a bit of research already."

She couldn't read minds or auras, but Gracie thought she read Nick well enough. His heart was in antiques, but his pockets required cash. She certainly understood that dilemma.

"You'll have time to work on Bertie's website?"

"Of course! I won't be starting in my new position until after the first of the year. There's plenty of time to have the sale up and running and send a publicity blitz."

So many things she should say but frustration stopped her tongue. She didn't even know why she was disappointed. Men came and went. She didn't need them.

Nick left. Aster ran in to show her a gift she'd made of popsicle sticks. Gracie hugged her daughter. Aster had to be the most important part of her life, and she was fine with that.

Setting aside her useless attempt at writing, she followed Aster back to the parlor. The eccentric Christmas tree with its gleaming old-fashioned lights harbored a mountain of equally eccentric gifts. The ones from Great Aunt Val had arrived wrapped in burlap with gingham bows. Others were wrapped in comics or fabric scraps from the attic. The recycled gift wrap competition had reached the absurd but reassured her a little. Her family would always be her family.

Trying not to fret over how she'd buy her mortgage back, Gracie joined Pris in the kitchen to prepare lunch. She supposed she could live with Evie. Would the mortgage company pay her what her house was worth? Maybe that could be Aster's college fund.

"The parade's tomorrow!" Aster cried in excitement, nearly knocking her milk off the table. "Will there be Thanta Clauth?"

Dante's twins looked up expectantly, their dark eyes gleaming. They still weren't very talkative, but they were learning to participate more. "Santa?" Nan inquired.

"Parades always have Santa," Loretta declared, from her lofty, eleven-year-old position. "And bands and candy. Mr. Nick said he might even find elves."

Nick said. . . ? *Forget it, Gracie.* Nick was a generous man who happened to have a little time on his hands. He'd be gone in a week. His travels would probably take him home, and she'd never see him again. He might even start his antique shop in London, where he could date supermodels. Men like that didn't stay in Afterthought.

Maybe Layman would rename the town after he owned it all. *Forethought* probably wouldn't be any better. *Forthright* would be nice but certainly not accurate for a town filled with secrets.

Evie blasted in, jangling keys. "Planning commission meeting convening at the Barn this afternoon! Anyone with ideas is invited. Mr. Patel will be there. Larraine says she'd like to meet Mrs. Walker and see if she can help. Where's Nick? This is right up his alley."

Everyone turned to Gracie. She tried not to stab the peanut butter sandwich she was cutting. Without looking up, she announced, "He's in Charleston looking for a home. He has a new job."

After various polite expressions of interest Gracie couldn't answer because she'd been too self-involved to ask, the conversation moved on. She tried to move with it.

So, she was probably losing her home. *Plus* the only man she'd had any interest in for years. And writing was probably a waste. Evie's mysteries were too weird to write about anyway. She should just go strip wallpaper.

But when it came time to visit the Barn, Gracie left Aster with Pris and climbed in the Kia to follow Evie and Jax to the crime scene.

That's all this meeting was, she reminded herself. Sammy had died there, and Evie simply wanted company in case his spirit energy lingered. Without Nick, no one wanted all those crappy *antiques* that were basically junk.

Larraine and Reuben were just climbing out of her Mercedes when they arrived. Mr. Patel's old truck was already in the lot, but he wasn't in sight. Gracie hoped they weren't raising his hopes for nothing. At least Judge Satterwhite owned this building, so maybe all would be well.

Jax unlocked the door. It already smelled musty inside. Gracie found the overhead light switch, but the place had never been well lit. One of the fluorescents appeared to be dead, which didn't help.

"Icy," Larraine commented, drawing her fur around her. The mayor looked more the part of the fashion designer she was than the politician she played.

Jax hunted for a thermostat, but they all knew by now that cold pockets meant spirit energy. Evie was already tuning in.

Restlessly, Gracie hunted down the old books she'd seen in here last time. She could probably pay Mrs. Walker for them if she found anything good. Was Sammy's mom coming?

Even as she wondered, the older woman tentatively stepped through the open doorway. Probably in her sixties, she looked much older. Her hair had turned iron gray, and she wore it in a frazzled bun. Her flowered cotton dress looked as if it had been fashioned from a sack. Although her shoulders were stooped, she walked without a cane.

Before she could turn to greet Sammy's mom, Evie screamed Gracie's name—and the shabby shelves of books Gracie had been perusing toppled.

$$\sim$$

CURSING, JAX KNEW HE WAS TOO FAR AWAY TO STOP COLLAPSING SHELVES, BUT HE and Reuben rushed toward Gracie anyway, while Evie shouted at an evidently angry spirit.

To his shock, the tumbling shelves abruptly fell sideways, missing Gracie by inches. Books flew everywhere. She seemed more concerned with rescuing them from thin air than saving herself.

Rescuing. Floating books.

Jax sighed and grabbed Reuben's arm. They watched with fascination as books drifted to the floor, undamaged.

Looking briefly embarrassed and apologetic, Gracie dropped to her knees and began gathering her bounty.

"Well, I never," Sammy's grief-stricken mother exclaimed from the doorway. "I had no notion this place was so dangerous!"

"They've been neglected too long," Larraine explained, while watching the scene with her carefully shaped eyebrows raised.

Jax checked on Evie. She leaned against the front counter, ostensibly talking into her phone. The cold pocket wafted away from the bookshelves, so maybe Sammy's spirit was listening.

He crouched down beside Evie's timid sister. "Need some help?" He knew Gracie could play card tricks. He'd never seen her float books, but he was fairly certain that's what had just happened.

Reuben brought over some old boxes and began stashing the old tomes inside.

"No, no, I'm fine. I wanted to see the titles. Yes, go look after Evie. I'm guessing Sammy is unhappy." She seemed nervous, but then, she usually was.

Jax left her with Dr. Reuben discussing the merits of some old fantasy novel. How a man who looked like an embattled African warrior could be such a nerd was hard to navigate.

Keeping an eye on Evie, who wouldn't appreciate his hovering, he returned to Larraine and Mrs. Walker.

"You said you have the lease agreement Sammy signed when he rented the barn?" He hadn't worked out a plan yet for untangling Layman's greedy scheme, but he was gathering a base of knowledge.

Mrs. Walker nodded and produced a manila folder from her oversized purse. "The judge was generous. He knew I needed my Sammy nearby. And no one else would want this place. My husband's family used to sharecrop these fields. But farm prices got so bad—"

Jax tapped the legal papers from their envelope.

Mr. Patel finally stepped inside, scarcely hiding his eagerness. "There is much space! We could have farmer's market. Crafts, maybe. Rent booths!"

Worrying about financing a project like that was someone else's problem. Larraine leapt in while Jax kept a wary eye on Evie, who appeared to be following the path of a distressed ghost and not doing much talking.

Mrs. Walker watched everyone anxiously. "I need to get back to the grandkids. They're all excited about the parade. Could I just leave them papers with y'all? I don' know much about business."

"We can probably draw up a sublease. But we'll need to find someone to buy your son's inventory," Jax tried to explain. "Do you want us to talk to the judge and let him decide what's fair?"

She nodded. "He's a good man. He'll do what's right." She hobbled out as if sensing the supernatural activity. She probably wouldn't appreciate knowing her son lingered.

"Block and his buddies want to put Mrs. Walker and others in a trailer park on the swamp land back there," Jax told the mayor once she let Patel wander off to measure space. "How much of this do you already know?"

Larraine dropped her usually upbeat expression and allowed herself to look momentarily weary. "I told you I need more alcohol than you're providing to go into this. We'd have to go all the way back to high school. Have you looked at those yearbooks?"

Jax dragged his memory back to the twenty-five-year-old pages he'd studied. "You and the Walker brothers and Rhodes all went to school together. Turlock Sr.'s law firm and Block's real estate agency sponsored sports teams for your class, but their kids were too young to play those years. You said your class was mean, but I saw no evidence in the books."

"No, you won't. Unless you read the fine print, you won't notice Judge Rhodes and I were top of our class in eleventh grade but aren't listed graduating in senior year. We were kicked out in our final semester. And Bertie, of course, dropped out early. Sammy graduated only because he was our star football player."

Jax raised his eyebrows. "Neither of you graduated?"

"We took the GED. Money was tight for all of us back then. Turlock and Block were already on their way in the world, or pretending they were Big Important Men by running up debt. Kids didn't know that sort of thing. We just knew they were offering a scholarship for the best all-around student. There were only twenty-five of us in the graduating class."

Jax grimaced. "And so you all started eliminating each other instead of standing out on your own."

Larraine shrugged. "What chance did a gay n. . ." She pulled up short on the epithet and continued, "Even if I busted my gut being best at everything? Besides, I was into fashion, not sports. I never had a chance. I just did my level best to see that everyone else played fairly. And they didn't."

"And your notion of fairness?" Jax appreciated Larraine's world view, but she'd had to be tough to survive.

"I reported Rhodes for cheating. He'd been doing it for years, but it didn't matter until then. I showed them where he'd copied my answers, right down to the mistakes. He claimed I was the one who copied. Since I'd taken at least one of those tests early, that was bogus, but they expelled both of us."

She refrained from adding what Jax understood—that school officialdom would have been happy to be rid of a poor, gay, Black troublemaker. She was just fortunate—or extremely determined—that they'd also been forced to kick out the upwardly mobile white guy. Evie's family may have been involved. Mavis had been Larraine's mentor by then.

"Out of curiosity, who won the scholarship?" Jax tried to wrap his mind around a cheating judge, how someone might use that scandal, and how it applied here, but the result had multiple outcomes.

"Nobody. I forget the excuse. Poor school spirit or some such, but my bet is that Block and Turlock weren't raking in the profits they'd expected from that promotion. Now tell me why I'm really here." She waited expectantly.

Jax produced his notebook computer to show her the LLC file. "With Block's demise, Franklin Layman inherits mortgages on half the town. He can recall them anytime. And we've uncovered plans to demolish Main Street for one of his malls. How much do you know about that?"

Larraine rolled her eyes. "Turlock has been on my case about the zoning ever since I forced it down the council's throat. Apparently they didn't realize they were ceding control of development to the voters."

Jax snorted. "Because, until recently, the voters didn't care and let them do whatever they wanted. You woke up the town. So Turlock is in on the scheme?"

"He's been standing in Block's shoes for months. I don't know what he has invested in this project now that his pal is dead. Maybe we should ask him." She glanced at her mobile and uttered an expletive. "I know I charged this thing before I left the office."

Jax handed her his battery recharger. "It's Evie. You might want to go to your car to make calls, or she'll drain this the moment you connect."

"Tell Reuben I'll be right back." She took the charger and sailed outside.

Jax would have liked to hear the conversation with Teddy Turlock Sr., but Evie would be wiped soon. He turned to watch her. He might not be able to call spirit energy, but he could be there after they drained her.

"Drug dealing is not the same as cheating in high school, Samuel!" Evie whisper-shouted. "And blackmail isn't any better. Two wrongs don't make a right."

Blackmail. That introduced an interesting new perspective. Jax would be happier if he thought she was talking about Layman being blackmailed, but Sammy wouldn't have known the wealthy businessman. It had to be a local.

Jax watched Gracie shyly float a book toward the always-curious Dr. Reuben. He wanted to wrap up this case so everyone could go back to enjoying the holiday. And so he could have Evie's full attention and pin her down to a wedding date. At this rate, he was contemplating Las Vegas. Her family would kill him.

"I'll give your Mom your love, Sammy. And your kids. They're going to be fine. We'll look after them. You need to move on. Bertie will need your help."

Jax was ready the moment Evie slumped. She'd terrified him the first time she'd done this. His pulse still accelerated. But he knew she was simply drained, more so if she'd just sent Sammy to the next plane.

He cuddled her close and took a seat on a rickety Bentwood rocker as she stirred.

The distinct crack of a rifle shattered the brief moment of peace.

Twenty-four

His earlier glee diluted by hours of hunting for an apartment he couldn't afford if he had to make car payments, Nick pulled off the highway at sight of the collection of family vehicles at the Barn. They must still be deciding what to do with the inventory.

His brain bubbled with suggestions. Creating ads and marketing slogans came easily, but he loved hands-on work. Gracie probably had a low opinion about that, given her bad experience.

He wasn't entirely certain why he worried about her opinion, except he'd spent these last hours trying to imagine Gracie in the apartments he looked at and failing. She needed her little cottage and yard and her family. He needed an understanding, independent woman like Gracie, one who wouldn't mind a modern apartment with a swimming pool for a courtyard —in a bad part of town where schools probably sucked.

He was starting to remember how he'd become mixed up with his family's bad lot who waved cash.

He slid the Harley between Evie's Subaru and Gracie's Kia. While he watched, the mayor in her fur coat climbed out of a Mercedes near the front door. He'd driven fancier cars. He was no longer interested. Luxury cars only had two purposes—to impress and to guzzle gas from one place to the next. He'd seen the result of showing off wealth. It was unhealthy for the budget and one's morals. These days, he simply needed wheels.

The abrupt silence of the bike as he switched off made the loud crack even louder. Nick froze. He was a city boy, but he'd been on a pheasant hunt with a sponsor once. He was pretty certain that had been a gun. Did people shoot birds here?

In answer, right before his eyes, the mayor slumped to the ground between the barn and her car.

Bloody friggin' hell. What did he do now?

Instinctively, he hit the emergency number on his mobile while ducking between the Subaru and Kia. Reporting his location to the dispatcher, he tried to scan his surroundings. He had a vague memory that the dispatcher wasn't local.

The barn door flew open and Reuben dashed out. The gun cracked again. The computer nerd flattened beside the Mercedes and Nick lost sight of him.

He wasn't a military man. He didn't carry a gun. Where was Jax?

Another gun shot hit the dirt in front of the barn door when it opened again.

Back door. There was a back door—

The gun fired again. Nick couldn't see where it hit. Could the sniper see the back door too?

His gaze traveled up the hill to the burned-out fruit stand. A sniper up there could see half the county while hiding behind those block walls.

Maybe they would go away if no one else emerged. Except he heard no sirens and the mayor could be dying.

He tried calling Gracie to warn her to keep everyone inside and got voice mail. The same with Evie and Jax. Bloody hell.

The gun spit two more times. Still no siren.

Cursing, Nick climbed back on the bike. Leaning low, he throttled the gas into full speed, scattering gravel like shrapnel. How far did guns reach? Obviously, pretty far to have hit the mayor. He knew nothing of weapons except some carried multiple rounds of ammunition. Surely no one would shoot into traffic? He hit the highway behind a hay truck and a semi.

He veered into the fruit stand lot as the first siren screamed down the highway. Before he could figure out what he meant to do, a scooter sputtered into life and rolled away—straight down the rutted hill behind the stand and into the muddy field beyond.

Anger dictated revving Jax's expensive Harley into running the sniper down, but the sheriff's car screaming into the lot below held him back. Torn, he hesitated. He never wanted to be arrested again. Twice was more than enough. And if he took off down that hill with his record. . . They'd think he was a sniper and shoot him.

Cursing, he stuck to his civic duty. He roared back to the parking lot and pointed out the direction of the sniper to the man in uniform.

While the lawman called in his report, Reuben rose from the gravel, hand extended. "You have a working phone? Give it to me."

Startled, Nick did as told, and watched with relief as the fur-coated mayor warily stood up behind the massive Mercedes.

An ambulance roared in, and Reuben all but shoved the mayor toward it while shouting directions at his partner on the other end of the line about trajectories and blockades.

Jax peered warily from the Barn door, then stepped out at sight of the official cars roaring into the gravel lot.

Nick finally had time to think clearly enough to remember Gracie and her family must be inside. His anxiety elevated. "Is everyone all right?" he shouted at Jax.

Lawyer man nodded, and Nick closed his eyes in silent gratitude to Whoever. He'd seen too much death lately. Then he crossed the lot while waiting for cautious Jax to survey their surroundings and scan the hill.

When Nick came closer, Jax said, "Our phones are dead. Damned good thing you arrived when you did. He had us trapped. How's Larraine?"

They both turned to watch as the mayor resisted the emergency workers removing her fur, and Reuben walked over to strip it off. Blood stained her silk shirt. She smacked Reuben. He ripped off the shirtsleeve.

"Well, now we know how that relationship works," Jax said, sounding exhausted and amused at the same time.

Nick didn't care how that relationship worked. Leaving Jax to talk to authority, he ran into the barn to see how Gracie fared. He found the sisters digging beneath the cash register counter, producing piles of old ledgers and papers.

Gracie shot him a look that could have been hero worship or irritation. He wasn't good at reading her expression. But she—and the others— appeared to be in one piece.

"Mr. Patel's in the workshop," Gracie called. "You might want to see if he's okay. He looked pretty shaken, but I'm afraid he might be building bombs."

Of course he was. Nobody in this town did normal things like hiding under the furniture. Nick trotted back to the workshop, assured the fruit stand owner that the sniper was gone and the sheriff had arrived. They discussed their plans for tomorrow's parade. Normality added a patina of calm, even if his insides were writhing with fury and fear. Who would endanger innocents while using the mayor for target practice? What was it with this town and mayors anyway?

What he really needed to do was hug Gracie and make certain she didn't have any bloody stains on her blouse. That might settle his rattled nerves.

Abandoning Patel, he returned to see what in hell the women were doing. Gracie cast him a cautious smile and returned to reading through old ledgers. Evie shoved a stack of books at him.

"Sammy seemed to be saying he was blackmailing his killer," Evie announced.

Sammy. Nick racked his brain a moment. Wasn't Sammy dead? Was there another Sammy? Then he recalled that Evie thought she talked to ghosts—ones who talked of blackmail? He struggled to make this compute while his hostess continued.

"I'm not entirely certain I understand who he was blackmailing or why. It has something to do with catching the drug dealer who hurt Bertie and keeping some cheater from evicting his mother. He couldn't give me names, although *turd* did come up in conversation," Evie said wryly. "I'm assuming that isn't another word for manure, and he meant one of the Turlocks."

"Shit, Evie. Just say *shit*. We're all adults here and this is what is called a clusterfuck." Gracie slammed a ledger down. "We're never going to find anything useful. We might as well start looking for new homes."

Nick almost fell over in shock. Quiet, proper Gracie did not use that language. She had to be really shaken.

He'd be shaken too if he had a solid, comfortable life and some wanker steamrollered over it. He took the ledgers Evie shoved at him and, giving in to their daft beliefs, sat on the floor beside Gracie. "Are we looking for naked lady pictures? Death threats? Signed confessions?"

"Anything that doesn't belong in ledgers?" Evie guessed. "You have to understand how small towns work. Sammy went to school with all the locals his age. He could have been blackmailing someone about stealing books from the school library in fifth grade. Or he could really have known about drug dealers and have proof."

Jax returned to hear this. "The mayor says Judge Rhodes cheated in high school. Others may have too. I've already done a search on drug convictions. We have arrests—the Shepherd twins being case in point. But we have no convictions."

"One assumes if the person being blackmailed had been caught and convicted, the news would be public, and they couldn't be blackmailed," Nick pointed out. "So chances are good this person has a clean record."

Sheriff Troy stormed in, halting in the doorway to adjust his eyes to the dim light. "Gladwell, you in here? We need a word with you."

Nick's insides sank to his insoles. He'd spent a lot of nasty hours in jail while the police in another county sorted out his cousins many crimes. Rising from the floor, he was grateful when Jax stuck to his side. Dealing with authority required marketing *himself,* something he'd never been good at.

"We need a precise description of what you saw." Troy started out with a simple request.

Nick knew from experience that it would get complicated from there. "I parked. I saw the mayor step out of her car. I heard a loud crack which I took to be a gunshot. I am not familiar with weapons and cannot tell you of what sort."

"Old-fashioned bolt action, no cartridges left behind," the sheriff said, probably for Jax's sake.

Jax nodded. "Precision hunting rifle, common, would be my guess. Not a .38 though. If it's the same killer, he has an arsenal of sorts."

Nick felt a little better that they were exchanging information. Did that mean he was not a suspect for a change? When the sheriff waited expectantly, he continued. "Before I could move, Reuben ran out and the sniper fired again. We all hit the ground. Jax attempted to leave the barn but the shots kept coming. I couldn't tell, but he may have been hitting both the front and back entries. Does a rifle have that many bullets?"

"As many as he can carry. It's how quickly he fired that matters. That was not military trained use." Jax shoved his hands in his pockets and frowned at the ceiling.

"But neither of you could see him?" the sheriff asked.

Nick shook his head. "I decided he had to be on the hill, possibly behind the fruit stand walls. That's pretty solid cement block up there. So I climbed back on the bike and headed up that way. I assume he saw me coming, but he'd have to shoot into traffic to reach me."

"You're the reason he fled. Otherwise, he had us trapped," Jax admitted. "Evie's ghost killed all our phones. We couldn't call out. The sniper had no way of knowing that, so I don't know what his plan was. To shoot us all?"

No wonder he hadn't been able to reach anyone. Ghosts killed phones? Nick didn't attempt to puzzle that out. "I'll stick my neck out here and assume if the mayor was his target, then he was making certain she was down for good or trying to get a better shot at her."

That brought a moment of silence. Nick glanced over his shoulder. Evie and Gracie listened with looks of horror. He swallowed hard. Perhaps he shouldn't have been so blunt?

Jax nodded agreement. "If Reuben hadn't gone out, Larraine would have stood up just to prove she was alive. Or climbed in the car and gone after the shooter. Or she could have bled out waiting."

"Give us what description you have," the sheriff said in resignation. "I have men tracking the scooter he escaped on, but he's long gone."

"I couldn't really see anything." Nick summoned what he could of his memory. "Small black motorbikes look alike to me. This one could have been the same as the thief at the art gallery used. I couldn't swear to it. I assume the shooter stood behind the wall, so he'd have to be tall enough to see over it. He was some distance away when he jumped on the bike, but I'd guess he was male. He was wearing a white helmet and a navy nylon coat. But I was concentrating more on whether I should take Jax's bike after him and not on what he was wearing."

"The Harley was too heavy, so good thing you didn't," Jax said. "At best, you'd have been bogged down. At worst, he would have shot you too."

That didn't make him feel a great deal better. If a killer was stalking the town, he should have gone after them somehow.

The sheriff's phone rang, and he gestured for them to wait. Listening, he nodded, grimaced, and rang off again. "Found the scooter covered in mud down in the old creek. It was reported stolen last week. I doubt we'll find prints, but they'll check."

Nick nodded. "Yeah, I'm pretty sure he was wearing gloves."

"Footprints?" Jax asked.

Sheriff shook his head. "Creek bed is all rock. All he had to do was walk down the creek and over to the sewer line, climb back to the road, and he's gone. I have men knocking on doors, but that's mostly empty warehouses back there."

The barn door slammed open.

"Merry, merry Christmas!" cried a jolly old elf, ringing a brass bell. "Is the party over? I just saw the mayor's car leaving."

~

"YOU SHOULD HAVE SEEN YOUR FACES!" EVIE CRIED, NOT FOR THE FIRST TIME, AS she rolled on the floor, laughing. "Admit it, you were all about to dive for cover when Santa entered!"

After Santa's interruption, she'd used Nick's phone to notify everyone that all was well. Then Jax had run out for hot drinks and snacks. Now her guests were hunkered down, working through Sammy's filing system—not Evie's idea of fun, so she leaned toward distraction.

Her sister grumpily flung another ledger on the discard stack. "We have a Christmas parade *tomorrow*. Mayor Larraine is supposed to ride in Judge Satterwhite's big white Cadillac convertible as Santa's helper, while the judge plays Santa. We could have snipers shooting at them! This is not funny, Evangeline."

Evie bit back a snicker. "But he was so obvious! The judge plays Santa every year. Even if you can't see his aura, you had to know it was him." She sobered at the mention of the parade, though. The sheriff had warned them earlier. "Reuben will have to tie up Larraine to keep her out of that car."

Attempting to fix voting machines and demanding recounts to keep a flaming liberal out of office were one thing. Shooting at Larraine. . . was quite another. But that didn't add up with shooting Block, who had been one of the world's most traditional office holders. Maybe the killer just didn't like government.

Jax had reported that Roark was searching for cameras in the warehouse area where the sniper had escaped. Reuben was tracking the cell phones of their various suspects, without results. Now that Sammy's ghost had passed on, Jax and Nick had their phones charging and were pounding at the screens. Evie hoped they had plans to keep everyone safe tomorrow. Disappointing a town full of kids—and Larraine was the biggest kid of all—would be a real bad start for the holiday.

"Nick's right," Gracie said in disgust. "We have no idea what we're looking for. Did Sammy specifically say his proof was in these books?"

"Sammy said he offered to buy his brother's unsold sketches after he learned that Bertie was following the *turds*. He thought the Turlocks were after his mother's home, and he wanted evidence, but what he meant to do with it, he didn't say. But Sammy specifically said he was blackmailing his killer, and *the proof is in his books*. But I'm not seeing any sketches in here."

Evie pushed around the debris they'd ferreted out so far, all the bits and pieces Sammy had shoved in between the pages in some filing system they'd never sort out. Once his spirit had communicated his fury, and been satisfied that his killer would be caught, he'd been persuaded into departing this plane. Evie thought the only reason he'd lingered was that he'd been too shocked and confused to move on. Sammy really hadn't had a purpose—like Bertie and Block.

Looking at this mess she'd hoped would solve the mystery, she wished she hadn't been so hasty, but Sammy had never been a smart man. As a ghost, he'd just been angry. He wouldn't have provided much help. She hoped he'd passed on to better things.

And as usual, he couldn't name names, only that he'd been blackmailing his killer. So maybe this had no relation to Block or this latest shooting. Blackmailers seldom came to a happy end.

"Here's a sketch of Sammy that Bertie drew as a young boy. It's old and probably not evidence." Gracie held up a small pencil sketch lacking the maturity of later ones.

Evie shook her head and studied fading photographs of the Walker siblings in various school poses. Invoices for the more expensive inventory he'd bought or sold. Invitations to a wedding from ten years ago. A certificate as runner-up in some gun show. High school report cards! Lordy, the things people thought important.

Gracie started on file folders. "I don't think he ever pitched an invoice. I'm guessing he couldn't remember costs, and he obviously had no bookkeeping system, so this was how he decided how much to sell something for. And then he'd forget he sold the item and never threw out the invoice. This is madness."

Nick clicked off his phone and reached for the file. "Let me see. I love knowing what things cost, and I have a steel trap memory."

"Have you and Jax talked Larraine out of the parade?" Evie knew that's what they'd been working on.

"We've found her the next best thing to the Popemobile." Nick clicked his phone photos and showed them the image. "It's in a used car lot in Savannah. Reuben has already ordered it delivered. Larraine can afford it."

"Bullet-proof glass." Jax pocketed his phone and began sorting through the debris file Evie had just rejected. "Satterwhite is insisting we use it if he's to play Santa, saying it's for his own protection. She can't argue that, not easily, anyway."

Evie leaned over and kissed his bristled jaw. "You are a man for all seasons, thank you."

"She has no idea where that phrase comes from," Gracie said grouchily. "She's just repeating a line she's heard."

Evie leaned over and pinched her sister. "I went to high school. I *remember* things. Just because I didn't read the book or play or whatever doesn't mean I can't hear. I am a professional human sponge."

Gracie dumped a file folder in her lap. "Here's all Sammy's school work from high school. It looks about like yours. Maybe he was ADD too."

Jax snatched the file away. "From *high school*? You did hear what Larraine said happened the year Sammy graduated?"

"High school kids cheat." Evie didn't mind having the file taken away. Reading wasn't the same as talking and doing. She could, if she had to, but then she couldn't observe everything happening around her, which she considered more important. She'd survived high school by having eyes in the back of her head. "We once had a contest to see who could cheat the most. It's a game unworthy of blackmail."

She might not read, but she understood what Jax was after. She continued, "Sammy said he wanted to stop Bertie's drug dealers, and he wanted to keep his mother's home. He suspected the *turd* was involved—except I don't know which one he meant. He didn't go to school with either of the Turlocks, too old for Jr. and too young for Sr. And how does any of this compute with Layman stealing our town? It doesn't."

"Someone just tried to kill the mayor," Gracie pointed out the obvious. "Does this mean someone is nervous?"

"Or that the mayor was the original target and not Block?" Nick suggested, flicking through invoices. "If you turn all your thinking around, that makes far more sense than shooting a man who was positioned to push through the zoning they wanted—if the current mayor were out of the picture."

They all stopped and stared at him.

Jax whistled and pulled out his phone again.

Gracie grabbed for the high school file. As a schoolteacher, she probably understood it better than anyone else. Jax didn't fight her for it. He was already reporting Nick's theory to the sheriff.

"Who would want Larraine dead?" Evie asked aloud, although Layman and Block were the obvious.

Without Larraine in the way, Block's handfed city council could have pushed through zoning changes for a mall, steamrollering right over the voters the way he had before. Layman really needed Block.

Evie had always thought that, which was why she hadn't considered Layman a suspect. But now. . .

"Turd, Turlock," she murmured. "Turlock Sr. wasn't fond of Block, but as a lawyer, he needed his business. So he was probably invested in Layman's mall and any new clients it brought. Teddy Jr. was at least aware of it, although I'd think it would wipe out his sporting goods store. Or maybe they offered his store a spot in the new mall. Any of them, as well as most of the town council, might want Larraine out of the picture for a shiny new mall, especially if they were offered discounted rental space."

Nick got up and paced. "This is how my cousins ended up in jail. Money and corruption go hand in hand when the players have no ethics."

"And we already know Block went to jail for lack of ethics." Evie gave that some thought. "And if Judge Rhodes is a cheat, his integrity is questionable."

"Anyone who did business with our late not-so-great mayor is questionable," Gracie said angrily, throwing down a ledger. "So we're right back where we started."

Twenty-Five

"THIS WILL NEVER WORK," GRACIE OBJECTED, AGAIN, THAT EVENING, AS THEY all gathered in the man cave. "This is the reason I'll never write your stories, Evie. They're all absurd and too complicated."

She watched as Jax taped a photo of Judge Rhodes on his cellar suspect wall. She'd never participated in these sessions of Evie's ridiculous Sensible Solutions Not-a-Detective Agency because she wasn't part of the team. But neither was Nick, and he was here now. She felt compelled to keep their madness to sensible levels, especially if they meant to involve children.

"The parade and Holiday Festival is the equivalent of bringing all the suspects into one room," Evie crowed, passing around a plate of Pris's assorted cookies.

Who would even imagine Pris as the sensible cousin? Even Iddy was down here studying Jax's silly story board. Her pet raven swung on the light fixture over the pool table, muttering to itself.

"Children aren't suspects! You're endangering innocents." Gracie contemplated the reaction if she made the kids stay home. It would not be pretty.

Exposing them to a sniper would be worse.

Reuben trotted down the cellar steps, and they all turned to him.

"How's Larraine?" Gracie asked the professor in a man-bun.

"Complaining loudly, refusing to take painkillers, and flinging things if anyone tries to make her sit still. I'm surmising she'll recover," he said dryly, grabbing a cookie and settling into his computer chair. "What have I missed?"

"Me, telling y'all you're insane and ought to be locked up. The whole town and a ton of visitors will be out tomorrow. You can't set yourself up as targets!" Gracie prayed they would listen. She knew they wouldn't. So she had to sit here and figure out how to save them all from themselves.

"The craft and food fair is in the morning," Evie said soothingly. "Everyone will be out in the street having a good time while we set up. At noon, we'll hold the gallery exhibit in the courthouse where Bertie and Blockhead can tune in, when everyone is at lunch or resting or preparing for the parade."

The Holiday Festival was supposed to be a pre-Christmas Eve shopping rush and family outing, not a hunt for a killer. Ghosts weren't exactly holiday spirits unless Evie thought she was re-enacting *The Christmas Carol*. What would Bertie be—the ghost of Christmas present?

The discussion gave Gracie cold shudders. "Where will the kids be?" she demanded, not in the least fooled by her sister's plotting. Evie had no respect for danger and no attention span for planning.

"Pris is manning the chocolate booth, so Dante will have the twins. You can lead Aster around with him. We don't need you to help set up the exhibit. Loretta will be with Mavis, and then she's going down to the school to help finish up the floats and rehearse for the play. If you mean *all* the kids in town, they're pretty much doing the same thing. It's not until the parade at two, when the mayor shows up, that we need to worry. So we have to bring this to a close before then."

"You can't really expect a stone-cold killer to accept an invitation to see Bertie's sketches!" Although, yeah, that almost made sense since someone had been attempting to steal those sketches. That didn't make her any happier.

"It's all we have," Nick said, working on his laptop, printing out publicity flyers. "Maybe you ought to stay with Pris in the chocolate booth and be our guard post."

That's what she wanted to do. But if she meant to write Evie's stories. . . She was crazy to even think it, but she wanted to see what happened. She was tired of being left out. And she was recognizing that it was her own fault that she was always left behind. She was a wimp, a yellow-bellied doormat letting others walk all over her.

She needed to broaden her comfort zone. So she squirmed and listened.

"If we're ready to start. . ." Jax taped up a photo to the wall. Evie's normally unflappable fiancé was looking a little harassed. "We need to determine our most likely suspects and make certain they attend our little event. Judge Rhodes was there when Block was killed. He'd just ruled on the zoning laws in Larraine's favor—does that mean he's against the mall, doesn't know about it, or that she threatened him with his high school infractions and he caved?"

Gracie tried to picture their stylish mayor threatening the dull, conservative judge and couldn't rule it out. Larraine's flamboyant confidence would have Rhodes strangling on his necktie. And with all this talk of blackmail. . . Who knew what the mayor might be holding over his head?

"We have Bertie's sketch of Layman handing Rhodes cash, so Rhodes definitely knows Layman. And Rhodes hates the old courthouse and is presumably in favor of new everything." Evie perched on the pool table and nibbled her chocolate chip cookie. "But if he ruled in Larraine's favor, then maybe he's honest."

"According to the yearbook, Rhodes won gun competitions," Nick added. "That was his sport and probably put him ahead of Larraine in the scholarship competition."

"Both Turlocks were at the courthouse and have gun licenses." Jax taped up a photo of father and son. "Teddy Jr. sells guns in his sporting goods store. He tested positive for drugs in a rifle team competition in college. He was later arrested for selling, but his father pulled strings and got him off."

"I did not know that," Evie said.

Gracie could have said the same. This town really held its secrets. "So that's why he's running a sporting goods store instead of following in his father's footsteps?"

Raven hair braided, Iddy crossed her long legs on an overlarge bean bag cushion. "That, and he's an idiot. Maybe he smoked his brains, but his ex-wife confided that he flunked his LSAT. She thinks he's still selling pot, at least. Or lying about store profits, because she couldn't get a decent settlement based on the store's income. Or lack thereof. But he's never short of cash. He laid down a bundle for that Corvette."

Ah, so that's why Iddy had been recruited. As the only veterinarian in town, she knew everyone with animals, which included most of the county. Gracie only knew people with kids.

"Teddy Turlock Jr. and the Shepherd twins went to school together," Gracie offered, reluctantly joining in. "I was a freshman when they were seniors. They were caught smoking behind the bleachers several times, but they were all on the football team and just got rapped on the knuckles."

"Toby and Verity were in your class." Evie swung her foot. "So they probably knew about that too. Are we trying to say Teddy Jr. or the Shepherds gave drugs to Bertie? Were they all at the Corvette party for *drugs*?"

Reuben and Roark looked bored. Small town gossip wasn't their thing. Gracie gathered hacking computers was more to their liking, or maybe spying. They were simply waiting for action, not gossip.

"You're the one who first said the Shepherds sell pot," Jax reminded Evie. "How do you know that?"

Evie pointed at Iddy.

Their cousin shrugged. "The Shepherds won't let me near their dogs, but I've trained La Chusa to keep an eye on them. Because the dogs bark all the time, I was afraid they were chaining the animals and neglecting them. I'm pretty sure what the raven is seeing are marijuana plants."

Gracie sighed in admiration as Nick's square-boned model face frowned impressively as he asked, "So in the sketch with the Corvette, they were all having a pot party? Do we now have to suspect the mayor's tree-hugger son and the woman who gave us the gallery consignment?"

Evie shook her head negatively. Gracie intervened. "Even I could tell that Verity was scared when she gave us those sketches. She was the one who framed them to hide the Main Street drawing. Since her mother and Layman have a relationship, she may even have helped Bertie steal it. We just don't know when or how."

"The two tree huggers had to know something was going down," Reuben pointed out, flipping through his laptop and studying his notes. "Verity's mother is dating Layman, and Toby is Block's son. They probably overheard conversations. So they paid Bertie to follow the Turlocks all summer."

"Toby would be totally against a trailer park on the swamp, and his aura seems clear. I don't know Verity's place in this." Evie studied the gallery of suspects.

"So why were they all together at the pot farm?" Nick persisted. "Wasn't Bertie about ten years too old for that lot?"

"Physically, maybe, emotionally and mentally, probably not," Gracie tried to explain. "Bertie was talented, but his brain never matured as it should. Didn't Mrs. Satterwhite say that the Shepherds tried to buy her farm?" And Evie claimed Bertie and Sammy's ghosts were afraid of their mother being evicted. Gracie couldn't see the connection to the Main Street project that would evict her and her neighbors.

"Spying," Jax said enigmatically, slapping a copy of the Corvette sketch on a different part of the wall. "Verity and Toby suspected something was up. They know these guys, went to school with them, knew the Shepherds did drugs and couldn't buy farms."

"Speculation," Roark argued, munching on what appeared to be beef jerky instead of sweets. "You ain't goin' nowhere wit' dis."

Evie jumped down from the pool table and grabbed the yarn Jax had been using to connect photos. She taped one end to Bertie. "Bertie died from dirty drugs, not pot." She taped another end to Teddy Jr. "The Shepherds might be growers, but Jr. is the most likely dealer, possibly of more than pot. His father backed Block and probably has grand delusions of working with a billionaire now that Block is gone. Jr. owes his dad big time for keeping him out of jail and maybe for setting him up with the sporting goods store." She slapped the end of the thread leading to Turlock Sr.

"If the younger lot were partying with Bertie, they knew he was living in the attic." Gracie's insides roiled as the amorphous theory took shape. "If one of them wanted to use the attic to be rid of Mayor Larraine, they had to remove Bertie. If Jr. invited him to a pot party. . ."

"But it wasn't pot that killed him," Evie corrected. "The coroner's report says opioids and fentanyl did."

"I'm betting the younger lot were all about Bertie's sketches," Nick said into the silence that followed. "They have no money to invest in grandiose land grabs. But Jr. may have mentioned something about his dad and the swamp that made the tree huggers suspicious. They probably thought they were being altruistic by jump-starting Bertie's career, giving the poor brain-damaged bloke a direction to wander and sketch in hopes he'd see something. The Corvette party may have been where they explained Bertie's presence with some feeble excuse."

"Let's quit guessing and nail Toby down." Jax was already punching a contact on his phone. He put it on speaker when his client answered. "Attorney-client privilege. Are you alone?"

At Toby's affirmative, he asked, "What was the Corvette pot party about last summer?"

The other end was silent. Evie stuck her hand out for the phone. Jax shook his head and refused.

Toby finally spoke warily. "The swamp. Why?"

"Let's pretend I believe that was your only goal. Why would a trio of potheads be of use?"

"Trio?" Toby asked dryly. "Which one are you leaving out?"

"Bertie. He claimed to be clean. The Shepherds are growing and Teddy

Turd Jr. is selling but Bertie was no longer using. Where's the connection with the sketches?"

More silence. Jax outwaited him.

Itchy all over, Gracie got up for another cookie.

"What's this about, Jackson? Is it related to my father's properties?"

"Layman now owns your father's properties unless we prove fraud is involved. Was that your goal?"

Gracie pursed a whistle. So this was why Jax was a lawyer. Pity he wasn't still earning the big bucks.

The late mayor's son sighed and gave in. "Originally. Verity saw one of Bertie's sketches of us and thought he might be marketable. So she bought several and showed them to me to learn more about the subjects before she took them to the gallery. One sketch showed Teddy and the Shepherds at the fruit stand, except they were looking at the swamp and not fruit. This was abnormal behavior for pot dealers. I got suspicious and asked Bertie about it. He said the Shepherds were trying to evict his mom for some housing thing."

Gracie caught herself biting her thumb and sat on her hand.

"About that time, Verity overheard her mother's boyfriend talking about a project in Afterthought keeping him in town. My dad was in jail and his lawyer wouldn't give me the time of day, but I figured Turlock knew everything Dad did. So we tried his son—"

"Who smoked what few brains he possessed and could be pumped. I'm getting the picture." Jax wrapped yarn around his fingers.

"Bertie was our cover, so to speak. We said we wanted to launch his art career, so he was going to be sketching around town. Since he wasn't doing drugs anymore, we wanted them to believe he was harmless."

"Except he'd already been sketching, hadn't he?" Jax asked.

"Yeah, and that came back to bite us. Once he got off drugs, Bertie was prolific and showed his treasures to anyone who asked. He sold some to his brother and who knew who else. Not long ago, Teddy called and yelled at me and demanded we hand over the lot. I told him Bertie only gave Verity the ones he wanted sold. He'd have to ask Bertie where they were." Toby sounded sad.

Gracie watched Evie sit on her hands too. She suspected her sister was trying not to snatch the phone.

Luckily, Jax understood her struggle. "For what it's worth, I don't think Bertie died for your sketches. I think he died for the architectural drawing Verity hid behind one of them."

"Not making me feel better," Toby said gloomily. "We don't know how Bertie obtained that drawing. He had utterly no idea what it meant. He was just excited about the buildings and the perspective. He wanted to do something similar from the courthouse roof."

"But that's when you realized what your father was up to?"

"I knew he'd sold us out somehow, but he refused to tell me details. He just said he was restoring my inheritance, which I never wanted in the first place. Generations of dirty dealing should have been returned to the community. I was hoping you'd find at least some funds somewhere. But if Layman now owns everything. . ." His sigh was loud enough to be heard through the speaker.

If Layman now owned everything, they were up a creek without a paddle. Hiding her tears, Gracie got up and walked out.

Twenty-Six

WEARING REINDEER ANTLERS, A ROUND RED NOSE, AND A BAGGY BROWN TUNIC, Loretta hugged Evie the next morning. "I'll be fine. I'll stay with Mavis and the aunties and then go straight to the school. I'll run if I see any bad bubbles."

"Right. Bad bubbles to be avoided." Although pointing them out to authorities wouldn't float, as Evie well knew. "But I want you to have fun." Evie hugged her ward and sent prayers to Whoever watched over them. She was more aware than most of the spirits lingering beyond the Veil. She just hoped maybe Loretta's parents hovered protectively.

"I'm already having fun! No one knows who I am in this costume. I can't wait for the parade!" She skipped off down the street without a care in the world, as it should be.

And every person in town turned to smile at her because millionaire kids never went unnoticed.

Fighting her trepidations, Evie went in search of Pris. If a killer was after one of Bertie's sketches or the mall drawing, everyone needed to be in position and well-rehearsed once this art show got going.

Her cousin was already handing out hot chocolate to workers setting up booths around the courthouse square. Pris had recruited some of her former staff to sell cookies and cupcakes. Evie hoped she would open a café if she stayed. The booth was doing a booming business.

"Is Dante a wreck yet? Will this send him fleeing back to Italy?" Evie asked, reading the intense colors in Pris's aura and thinking the green streak in her hair almost matched.

"The idiot man is actually *enjoying* the skullduggery. He's leading two innocent children wearing antlers around, feeding them junk so they're hyper, and handing out Nick's art show flyers. My mind will be blown before noon." That was Pris's reminder that her psychic abilities went into overload in crowds.

"I don't want you reading minds. Just let us know if you see or sense anything unusual. Take the kids home before noon. Sheriff Troy will be with us by then."

They were both aware that Gracie and half the town stood to lose their homes and businesses unless they put an end to Layman's plans. Larraine might never walk safely down the street again unless they caught a killer. But one did not necessarily lead to the other. Working without any evidence except a ghost's warnings had its difficulties.

They needed to know what Bertie's sketches had to do with a killer, if anything. She simply didn't believe in coincidence when it came to death. Had Sammy died for his brother's sketches or was it a simple blackmail situation? Then—had the mayor been blackmailing too? If they ruled out the sketches as motive. . .

She was pretty certain they couldn't rule out the pièce de résistance, the mall drawing. She just prayed the ghosts would speak up or she could read a killer's aura before he killed again. With all the spinning wheels she had to put in place, one trap at a time was the best she could manage.

Evie located Iddy next. Her vet cousin was setting up an Adopt-a-Pet area in the sheltered spot beside the courthouse steps. Evie crouched down to tickle a beagle puppy behind its ears and watch it squirm with joy. This was what the day should be about, not ghosts and evildoers.

"I'm heading up to check with our resident spirits. Are you good here?"

No-nonsense Iddy hadn't bothered with costumes. She wore her usual work clothes of jeans and tucked-in shirt and boots, with her heavy blue-black hair caught back in a rubber band. She helped an owl from its perch to her wrist, where it bobbed its head at Evie as if answering her question.

"I have a few critters upstairs as well as down," Iddy said. "I can't say how much help they'll be, but I should receive an image of any disaster."

"Since the sheriff will be with us, I'm not sure who else you can call, but we'll hope this all goes down quietly." Evie couldn't imagine how. She suspected even Bertie would be agitated to see his work displayed.

At least neither spirit had displayed poltergeist tendencies. Yet. A building with slamming doors and flying files would be condemned pretty fast.

Satisfied her outdoor troops were in position, Evie entered the courthouse. She was worried about Gracie. Her normally quiet, cautious sister had developed unusually intense colors similar to Pris's lately. Lust for Nick was part of it, she supposed. It was about time Gracie stopped being a nun, and the Brit was cute. But this business about writing a book and going with Nick to investigate galleries. . . Just a wee bit scary.

Viking Verity had a crew of helpers carrying easels to the upstairs rotunda. The leaflets and the last minute changes Reuben had made to the festival website specified the exhibit opened at noon. Evie didn't fool herself into believing criminals paid attention to rules. The sheriff had men on the watch. So did she.

Upstairs, the rotunda was relatively warm. The courthouse haunts had gone into hiding with all the activity. That wouldn't last now that Evie had arrived.

Hiding behind a website was no longer an option. They needed to know who wanted Bertie's work, and they needed to know before anyone else died.

She found Jax with Roark studying schematics—they'd jumped on the blueprints she'd shown them. There'd been changes since her father's day, but it gave them a start. "You need drones to spray pepper and guns in the wall to shoot Tasers," she suggested facetiously. They needed to chill.

"Lasers," Jax responded without looking up. "Dream bigger." He looked good, if not Christmasy, in his chocolate-brown cable-knit sweater over a collared shirt. She couldn't believe she planned to marry a preppy!

She was about to leave him to his consultation when he caught her waist, held her close, and planted kisses down her neck until she couldn't think straight. Would she ever get used to this brilliant man wanting *her*? Probably not in this lifetime.

"Stay out of the crossfire, please," he whispered. "Hide under a bench, anything. I don't want to lose you."

She hugged him back, cuddling close. "Ditto, Macho Man. But there's no reason for guns if Larraine isn't here. We're all just art lovers."

They both knew that was a lie, but it was all she had. She couldn't speak for the ghosts while hiding under a basket, and the whole point here was to get a ghost's perspective. She doubted anyone but Jax fully understood that.

Reuben was with Larraine in her secure office at city hall down the street, but he had access to the cameras Roark was installing. Evie could hear him in Jax's earbud, directing camera angles. She kissed Jax's jaw and wandered off to check the positioning of Bertie's artwork.

In his usual denim work shirt and jeans, Toby had set up the architectural drawing of Main Street USA in the middle of the hall, with a cloth over it. Bertie's lovely watercolor collage blocked it from view. Evie admired the details of the painting, waiting for Bertie to announce his presence.

Instead, Gracie, in a festive red sweater that looked good with her blond hair, joined her. "I called Mrs. Walker and told her what we're doing. I don't know if she'll come, but maybe some of Bertie's family will."

Evie nodded and swallowed a lump. "Having his family see this display would be the next best thing for Bertie. Poor guy deserves a Christmas. I thought you were taking Aster around the fair."

"I am. I just wanted to see the set-up first. I'll be back in an hour or so. We're helping Nick and Dante pass out flyers advertising the show. Are you okay? No apparitions shoving anyone around?" She'd pulled her hair up in red ribbons and left curls dangling at her nape—a far cry from her usual neat bob.

Evie thought she should have dressed up a little more too. Her reindeer sweatshirt would have to do though. "I don't know if either spirit has gathered enough energy to do more than slam doors. They're not exactly live wires. All I can do is wait and see. Ghosts usually find some way of expressing themselves if disturbed."

"Then I hope you can hide in a closet if they do. I'll see you later." She took the stairs down.

"Charging admission is a good way of eliminating lookie loos." Looking good in fitted jeans, Toby stepped back from the main easel to examine the hall with a critical eye. "Who gets the funds?"

"Bertie's family, of course. If we sell anything, Verity receives her fee and the balance goes to his family. Do you think they'll sell?" Evie had once considered Toby the coolest guy in school, probably because he was new and hadn't really picked up on her ADHD.

A little experience made a lot of difference. She could now see that he was a nice guy, nothing more. She supposed it said something for his character that he'd turned out well despite his years of privilege and his blockheaded father.

"Verity will do her thing," he said. "She'll label the mantel collage not for sale. The rest will have price tags. None of this will prevent Layman from owning the town."

"I know." Evie bit back her sadness. She preferred action to grieving. "I know you don't believe, but I'm hoping your father's spirit will point out the bad guys, even if he can't name them."

"I don't believe killers will show up, much less any of the rest." Toby walked away.

Well, there was that. The sketches were the only bait she had. And they weren't even drawing out ghosts.

⁓

AROUND ELEVEN, WITH ALL HIS FLYERS HANDED OUT, NICK CHECKED THROUGH his phone for the various online news sites to see if his press release had hit any of them. Several of the locals had added the exhibit to their event calendars, but it was too late for the bigger sites. He had an e-mail from a reporter about the art website and Bertie. That would be too late for today's events but if all went well, might sell a few sketches later.

He had no idea if any of his publicity had reached Layman or his cohorts. He was counting on small town gossip and the town council passing the word.

He was counting on a killer coming to see the sketches. He was now officially insane.

He bought hot chocolate from Pris, who was packing up her booth. "See Gracie?"

"Upstairs already. Take her a cookie. Her anxiety level has reached nuclear." She wrapped the last of her confections, added them to a carry bag, and handed it over.

"Thanks. I'm not sure she appreciated the hot dog lunch." He'd decided hot dogs were an acquired taste. He should have tried the barbecue.

Way to deny insanity—think about dead meat.

Holding the bag, he entered the courthouse. Downstairs was relatively quiet.

The ticket seller wasn't in position yet, so he proceeded upward.

Despite the early hour, a crowd had already formed. He searched for Gracie, finding her in a brilliant red sweater, shivering near one of the courtroom doors. He handed her his hot chocolate and admired the silky blond curls escaping her ribbons. "Is there time for me to run back and fetch a coat for you? It's colder in here than out."

Gracie nodded toward her reindeer-adorned sister pacing with a phone to her ear. "Hope you brought a cell phone charger. I think Evie's apparitions have shown up. Stick around for the show."

He shrugged off his blazer and dropped it over her shoulders. His wardrobe tended toward black, not exactly a holiday color, but his turtleneck was warm. "I'll be better prepared for action this way. Name the players, please."

She handed back the hot chocolate while rummaging for the cookies. "The slight man with the dyspeptic expression and the only one wearing a suit and tie is Judge Rhodes. You've met Judge Satterwhite—the older man with white hair, wearing a Santa hat? He dons his Santa suit in his office, but he's here early."

"And I recognize cowboy boots and leather jacket as Layman. He's not looking happy for a man who owns the town."

The gazillionaire had shown up! Nick would feel triumphant except Layman was glaring ominously at the collage on the center easel. Did he know it hid his architectural drawing?

"Shh, I don't think we're supposed to know about him owning the town. I bet he's hunting for the drawing that would expose his evil schemes. He's talking to Turlock Sr., the guy wearing the gray sweater over a shirt and tie. I'd scowl, too, if Turd got too close."

The late mayor's lawyer left the scowling gazillionaire and crossed over to talk to an older man in a faded blue suitcoat and no tie.

"Hank, chair of the town council, once former Mayor Block's good buddy," Gracie murmured.

Nick recognized the hardware store owner but hadn't made the connection. He'd seen Layman in the store complaining about zoning laws. Interesting. "I see Verity, our art gallery hostess, has disappeared. She doesn't want her mother's sugar daddy to see her?"

Gracie shrugged. "She's scared for some reason."

"Which one is Tobias Block? Is he here?"

"Long-haired surfer dude leaning against the wall, watching the world go by. Or listening to Evie talk to ghosts, since he seems a trifle bewildered." Gracie munched her cookie. In between bites, she pointed out the various town council members who appeared to be nattering more than studying the artwork.

The sheriff had positioned himself inconspicuously in a niche behind the easels and was talking into his phone. Nick hoped he was lining up reinforcements and had a battery charger, if reports of ghostly energy draining phones were reliable.

If ghosts existed, they'd better be good guys, because he was thinking the bad guys had them outnumbered.

Gracie coughed and nearly spit out her cookie as two muscular, pot-bellied men entered, smelling of manure and skunk.

"Shepherd twins?" Nick surmised. He recognized the stench of pot.

She nodded and gulped the chocolate.

"Now all we need is Teddy Turlock Jr., right?" He didn't think anyone here looked like the man who stopped by the garage hunting for Bertie's sketches. . . and offering him a job.

"He was here a minute ago. I suspect he called the Shepherds. They're not married and don't have kids and never come to these things. Look at Iddy's raven."

Nick turned to watch the bird flapping its wings and bobbing its head menacingly. "Is it preparing to peck out eyes?"

Gracie glanced at the ceiling and Nick followed her thoughts. The canister lights were all in place. The hole had been plastered over. No gun aimed at them. That wasn't the reason the bird was upset.

OK, now he was believing in birds as security guards.

A brisk wind swept through the hall, catching the larger sketches. They toppled, taking the easel with them—revealing Teddy Jr. talking to his father. The raven screamed and returned to its perch on an old light fixture. The Turlocks looked startled.

"I think Bertie has something to say to you, Teddy." Evie called gleefully from near the janitor's closet. "He's remembering who invited him to a party he never got to attend."

"Here we go," Gracie whispered in horror.

Had the slightly dodgy sporting goods store owner killed Bertie? *Why?*

Twenty-Seven

"YOU'RE NUTS!" TEDDY JR. PREDICTABLY SHOUTED, HEADING TOWARD THE STAIRS, wearing one of his store's designer nylon jackets in blood red.

Easels mysteriously toppled with every step the lawyer's drug-dealing son took. He tried to walk around the flying canvases—while everyone in the rotunda gaped.

Evie mentally cheered Bertie's spirit for finally gathering the gumption to act out.

"Bertie's mad," she called after Teddy. "He wanted to party and ended up dead. How did that happen?"

"How the hell am I supposed to know?" Jr. cried, leaping backward as an easel just missed smacking him on the hip of his saggy jeans. "Druggies are delusional."

Evie grinned. He was talking as if Bertie were really here—which he was, in spirit.

Looking good in black, Nick helpfully returned the easels and sketches to upright, placing himself between Evie and Teddy.

She watched the angry wisp of Bertie's gray spirit attempt to swing a skinny fist at the sporting-goods store owner. The artist had never been much of a fighter when alive, but his energy succeeded in making his victim shiver in his nylon jacket and spin around, searching for another way out.

"Who put the needle in your arm, Bertie?" Evie asked, just because that had been bothering her.

I quit needles! Bertie insisted. He showed a little more substance than usual as he paced back and forth through Teddy. *I got achy. He gave me pills so we could go to the party.*

Oh dear, Bertie had never been bright either. This wasn't fun anymore. "Sheriff, Bertie says Teddy gave him pills when he got achy before the party. I don't suppose there's any way of telling the difference between pills and needles in the system?"

"I didn't do anything!" Teddy shouted. "I just wanted him out of the attic so I could find the sketches!"

Ted's kid was always a shit head. Sounds like a confession to me.

Evie pinched her nose to hold her focus as ex-mayor Block materialized near the railing where he'd died.

Did my lawyer's brat shoot me? Is that why he was in the attic?

This was taking distraction to new levels. How did she listen to two ghosts while transmitting all this information to whoever needed to hear it? At least Block was finally acknowledging he was dead.

Jax offered his strength by gathering Evie against him. She ignored the former mayor and returned to the Teddy/Sheriff conversation. "How did you persuade Bertie out of the attic? Did you find any sketches?"

"I told him we were going to a party," Teddy said grudgingly, realizing his error in admitting that he wanted the sketches. "He said he had a headache. I gave him a few pills, told him to rest, and that I'd take his sketches down to the car so he could show them to others. I didn't kill him! He fell asleep, and I left him there."

"And he never woke up," the sheriff said. "What kind of pills?"

Evie kept her eye on the two ghosts while half listening. Bertie wasn't happy but aimlessly studied his artwork. Block. . . seemed to be waiting for something. He always played his cards close to his chest, even in death.

"Nothing big, just a little painkiller to take the edge off! He must have already had drugs in his system." Teddy Turlock Jr. edged toward the front stairs.

Silver-haired Turlock Sr., looking stuffy in gray sweater and tie, glared at his son with scorn but remained silent. Evie suspected, as a lawyer, he ought to be telling Jr. to shut up, but maybe he was tired of dealing with his antics.

Kid ain't his, Block offered, as if he'd heard her thoughts.

Evie pretended to talk into her dead phone. "How do you know?"

She would let Jax and the sheriff persuade Jr. into incriminating himself. Translating ghost speak was her job.

They took those DNA ancestry tests last year. No relation. Block's aura drifted from the railing to walk through Turlock Sr., apparently for amusement. Evie hadn't realized the ex-mayor found anything humorous except grabbing up land. Turlock shivered in his thick sweater and headed over to talk to Judge Rhodes.

He killed me? Bertie asked plaintively. *I thought he was my friend.*

"You have to be careful how you choose your friends, hon," she murmured to the specter. Jax's arm tightened around her.

In a louder voice, she asked, "Where are the sketches you took from the attic?"

Teddy Jr. grasped the question as if she'd thrown him a lifesaver. "I gave them to Dad. He said Bertie had stolen a valuable drawing, but all I found was his scribbling."

Bertie knocked another easel into him, catching Teddy Jr. in the back of his nylon coat and causing him to stumble. *Not scribbling! Art! The lady said so!*

Too much distraction. Evie focused on Teddy's father, since that was where Block's spirit stood. "Does that mean you have more artwork to contribute to the gallery exhibit, sir?"

"Me? You're talking to me and not one of your phantoms?" the lawyer asked with a sneer. "I can't believe we're allowing the use of a public courthouse for this obvious marketing ploy for your fake little shop. Albert was a homeless addict. Watching you sell his feeble crap while you pretend to see ghosts is a waste of our time."

Turlock Sr. started for the stairs, retreating from Block's icy vicinity. Judge Rhodes, most of the council, and Layman appeared prepared to follow.

In a blast of energy, Bertie whacked the big easel, hurling the collage and the Main Street sketch at them.

Him! It's him! He was the one who woke me up! He had a gun!

GRACIE NEARLY JUMPED OUT OF HER SKIN AS EVIE SHOUTED INCOHERENTLY, "Bertie says *he* woke him up and that he had a *gun!*" before slumping in Jax's arms.

Poor Jax looked rightfully terrified and appeared ready to give mouth-to-mouth resuscitation.

Who, Evie, who? Gracie wanted to scream, once her heart started beating again. She knew her sister was fine, just drained, like all their phone batteries. It happened.

Everyone froze and stared at the large drawing on the floor of the rotunda.

"Uh oh, this is about to get ugly." Gracie gripped Nick's arm as Judge Satterwhite lifted the previously concealed architectural drawing that the ghost had sent flying.

Studying the professional print of a mall, the white-haired judge muttered an expletive before asking, "What is this?" He held up the Main Street portrayal. "Bertie didn't do this. Turlock, is this the drawing you claim Bertie stole?"

All those departing stopped to look.

Gracie could swear the two Turlocks turned three shades of gray. Layman reached apoplectic purple. She was beginning to understand Evie's penchant for colors.

The sheriff looked up from remanding Teddy Jr. into the custody of one of his deputies. "Is that one of the drawings you took from Bertie?"

Looking defeated in his saggy jeans and nylon jacket, Teddy Jr. shook his head. "That wasn't in the attic. It used to be in Dad's office, but Bertie stole it while he was spying on us. I tried to get it back but couldn't find it."

Losing his surfer dude carelessness, Tobias Block finally straightened into an angry straight arrow. "It's an architectural drawing Bertie found while following Mr. Layman around town."

The chill factor dropped ten degrees. Gracie glanced at her sister. Evie still rested against Jax, but she was following something with her gaze. The ghost of Toby's father, the man behind Layman's mall project?

Still muttering un-Santa-like language despite his fuzzy hat, Satterwhite held it up for all to see. "Look familiar to anyone?"

Gracie watched with interest as proper Judge Rhodes in his blue suit eased toward his courtroom door. She considered stepping in front of it, but Nick beat her to it. She sent him a tentative smile. It was easier to be brave with someone at her side.

Rhodes glanced anxiously at the backstairs, but the Sheriff was there with Teddy Jr.

Who woke Bertie up? And what did *woke* mean? Bertie died while asleep. Did Evie mean someone woke Bertie's *ghost*? Nervously, Gracie studied all the familiar faces. None looked happy. Or guilty. Pris should be here to read minds.

"Mayor Block wants to say something," Evie called from the bench when no one responded to the judge's question. "He's angry and cursing and not very coherent, so you'll have to pardon my loose translation. I don't use that language."

"Block is dead." Stiff and stern as only a judge can be, Rhodes objected. "This is ludicrous. That's a perfectly reasonable rendition of a transformative addition to our town. It will put Afterthought on the map and land prices will soar. We'll all benefit. People will have good-paying jobs. We can't relive the Civil War forever."

Ah, Gracie thought, there was one person who admitted knowing about it. How many others? How could she ever write a mystery when her stomach tied in knots trying to solve the puzzle? And find a killer!

"Afterthought wasn't much more than a few plantations and farms, a church, and a saloon during the war," Santa-Satterwhite said with scorn. "Our fathers built this town with hard work, not slave labor. We built businesses we can pass on to our children, businesses that hire our neighbors so we can share the wealth."

He shook the drawing until it rattled. "Corporate behemoths like this drain us of our livelihoods, send our money to make rich men richer, and make part-time, minimum wage slaves of our young people! Is this what you mean to put on my mother's farm? Then we can just tear up this little piece of trash now, can't we?"

"That's not yours to destroy," Rhodes cried. "You're all so buried in your past, you can't see the future Mr. Layman has promised!"

Shifting his big shoulders beneath his leather jacket, Layman scowled at being named. "Tempest in a teapot, folks. Ghosts and this little girlie don't know anything. I'll take the drawing with me, and y'all can go back to enjoying the party."

Gracie couldn't stand it. If no one would declare it out loud, she would. She couldn't let that creep sneak around and steal her home and say *nothing*. "Tell us where you really mean to build that mall, Mr. Layman! Your Honor, take a look at the courthouse in the corner of the drawing. That's not your family's property. That's right here on Main Street, like the drawing says!"

Satterwhite looked and threw down his Santa hat in fury. Tobias Block grabbed the print from him and held it up so others could crowd around. Gracie watched as Nick whispered to a stranger. Had he called reporters? A few of the council members studied the drawing and muttered. Had they *not* all been in on the scheme?

Several phones—the ones presumably with battery backups—pinged around the room. Gracie glanced at a text from Reuben: LARRAINE ON HER WAY WITH MRS. WALKER

Oh shit looks passed across half a dozen faces. Larraine was supposed to stay away! She must have tied Reuben in knots to escape his custody.

"Wait a minute, if this is down the street from the courthouse, it takes out my office building!" Geoff Hayes, Jax's landlord, cried in shock. He'd always been good buddies with Block and the council. And he didn't know about it?

"Mr. Block is saying none of this can happen if you pay off your mortgages, but your property isn't worth the paper it's written on, if that makes sense?" Evie curled up on the bench, giving Jax freedom to move.

Jax continued to hover protectively over Evie, while Roark paced near the front stairs. The sheriff still guarded the back. Gracie was pretty sure Evie's team had hidden cameras filming everything. That wouldn't stop a killer with a gun. She leaned against her hands to keep from chewing nails.

"This isn't a happy crowd," Nick whispered in her ear.

"Understatement," she retorted. "Who was that you were talking to?"

"Art critic from the paper. I think Verity called him."

Gracie couldn't concentrate on selling Bertie's work while her house was at stake.

"My office is worth something to *me*," Hayes shouted. For an accountant, he was dressed quite festively in red tie and green sweater. "Who came up with this?" He turned on cowboy-wannabe Layman. "I thought you wanted the Satterwhite farm for your damned shopping center."

"He only considered outside of town because Mayor Larraine blocked him with zoning in town," Evie called. "Block says y'all were supposed to get rid of Larraine."

Get rid of Larraine? Vote her out—or kill her? Gracie sucked in her breath. Jax spoke before she could phrase any question.

He sounded very controlled, as if suppressing fury. "Who arranged for the zoning lawsuit to be finalized the same day as Block's bond hearing?"

Ah, she breathed in relief. Leave it to Evie's lawyer man to grasp the logistics.

"I set Arthur Block's hearing according to his lawyer's schedule." Looking very un-Santa-like, Judge Satterwhite's wrinkled brow pulled down ominously as he nodded at Turlock Sr.

Heads turned to watch late Mayor Block's silver-haired lawyer. Turlock Sr. shrugged and admitted nothing. *Conspiracy and secrets,* Gracie thought. Old-fashioned honesty and democracy vanished when greed prevailed.

"Judge Rhodes?" Jax demanded when the younger, visibly angry judge didn't speak up.

"Why does this matter?" Nick whispered.

"Block's killer must have known Block and Larraine would be here at the same time, and there would be a crowd to cover his movements," Gracie whispered back.

Looking pale and furious in his blue suit, Rhodes finally replied, "The zoning law should never have been passed! The council should have rejected it instead of letting that faggot bully them."

Gracie winced at the slur, remembering Rhodes and Larraine had gone to school together. The mayor had probably put up with those insults every day as a kid. Instead of breaking her, as the bullies intended, it had apparently made her stronger—and taught her their tactics.

"So in retaliation, you set the zoning hearing for the same day as Block's release, knowing he'd have a mob of supporters and a news conference right outside your door?" Jax pushed harder.

Nick whispered an expletive.

Before anyone else could react, Rhodes' necktie flew up in the air and slapped him in the face. He screamed and struggled to catch it—while his suit coat blew erratically in a nonexistent wind. He grabbed at his carefully combed hair, but the wicked breeze revealed his receding hairline.

Everyone watched in astonishment as the judge danced and swung at an invisible attacker.

"Bertie says you're the man *with a gun* who woke him by kneeling on him," Evie cried over the murmurs and snickers echoing through the rotunda.

Iddy's raven screamed and flew over the judge's head, visibly shaking him more.

"Stop it, stop it! Let me out of this circus!" His usual impassive expression now bordering on frantic, Rhodes aimed for the front stair, evidently expecting the towering, muscular Cajun to give way and let him pass.

Roark did no such thing. Arms crossed, he stoically dared anyone to squeeze by.

"Bertie insists *you woke him up*," Evie said helpfully. "And it's *you* he's hitting on, Your Honor, not Teddy. Do you remember waking up Bertie, sir? Maybe when he was in the attic?"

"Dead men can't talk!" Rhodes had developed a gray tinge beneath his pale skin. "I didn't wake up anyone! That damned queer is the criminal here." He swirled and headed for the back stairs and the sheriff. "You can't hold me. This is a free country."

"Our beloved former mayor's spirit is calling you a pathetic loser," Evie shouted after him. "Block is saying it's all your fault if the mall plans fall through, and Layman owns the town."

Layman leaned against the railing, cowboy boots crossed, looking bored. Gracie contemplated smacking him upside the head with his mall drawing, but she feared the riot of noise below was Larraine's arrival.

"I don't like this," Nick whispered. "Judge Rhodes is about the right size for the man who shot at Larraine at the Barn."

To her dismay, he started easing in the judge's direction. Could he stop a judge from leaving?

An eerie wail filled the rotunda as the sheriff vacillated between his respect for the law, his disbelief in ghosts, and his desire to nail a murder suspect.

Unlike the sheriff, Gracie had no reason to doubt her sister, but she did doubt her own ability. Shakily, she realized it would be cowardice to let her fear allow a possible killer to walk away.

If she got it wrong, they'd put her in jail. Hating the idea of scatter-brained Evie raising Aster. . .

Her child couldn't live in a world run by killers.

She had to do it. Concentrating, she levitated the easel closest to Judge Rhodes and flung frame and easel at the back of his head.

He stumbled and hit the floor.

Twenty-Eight

Nick watched in astonishment as the large, framed mantel collage, *plus* the easel it rested on, literally *flew* at the fleeing judge. The ghost had learned to do more than wail and create wind? Because that wasn't a wind—no actual draft blew through the hall.

Remembering the evening in Gracie's cottage and books and shelves that had righted themselves—He glanced back at Gracie, who slid down the wall and covered her eyes.

Right. Catch a killer, Nick. Discover insanity later. While everyone else froze, he eased closer to Rhodes's prostrate form in his fancy blue suit, now coated in dust from the dirty floor. Did he sit on him?

Before anyone could act, Mayor Larraine sailed up the front stairs in all her glory, an ermine boa at her throat and a fur-trimmed red pantsuit skimming her curves—red hot Mrs. Claus or jolly elf?

Beside her walked the timid farm woman he'd seen at the Barn—Bertie's mother. With her hair brushed into a tight bun and wearing a loose-knit sweater too large for her and a wool skirt that brushed her shins, Mrs. Walker appeared terrified.

Rightly so. The instant Larraine pushed past Roark into the rotunda, the air turned frigid. If he believed the women. . . the former mayor's ghost?

"My, my, Rhodesy, crawling on your belly where you belong?" the mayor sang cheerfully as the judge attempted to push up on one elbow. "Don't bother getting up for little ol' me, although you might want to show respect to Mrs. Walker here. She's been through a lot, what with both her boys gone."

Near the back stairs, Rhodes wobbled to his knees and reached for his coat pocket. Worried, Nick eased closer.

On the other side of the rotunda, Evie screamed, "His aura is fiery, duck!"

Closest to Larraine and Mrs. Walker, Jax and Roark pushed them to cover. Given excuse to take action, Nick reacted instinctively. He tackled the judge and toppled him again.

For his efforts, a gun exploded in his ear.

Deafened, he still recognized distant shrieks. The suited man beneath him struggled and cursed. Without considering how the law would look on assaulting an officer of the court, Nick plowed his fist into the jaw of the shooter who'd nearly taken off his ear.

Rhodes flattened. Apparently, Nick's pub days hadn't been wasted. Coughing on the stench of gunpowder, he rolled off and onto his back while shaking his head to clear his ringing ears. Before he could stand, Gracie fell on him, weeping. Was he dead? Maybe he was now one of Evie's ghosts. Except Gracie felt pretty damned alive, and he was responding accordingly.

"Good job, Gladwell." The sheriff spoke roughly as he snapped hand-cuffs on the unconscious judge.

Only then did Nick realize the screams and commotion had escalated. Holding one hand to his ear and the other around Gracie's waist, he rolled her off him so he could sit up. "What happened?"

Gracie propped him up so he could observe the spectacle. She was whispering, but he couldn't hear through the ringing.

Behind Jax and Roark against the far wall, Larraine and Mrs. Walker covered their mouths in shock. They weren't looking at Rhodes and his gun, as they damned well ought to be. The judge was a menace to everyone here.

At least the sheriff had the sense to remove the judge's gun while calling for backup and an ambulance. An ambulance? Nick didn't think he'd broken any bones. He glanced at Rhodes, who'd woken and started sobbing. He looked whole.

Everyone else was looking elsewhere than at Rhodes as well. Shaking his head to clear the confusion, Nick followed their gazes to the railing where the cowboy-booted developer had been standing earlier.

Roark and Jax abandoned Larraine and ran down the stairs, which gave him a cold chill. Nick swiveled his gaze back to the railing. Evie stood there, arguing into her phone—or talking to ghosts? She didn't appear worried about Jax, just harassed—and maybe a little shocked?

Was the railing *broken*?

He could hear Reuben shouting below. Larraine's bodyguard had arrived and wasn't happy about something.

"My ears are ringing," Nick told Gracie when she tried to explain whatever was happening.

Tears crawled down her cheeks and she spoke louder. "It was a big gun. You could have been killed!"

A big gun. A judge with a big gun. Right. The world kept spinning.

"Is everyone all right?" he finally had the sense to ask, now that he was assured he wasn't deaf or dead.

"Not Layman," she whispered. At his questioning look, she spoke a little louder. "The bullet missed Larraine and hit Layman. He slammed against the railing and it broke."

Shaking her head, Evie crossed the rotunda to stand over them.

Or maybe over Rhodes, who refused to stand up despite the sheriff's urging. "Mayor Block's spirit says you're a fool who has never been able to hit the broad sign of a barn, and if you're the best Layman can find to help him, he deserved what he got. I think he's trying to spit on you."

Rhodes only groaned and sobbed.

Larraine wandered over to join them. "Mr. Gladwell, you're an excellent example of the kind of citizen we need in this town. I hope you will be staying."

Well, no, he needed a job and money and. . .

The mayor didn't wait for his reply but turned to the weeping judge. "That's where cheating gets you, Rhodsie. You were never more than second best and probably worse. I'll have to agree with our spectral ex-mayor, you're pathetic. I can understand wanting to shoot *me*, but poor Sammy? Why?"

"Blackmailing pigs," Rhodes retorted. "Both of you."

The sheriff belatedly began reading him his rights.

Nick figured a judge ought to know them by now.

Not releasing Gracie, he stood and attempted a dizzy bow to the mayor and Bertie's mother. "Ladies, this is not how I wished to introduce you to Albert Walker's exhibit, but if you will excuse the dishevelment, may I show you his crowning masterpiece, the one he intended to adorn your mantle, Mrs. Walker?"

∽

EVIE LEANED AGAINST JAX AND WIPED TEARS FROM HER EYES AS MRS. WALKER studied Bertie's masterpiece. She whispered to the sad wraith clinging to his work, "You did good, Bert. Your mom loves your gift."

Bertie nodded. *I wasn't a real good son. What did that person mean about shooting my brother? He's not stupid like me.*

She'd hoped he hadn't heard Larraine and Rhodes talk about Sammy. "Sammy's on the other side, waiting for you. Would you like to join him? I think your mom will be all right now. Judge Satterwhite won't let her lose her home. And your art will give her some nice spending money."

Bertie studied the police carting away a judge and people coming up the stairs to see his work and everyone talking excitedly. *Seeing my brother isn't stupid, is it?* he asked hesitantly.

"Visiting family is never stupid, wherever they are. For good or bad, they're part of who we are." Evie opened herself up the way she'd learned as a child in this courthouse.

Bertie hesitated, then let go, and vanished.

Jax rocked her on the bench as she cried a little for a lost soul who had never been given much of a chance.

"Teddy Jr. gave Bertie pain pills. Is that enough for an overdose?" she asked, closing her eyes so she didn't have to see auras right now. Fear and agitation and excitement created dizzying, gyrating rainbows.

"If Bertie had been off drugs for a while, his system wouldn't take the levels he was used to. And if Teddy had a bad batch laced with fentanyl— that stuff can kill non-users instantly. He'll plead not guilty and make a deal —unless his father refuses to help him. No guarantees there. Why don't I take you home, let you rest before the parade?"

"Can't. Block's still here. I hope the fall didn't kill Layman. I really don't want to deal with his polluted spirit." She shivered at the thought.

He texted someone while she rejuvenated with the happy energy of excited people finding themselves and their homes in Bertie's artistry.

"Alive, barely," Jax reported. "They'll take him to some fancy hospital far, far away. No ghosts here."

She nodded. "OK, here goes. I need to see what Block wants, and if he'll go away."

"Can't it wait?" Jax asked in concern. "You're more drained than I've ever seen you. That can't be good."

"Layman still owns us. Block is still here for a reason. He was never an evil man. He just thought his vision of what the town should be was more important than anyone else's. As history shows, it's not exactly an unusual attitude." She sucked in more of Jax's love and concern. She wished she could plug herself into an electric outlet. People energy would have to suffice.

She opened her eyes and located Block's spirit hovering near the broken railing, looking a little more gray than usual.

Pretending she was still talking to Jax, she addressed the late mayor. "So, if Layman dies, his heirs inherit the town? How can that work if Toby can't inherit it?"

Block drifted from the railing to watch his son talking to Verity, who had reappeared once Layman had been carted off in an ambulance. *I'm not dumb either*, he said with sarcasm that indicated he'd overheard her saying he wasn't evil. *I tied those mortgages up every which way but loose. You'll find the signed documents inside the cover of the black book. My partner isn't the man I thought he was.*

"Gods do not walk among mere mortals." Evie quoted one of R&R's games or thought she did. It sounded good anyway. "Although there are days when I think demons might. Maybe gods are quieter."

Block snorted. Or maybe it was Jax. She was getting a little fuzzy brained.

It's easy to buy people when you know what they want. My billionaire partner told the judge he could invest in the mall project, be one of the directors, make him important. That's what the dupe wanted—for people to look up to him. Except there was never anything there to look at. Looks like even a dippy fashion designer under-stood that. He didn't sound happy.

"Can we tell Toby about the document in the book cover?" she asked, so Jax knew what she was hearing. He stiffened to alertness but continued to hold her rather than running off to check the book, bless his heart. And she meant that for real.

Block glanced at his son, who was talking to Mrs. Walker. *He'll give it all away, the idiot. Make that lawyer fellow of yours show him how it makes more sense to put the money toward building the town, at the very least. I could have done so much more. . .*

So much more damage. . . But Evie refrained from speaking her weary thought. "We'll do what we can," she promised. "Are you ready to move on to the next plane?"

"What?" Block looked startled, and his aura lit up again. "What plane?"

"Beyond the Veil, to the Pearly Gates, whatever." She was just a little irritated at his obliviousness, a sure sign that she was worn down.

Or hell? the former mayor suggested. *Nope, not ready. You're stuck with me a while longer.*

He vanished.

"Oh, hell," Evie muttered, before passing out.

Twenty-Nine

EVIE'S EYES ROLLED BACK IN HER HEAD, AND HER BODY FELL LIMP IN JAX'S ARMS. He freaked.

Clasping her chilly form, fighting down panic, he shouted, "Evie, damn you, *wake up!*"

He'd seen her slump with exhaustion, but this. . . Swallowing sheer terror —she was cold, dammit!—he tried to wrap her as closely as he could, but *she didn't stir.* Evie not moving was a terrifying experience. She even twitched in her sleep.

What the hell did he do now? First-aid classes didn't teach ghostly energy drains.

This was what he'd feared from the first—that he'd lose her to her determined pursuit of justice. He just hadn't expected to lose her to a corrupt ghost. Clenching his molars to keep from screaming, he tested her pulse. It beat faintly.

Friends and family came running, but they were as helpless as he was. The raven squawked and flew off, presumably to report to Iddy. Evie lay unmoving.

Every damned phone up here was dead despite the backup batteries and chargers he'd provided. Evie and her ghostly friends had drained them all. Mayor Larraine flung hers at a wall and shouted over the railing for medics and an ambulance.

"Half the town will be up here in a second," he whispered to his unconscious burden. "You'd better wake up soon if you don't want Loretta to see you like this."

That produced a slight stir, at least, allowing him to take a breath. She was still in there somewhere.

Fighting real fear that he might lose this precious life because he knew *nothing*, Jax stood, carrying Evie with him. R&R rushed to clear his path, pushing back well-meaning onlookers. They formed a phalanx down the stairs and through the crowd.

Outside, people were claiming their favorite positions along Main Street to watch the parade, unaware of the drama inside the courthouse. The school chorus sang "Up on a Housetop" to the accompaniment of the school band.

Evie snickered.

Jax nearly dropped her. He forced himself to take a deep breath before speaking. "When we marry, Evangeline Malcolm Carstairs, one of our vows will include paddling you every time you make my heart stop."

Her lashes flickered. Reuben and Roark looked at him as if he were crazed. Gracie gave a *hmph* and returned inside to the art display. Iddy wasn't in sight, but Pris and Mavis were running toward them, following the raven.

"Your mother is almost here. Sure you don't want to recover?" If she could hear him, that ought to rate a reaction.

It did. She squirmed a little.

"She needs a battery charger," Jax told his worried friends. He didn't know how else to explain the inexplicable.

"Her mother ought to do it," Reuben said wryly, watching the hurricane in a candy-cane decorated caftan flying toward them. "I'm going back to rein in Larraine before she brings in helicopters." He took the steps two at a time.

"Down," he thought he heard Evie say.

"Toppling won't help," Jax cautioned. And then he heard the puppies Iddy was attempting to give away. Nothing had more energy than a puppy except two puppies, or three.

Recognizing that he'd totally lost his logical mind to Evie's irrational and wholly unscientific realm, he trotted down the stairs to the Adopt-a-Pet booth. Grasping his intent—Evie was the town dog walker after all—Iddy threw a stool in the middle of the pen. Jax stepped over the enclosure and took a seat.

Beagles, mutts, and wiener dogs jumped all over them.

Evie wriggled with them.

By the time Mavis arrived, huffing and puffing, Evie was giggling and pushing off cold noses.

Mavis glared at Jax as if this were all his fault. "Inappropriate and undignified, but if it works. . . She's all yours." She stalked off to talk to one of her witchy friends.

Watching Evie laughing like a toddler at the puppies, Jax thought about it, and decided, yeah, he was good with that. Evie kept him alive.

Pris arrived in less of a hurry. She shrugged at the sight. "She should have been raised in a pound. Get some food in her. She didn't eat lunch." She, too, drifted away, unconcerned.

"My loving family." Evie struggled to sit up.

"I should leave you here and go find food." He threatened to dump her into the whirling tornado of yips and wagging tails.

"The schnauzer thinks you smell like home and wants to go with you," Iddy called from the other side of the fence. "He's used to cats. Psy won't bother him."

Kissing Jax's cheek, Evie rolled off his lap into the filthy pup pen. A tattered gray-haired dog with a lopsided ear leaped on her. Jax sighed as she cuddled the mangy pup and grinned up at him. "Can I take him home, pretty please?"

As if he could deny her anything.

THE FAMILIAR HOLIDAY PARADE OF HORSES AND CARS AND MARCHING BANDS calmed Gracie's jangled nerves. What had she just done?

Flung a huge frame and easel with her mind! She'd knocked down a *judge*—

And no one had even noticed.

She didn't know whether to be relieved or insulted. All the years of hiding her terrifying talent—and no one cared that she was dangerous—or at best, a destructive nuisance.

But Evie's ghosts had played worse havoc and no one yelled at *her*. Friends and family hovered solicitously around her sister as if she were precious crystal. Which everyone knew sturdy Evie was not.

Gracie figured she'd puzzle out deliberate ignorance some other time. For now, she simply needed to be a normal mom and teacher. She hugged Aster, kept an eye on the littles so they didn't run in front of the horses, and helped them to catch the candy Larraine in her bullet-proof mayor-mobile flung by the bucketful.

"Is that a real fur the mayor is wearing?" Nick stood beside Gracie, studying the American fantasy of jolly elves and sleighs where they never had snow. Peach baskets, cotton balls, and boll weevils made more sense.

"I asked. Larraine said she wasn't wearing any nasty rodent around her neck. She knows a manufacturer who creates expensive reproductions for designers. That outfit will probably show up in her catalog next fall." Having Nick beside her made Gracie think things she shouldn't, especially since he was leaving for the city in a week. . . .

He'd held her longer than necessary when she'd cried over him, as if she might matter. Of course, he was all male. Men were like that. She thought. It had been a long time since she'd looked at one.

Apparently, she was still female. She wasn't immune to hormones, and hers were buzzing out of control. She didn't need this distraction if she was about to lose her home. "How are the art sales going?"

"Sales are doing so well, Verity is considering setting up a gallery here, maybe on the walls of a restaurant to start."

"We only have two restaurants," she pointed out. "I doubt Gertie's diner is a good gallery. La Raison is too dark and stuffy and only open for dinner."

"I might have mentioned that," Nick admitted. "And then I remembered your cousin's desire for a café. . ."

"Oh my, one more stick on the fire of Pris and Dante's relationship. He's so good for her. But a café would be too." Gracie sighed. Life was never easy.

"Mommy, is that really Thanta Clauth?" Aster tugged her hand and pointed at a Santa-costumed Judge Satterwhite driving his antique convertible Cadillac as if he hadn't just thrown a very un-Santa-like snit. Larraine's splashy candy display had temporarily diverted from the main attraction. Apparently the judge had decided he was safe with Rhodes and Teddy behind bars.

Watching a silly parade was far better than fretting over whether they'd actually caught a killer and if Layman was still alive and could still steal her home and ruin the town. As far as she could tell, they'd left everything hanging, which gave her icy shivers.

"Santa Claus is very real, if you believe in giving gifts to make others happy," Gracie assured her, wishing it were true.

Aster wrinkled her nose at that philosophy but nodded. "Can we go play with Aunt Evie'th puppy now?"

To Gracie's amazement, Nick lifted her tired daughter to his shoulders and offered his free arm to Gracie. "I think, after all the excitement, we all need a time out."

From her new height, Aster hugged his neck and waved at everyone she saw.

Warily, Gracie took his offered arm. "Are your ears still ringing? That was an enormously brave thing you did. Rhodes could have shot you!" His act had terrified her cautious nature on so many levels. . . She'd done her best to shut out the scene. But he was safe and whole and. . . she still shook in her shoes. She squeezed his arm tighter to reassure herself that he'd survived.

He shook his head. "I'm fine, and it wasn't as if I gave what I did any thought. Diving into bar fights was part of my youth. I now know it's stupid, but sometimes, instinct wins."

"Instinct. Is that what one calls it when one does something stupidly dangerous?" she asked, thinking of her levitation.

He slanted her a knowing look. "I may not have known you for very long, but I'm fairly certain you've never done anything stupid in your life. You are cautious to the Nth degree. Want to talk about that?"

"I have to be cautious," she said stiffly. Yes, yes, she wanted to talk but not yet. "I'm a single mother and have a child to consider. Have you found an apartment in the city yet?"

"I may have to live in a roach motel until I find something. First, I'm waiting to be charged with assault on an officer of the court. With my luck, Rhodes will be out on bail tomorrow and suing everyone involved."

She squeezed his arm again as she grasped the extent of his fears. Men weren't supposed to be afraid. They did stupid things like diving at judges and knocking them out. But then, she'd flung a frame at one *with her mind*. In front of everyone. "If they take you down, they'll have to take me." She didn't know if she was being stupid or brave by saying that.

"Right. Flying frames and all that," he said loftily. "I'll take the blame, if it comes to that. They may as well conclude I'm barmy."

Gracie laughed, relieved that he accepted what she'd done and wasn't questioning. "Too true. If they can't believe that Bertie saw Rhodes in the attic with a gun, how can they possibly believe in flying frames?"

But it was a sobering realization that a killer could be back on the street again for lack of evidence.

Thirty

"EVANGELINE, PUPPIES NEED REST JUST LIKE CHILDREN!" GRACIE SCOLDED.

Evie was rolling around on the Antique Barn's floor playing with her new companion.

Jax knew as little about raising children and puppies as Evie. He wondered if listening to her more experienced sister would make good practice. Unlikely, he decided, watching his fiancée with her over-excited schnauzer.

He didn't think either suffered from the play. It kept them occupied while everyone settled in and Roark put Jax's sister, Ariel, on FaceTime.

"Iddy claims the puppy's name is Morrigan," Evie said, holding the pup up. "But she's too small to be a goddess yet."

Iddy, as usual, wasn't here. She had to take care of her animals. But the rest of the team and then some gathered at Sammy's Antique Barn in hopes of uncovering evidence before Judge Rhodes bailed out. The DA would never believe Bertie's ghost, even if he could testify, which he obviously couldn't.

"Call her Morrie," Jax said, studying the dog dubiously. "Confuse people. Don't let them know we have a goddess on our hands."

Evie laughed, which eased the group's silent tension a little.

"The reward requires that we provide evidence to put ex-Mayor Block's killer behind bars, right?" Reuben asked, working through his laptop.

"Looks like the reward fund has met the goal and then some. That's over a hundred grand of inspiration."

Block's son, Toby, who was sponsoring the reward, and Verity, from the art gallery, had joined them but were spending their time looking through old frames and artwork.

Toby looked up at Reuben's assessment. "Money stopped coming in after they locked up Rhodes, but there's enough there to pay what was promised."

"Even with ballistics, a good lawyer will raise questionable doubt without more evidence. A judge with no record can claim he accidentally shot Layman while defending himself and get away with it. We need solid proof and motivation to prove he killed Block and Sammy," Jax reminded them, lest they start dreaming dreams and forget the task at hand.

"It makes no sense for a respected judge to shoot an antique dealer and a former mayor. It does sound as if someone stole his guns." Gracie had all of Sammy's account books stacked in order. She was systematically rifling through each book for papers stashed between the pages, leaving the invoices in place and setting everything else out for examination.

"Exhibit A," Evie said, holding up on one finger. "Sammy's ghost tells me he's blackmailing his killer and the proof is in his books." She pointed at the ledgers Gracie was working through. "And B, Rhodes seemed to be calling Sammy and Larraine blackmailing pigs. There cannot be blackmail without proof."

Jax was amazed she'd focused so well. They'd left the children in the care of Mavis and the aunts—which apparently even made Evie nervous. He needed to keep them organized and be quick about it.

He handed Nick the discarded ledgers to do his numbers and names thing.

Pris carried in nachos and ice tea. R&R doctored their tea from a flask. Dante was setting up his laptop.

"It's akin to doing research before starting an expedition," the Italian archeologist mused. "One starts with the earliest written documents of the history to be explored. I've compiled dossiers on each of the suspects and victims. We can photograph and notate anything else we discover into these folders."

"We need our cousin Orbis, the psychometrist," Pris complained, examining the stacks of junk accumulating. "I might read minds but not trash. Although I suppose nothing we learn by mindreading would be admissible in court either."

Entering late, white-haired Judge Satterwhite led his frail mother to a padded rocking chair.

"This used to be a derelict old barn full of rusting carriages and farm equipment when my Kenneth first brought me here after our honeymoon." Mrs. Satterwhite looked around eagerly.

That had to be almost seventy years ago. Jax thought some of the rusted junk outside probably dated to then, at the very least.

"Do you think you will be staying in Charleston?" Evie sat up and brought the puppy over for her to pet. "Your aura is looking much more peaceful."

Mrs. Satterwhite glanced up at her son. The white-haired judge was a study in impassivity.

"I'm staying in town for the holidays," she said stubbornly. "I'm closest to my Kenneth here. I'm hoping all this nonsense over the land goes away. I cannot imagine what those Shepherd boys or little Teddy Turlock wanted with land so poor it barely grows weeds."

Toby glanced up at the question. "They didn't. They were scouting for my father and Layman. I am trying to look at it positively and believe my father learned from condemning the mobile home park and was looking for places to move people displaced by the mall."

"*Scouting* and burning down a man's place of business are two entirely different matters," Judge Satterwhite said sternly. "I want to throw those boys behind bars, if they're responsible."

"If I discover that the Shepherds, or more likely, their drug-addled buddies, were responsible for burning out Patel, I'll provide you with enough evidence of their grow operation for the Sheriff to go in and clean house. But Teddy. . ." Toby grimaced. "Teddy Jr.is a wild card. We'll have to see what he tells the sheriff."

Jax wanted to produce the paper hidden in the back cover of Block's notebook, but it was a confusing legal document, and no one here would understand it clearly. Nailing killers had to come first.

"Rhodes has clammed up," Jax reminded them. "Without a confession, we have nothing. He won't break as easily as Teddy, who doesn't appear to know anything except about his father's search for the missing drawing and desire for real estate. Sheriff has a search warrant for Judge Rhodes' house. We can hope they find the rifle used to shoot Larraine. With Nick's description of the shooter, that might add to any sentence from accidentally shooting Layman. But other than hoping ballistics match, we have nothing to nail him for killing Block or Sammy."

And if they wanted a reward, it had to be for killing *Block*—except Rhodes had probably been aiming at Larraine when he hit the former mayor, Jax concluded. Rhodes had been there the day of the mob, but without cameras, no one could prove he had slipped up to the attic. *Opportunity* simply added to their circumstantial evidence. Proving Rhodes hated Larraine wouldn't prove he shot Block. A DA would require more.

Reuben had a video fired up on his computer. "We have camera footage in the warehouse area where the sniper hid. It's not clear, but a man meeting the description Nick gave is caught climbing into an SUV with darkened windows. We ran a partial plate and narrowed the list down to vehicles of that make. One of Layman's corporate vehicles tops the list."

"I heard from my mom that Layman died this morning," Verity reported. "That leaves him out as a witness."

Not mourning the loss of a corrupt developer, Jax whistled. "That puts Rhodes up for manslaughter, at least. That should raise his bond and keep him off the street a little longer."

He hoped. An irate killer with an arsenal roaming the streets, looking for the mayor or anyone else, would not be conducive to a merry holiday.

"We've sent the sniper info to the sheriff," Roark said. "They can maybe test da SUV for prints. Other than proving Rhodes was after Larraine, it won't help da Block case much."

Knowing Layman was dead made explanations much simpler and perhaps gave motivation to their search. Jax waved Block's black binder. "Evie's ghost said there were papers concealed in the back cover of this. I've already told Toby about them, and he's agreed that I can tell our trained investigators."

Their untrained and cynical *investigators* chuckled and glanced up from their self-assigned tasks.

Jax had locked up the original document in his safe but kept a copy, which he produced now. "Block—or more likely his lawyer—amended the LLC document. I won't bore you with the legal details. By the time this was signed, neither party trusted each other much, is my guess. It covers death, malfeasance, and so forth, and reverts the assets to the original owner in such case. Now that Layman is dead, all the Block properties should revert to Toby."

Evie didn't appear to be listening, but Tobias Block was. Jax hoped that meant he was earning his legal fees.

"Still sounds like the properties revert to Layman since dad died first," Toby argued.

PATRICIA RICE

"With both their deaths, the LLC dissolves. Layman's heirs still hold the lien on the properties, but you inherit the real estate and associated mortgages, as well as the liability of your father's debt to Layman's estate, just as we originally believed." Jax figured he needed to confirm this with Turlock, but he didn't think now was the best time.

Layman's death had solved a lot of problems. It was a damned good thing half the town had seen Rhodes pull the trigger.

"So my house is safe?" Gracie asked anxiously.

"I think so, unless Toby decides to call in the mortgages, which he may need to do if Layman's heirs demand payment," Jax warned.

He watched Nick squeeze Gracie's hand and figured something was in the air there. But at least this news should allow everyone to relax and enjoy the holidays.

"Block's spirit is hanging around because he's afraid Toby will give his inheritance away. He wants the money returned to the community, although I don't know how that's possible." Evie proved she listened even though she was teasing the puppy with a nacho.

"I don't know what money Toby could give away," Jax said. "All I'm seeing is the interest the mortgages earn, and almost all that goes to pay Layman. I think anyone with one of these mortgages should probably be talking to a more stable source about refinancing. Gracie, you should qualify and might even end up paying less."

She shook her head. "On a teacher's salary? I didn't qualify before. And banks want cash to refinance. I don't have any."

"If we collect a reward, you should share in it. You and Nick have done more than most of us." Evie gave up on the nachos and turned to the stack of junk they'd been removing from Sammy's ledgers. "Any of this making sense?"

The need for the reward was concrete and all the more personal with Gracie's plight. The desire to save the town. . . Jax itched for justice. From everyone's tense expressions, they all felt the same. Even Pris was thumbing through old newspapers Sammy collected for reasons known only to him.

Toby sat down to study his father's black book, but he was a do-gooder who knew as much about finance as Evie. Jax left him to it and crouched down to work through the pile of trash.

"Mrs. S, you taught back when Rhodes and Bertie and Larraine went to school, didn't you?" Evie asked, holding up an ancient photo. "Was Sammy in any of your classes? I know he was a little older than Bertie."

Mrs. Satterwhite took the faded school photo. "I retired about that time.

Bertie was several years behind his brother because he kept failing, but there was only a year or two difference in them. It was a mistake offering that scholarship. Teenagers can be cruel, and they were crueler those years than any time I can remember."

"So why would Sammy keep this photo? I don't see Bertie or Larraine in it. Do you recognize any of them?" Evie leaned over to sort through the various documents and photos in the stack.

Jax had no idea what she searched for. It all looked like useless memorabilia to him.

Evie's elderly neighbor donned her spectacles and studied the photo under the bright work lights. "As I told you, there were only about a hundred students in the school and only twenty-five in that class. That's Sammy in the back left corner. He was always larger than any of the others. Ralphie is the slender young man kneeling in center front."

Ralph Rhodes, the angry judge, Jax assumed.

"Judging by the insignia on their shirts, I'd say this was the rifle team. Theodore sponsored it, and I believed he coached it, but I don't see him in this photo."

"Theodore? As in Theodore Turlock Sr., the lawyer?" Jax asked.

"Yes, he was never good at sports like football, but he was an excellent shot. I believe he thought he was aiding less athletic students, although I would have preferred he sponsor a debate team for the bright ones." Mrs. S handed the photo to her son.

Turlock Sr., Block's lawyer, was a trained shooter. . .

But if Larraine had been his target, he wouldn't have missed.

Judge Satterwhite studied the photo. "Turlock attended a private school. That's where he picked up the rifle team notion. Arthur Block's parents were land rich, cash poor." He gave a nod of acknowledgement to Block's son, Toby, who shrugged at old news. "Arthur had to attend public school. Got a football scholarship. So he sponsored the football team."

Jax hated indulging in gossip, but apparently gossip was the grease that kept the town functioning. "What about Rhodes' family?"

Mrs. S waved her frail hand. "They were very competitive. I remember once when I gave Ralphie a failing grade on an essay, his father stormed in and told me I was senile and threatened to have the school board take my job if I didn't raise his son's grade."

Jax realized the room had silenced. Parental antics were old hat in his formerly privileged world, but he tuned in anyway.

Getting into her story, Mrs. S smiled in satisfaction. "I pointed out that the essay was about heroes of the Civil War, and Ralphie's essay only included Confederate generals. In class, I had them study both sides, and not merely soldiers, but the abolitionists, statesmen, and women like Clara Barton and Harriet Tubman. Then I told him, it was as if someone who hadn't been in my classroom in nearly thirty years had written that essay, and that's why his son failed. That shut him up. I had Ralphie's father in one of my classes, you see, and I recognized almost the exact same essay he'd turned in."

"Did Judge Rhodes' father get an A for his efforts the first time around?" Evie asked with interest.

"That was half a century ago, dear, so yes, he received an A for his grammar and spelling and the accuracy of his research. But by the time Ralphie went to school, the Civil Rights movement had changed our curriculum completely. We do occasionally move with the times, even if belatedly."

"So Judge Rhodes plagiarized his essay, and Larraine claims he cheated by copying her exam. That's a pattern, but not evidence of anything except ethical issues that ought to disqualify him as a judge if they'd happened at university. Not sure high school counts. Hardly blackmail material." Jax didn't like the notion of an ethically-challenged judge, but there was no reason Rhodes couldn't have learned his lesson. He needed *evidence* to present to the sheriff.

Nick held up one of the ledger books. "I will admit that I have not led a life of purest intention, so I make no judgment. But I'm familiar with the very many ways cash can be laundered, and there is an interesting pattern in Sammy's account books related to your Judge Rhodes."

NICK HAD NO PROBLEM WITH ALL THE ATTENTION ABRUPTLY FOCUSING ON HIM. He *did* have a problem with raising hopes. But if the old lady's tales held their interest, maybe his discovery could be useful in some way.

"Old fashioned cash and pencil," Roark said mournfully, picking up one of the ledgers. "Where did all the modern computer crooks go?"

Reuben punched his arm and gestured for Nick to continue.

"Sorry if I'm stealing your thunder, mate. But maybe you can find the modern equivalent in some of Rhodes' bank accounts." Nick passed the ledger to Jax. "Judging by these ledgers, every third Monday of the month since the Barn opened, Judge Rhodes has been in to pay cash for sterling silver flatware. Even if Sammy was finding the most expensive flatware in existence, a single set would not cost that much. And if he's buying a twelve-place setting on account, he's paid for it twenty times over. No matter how I juggle them, the numbers don't compute. The total per year isn't substantial for someone moderately well off, but to Sammy, it was probably what kept this place afloat."

"Evidence that Sammy blackmailed Rhodes?" Gracie leaned to look over his shoulder. She smelled of sugar and spice and everything nice that Nick was not.

"Sammy doesn't appear to carry silver, so that sounds right to me," Toby added from a table in the back where he and Verity had returned to examining the contents of boxes.

"What could Sammy possibly have known about a judge to make him pay through the nose?" Pris asked, grimacing at the ink on her fingers from the newspapers.

Apparently remembering something, Gracie rummaged through their piles of Sammy's clutter to produce certificates and photos. "Might these be related? If Sammy said proof of his blackmail was in his books. . . ?"

"And he said he was stopping a *cheater* from evicting his mother," Evie reminded them. "Sounds like Ralph was a bit of a cheat in school, although what that has to do with eviction I can't say."

Nick spread out the photos and tried to see what Gracie was seeing. She was good at putting two and two together. "Certificates for winning some rifle award. Score sheets. Images of the targets with bullet holes. Photos of the shooters." He lined target photos on top and certificates and score sheets below.

"Look at the target numbers," Gracie suggested. "They should match the score sheet and identify the shooter."

Jax joined them, reading upside down. "Score sheets identify the contestants by number. Certificates are given to those with the highest score."

Nick saw the problem instantly. "Names don't match. Numbers do but not the names on the certificates. Look, target #16 in the photo belongs to Sammy Walker. Score sheet #16 has the best score. But the certificate for #16 goes to Ralph Rhodes. Target #12 for Ralph is pretty sad."

"For three years in a row," Gracie whispered. "Sammy and Rhodes were cheating?"

Mrs. Satterwhite rocked in her rocker. "That's how it was those last years

I taught. Those who knew they weren't smart enough to earn the scholarship competition sold their other talents to the students who had a chance. It was dreadful. We finally had to put an end to it. I believe Ralphie and Larraine were the top scholarship contenders and both were expelled for cheating in their final year. I don't think anyone else came close."

"Are we saying Sammy was blackmailing Rhodes over a *high school rifle competition*?" Evie asked, not bothering to look at the photos. "Everyone around here probably knew about it. So why would it matter?"

"I didn't know about it. Sammy must have kept real quiet," Judge Satterwhite said. "Rhodes earned a partial scholarship to play on the university rifle team based on his scores. His supposed prowess earned him an invitation to an exclusive country club where he met the men who helped him obtain his current position. I imagine it's a matter of pride at this point, and that he'd pay good money to prevent his cheating from being known."

"Chances are good he cheated on the university team too," Jax added dryly. "If Sammy threatened to talk to the university coach. . . ?"

"Block claimed that Rhodes wants to be seen as a big man in town." Evie poked through the rest of the pile. "He wouldn't want his record besmirched."

"Not enough motive to kill," Nick argued, having been there and done that. His record for juvie car theft was far worse than cheating. "Pressure and stress might push him if there was another underlying cause. . ."

"Would Rhodes be involved with Teddy Jr. in any way?" Evie asked. "Because Sammy's ghost said he wanted to punish the *drug dealers* who hurt Bertie and the cheater who threatened his mother with eviction. Rhodes may be a cheat, but there's no connection to drugs or eviction. He just seems to be a pathetic loser."

Frowning, the former mayor's son settled down to study the pile of memorabilia. Nick handed him the stack of target photos.

Tobias flipped through them dismissively. "My dad would have pressured his lawyer, not Judge Rhodes, into doing whatever he could to acquire prime property along the highway. Judging by dates and Bertie's sketches, looks like Turlock Sr. may have had Teddy and his friends harassing Mrs. Walker and Patel so they'd move out and give Mrs. Satterwhite a reason to sell. Not sure how that applies to Rhodes."

"But I *own* this land. I certainly didn't file eviction notices," Mrs. Satterwhite said with confusion.

"Would there be any way to make Sammy think you did?" Evie sat back on her heels and hugged her puppy.

Nick grimaced. "Back home, no one budged unless an officer of the law brought an eviction notice and started hauling out the furniture."

"A formal eviction notice!" Judge Satterwhite leaned over Reuben typing at his computer. "I can get you into courthouse records. . . if you haven't already hacked them," he added dryly, glancing at the screen.

"Say you just gave me permission." Reuben turned the laptop so everyone could read.

Nick whistled in shock. "An eviction notice signed by *Rhodes*." Did that mean they were finally onto something? His luck never ran toward hundred-grand rewards.

The white-haired judge slammed his hand against the desk. The genial Santa didn't look so genial now. "Filing an eviction notice on *our property* is enough for me to bring him up on charges. *Our property!* What gave him that right?"

"Turlock Sr. would be my guess," Jax suggested. "He knew Rhodes' from his rifle team days. He might have known about the cheating. Rhodes may have helped him get Teddy off on drug charges. They knew each other's secrets and would have used each other as needed."

Toby nodded agreement. "My father and Turlock would have contrived some document, if only as a backup for whatever they wanted to do. It's one of the ways they threatened everyone out of the mobile home park. Rhodes provided the rubber stamp."

"If Rhodes' signature was on the eviction notice, Sammy blamed him for that, at the least. He knew Rhodes as a cheat, but that's still not sufficient reason for blackmail." Evie sat back and let the puppy lick her nose. "How soon will the sheriff have a ballistics report?"

"It's the holidays. Not soon." Jax scowled as he jotted notes.

Nick could almost taste that money. Gracie looked as if she would keel over in longing. They had to keep adding one and one and one and finding an answer. "If Rhodes' gun is matched to the one that shot Sammy. . . The two may have argued over blackmail *and* the eviction notice. It might have become heated."

Gracie watched him with stars in her eyes, as if he might have the answers. "Why would Sammy believe a judge did anything more than sign a legal paper that Judge Satterwhite authorized as the owner?"

Nick prayed he was on the right track. "On the day I bought Bertie's sketches. . ." He scrolled back through the pictures on his phone. "I showed Sammy the other work of Bertie's that we'd found, including the one with Layman paying Rhodes, and the one with all the men in the barbershop.

That was the third Monday of the month, *the day Rhodes always came in,"* Nick added, excitement building as he worked it out.

"More circumstantial evidence," Jax added, not sounding as dubious as before. "We'd need proof that Rhodes always came in at that *hour* every month. We'd need to know Rhodes whereabouts that day."

R&R dived into their computers.

"Could Sammy have threatened Rhodes with anything in those sketches?" Nick asked, flipping through his photos, anxious to find something, anything, useful.

Judge Satterwhite took the phone and scrolled through the images of Bertie's sketches. "Town council, both Turlocks, Rhodes, Layman. . . shouts conspiracy to the paranoid. Although I suppose Sammy had good reason to be paranoid by then. Bertie's death, an eviction notice. . . A simple man like Sammy was probably beyond furious and running on scared seeing all these powerful people lined up against him, especially if he was blackmailing one of them. But I don't see any evidence."

Evie screwed up her nose and looked as if she meant to pull straws from thin air. "Remember—Sammy's ghost claimed he bought his brother's unsold sketches after he learned Bertie was following the *turds*. He was looking for *evidence*. And he specifically said he was blackmailing his killer and the proof is in his books. High school cheating just doesn't make sense. Sammy had to have more."

Bollocks. Believing specters or not, Nick had to agree. "Blackmail ought to involve an actual crime. Bertie's sketches are recent. Sammy had been blackmailing his killer for years. . . possibly since high school since their ways would have parted afterward."

Gracie gave an excited whoop and hurriedly scattered all the memorabilia she'd just stacked in order. "Look at this!" She handed him a scribbled note with initials and dollar amounts. "This dates back to the year Larraine and Rhodes didn't graduate—an IOU signed by Bertie to RR for a bunch of strange letters."

"Not us," Reuben called from where he was bent over his laptop.

Evie patted the big guy's knee as if he were a dog.

Ignoring the puzzling byplay in his excitement, Nick read the note and whistled, then passed it over to Jax, who passed it around. The others studied the note and initials in puzzlement. They didn't have his criminal background.

"Sammy kept a handful of those old notes." Gracie handed him more. "I don't know what most of the letters mean, but RR might stand for Ralph

Rhodes? If we're tracing a crime back to high school? The dollar amounts don't seem like much."

"For a kid back then, probably about right. THC and MSIR mean marijuana and morphine sulfate, don't ask me how I know," Nick explained, feeling a little uncomfortable when everyone stared at him. But the idea of a reward to help Gracie pay off her house was worth any scorn. "I'd say Bertie gave these IOUs for drugs to someone with the initials of RR."

"Looking at this yearbook, Ralph Rhodes is the only RR in the entire class," Pris called, waving the yellowed magazine.

Silently shaking his head, Judge Satterwhite took the yearbook and handed it to his mother, who flipped sadly through the pages.

Studying the notes, Jax whistled. "To heck with high school rifle competitions. If Rhodes knew Sammy had these. . . It would take a strong offensive DA to pin them on Rhodes, but with the right argument, these are a powerful motivation for murdering his blackmailer. But why now? He'd been paying him for years."

Evie didn't look at the notes but shook her head. "Motivation for killing Sammy if they argued, and like Nick said, Rhodes was feeling pressured, maybe. But we still have no reason for Rhodes to kill Block or Larraine. Rhodes seemed to infer *Larraine* blackmailed him. Maybe to keep her zoning laws? What was she hanging over his head?"

The mayor's bodyguard looked grim beneath his man bun as he hit his phone contacts. Nick gathered he was calling the mayor. Everyone waited as he furiously questioned the fashion queen. From the look on his face. . .

"We have *proof* Ralph Rhodes sold drugs," Reuben shouted at the phone. "Just tell us what you're hiding!"

Could they really have solved a crime? Nick squeezed Gracie's hand. She squeezed back. "Red herring," she whispered, inexplicably.

Looking as if he'd like to chew nails, Reuben clicked off. "Yup, the drama queen blackmailed Rhodes, not for money, but into upholding her damned zoning law. She has better proof than old IOUs that Rhodes financed his education by selling drugs. She kept the evidence close until she needed it. If we promise to keep the judge locked behind bars, she'll happily hand it over."

Jax glared at Reuben. "I can see why people want to kill your girlfriend— that's motivation for Rhodes and everyone else involved to murder her. Tell her to take the evidence to the sheriff right now. . . along with any other blackmail material in her possession!"

Gracie flung her arms around Nick's neck. "The Tale of Two Blackmailers," she murmured happily.

He had no idea what she was talking about but any attempt at thought evaporated with all her lush curves pressed against him.

Thirty-One

"ASTER, SETTLE DOWN AND TELL MR. GLADWELL THANK YOU." A TRIFLE rattled at the perfect gifts Nick had chosen for the children, Gracie pushed her hair behind her ear and wished she'd bought more clever presents than socks.

She was fortunate to have any brains at all after last night's make-out session—he'd called it snogging. Honestly, if two grown adults couldn't come up with better words. . . Every part of her tingled just remembering.

"Thaint Nick, I love you!" Aster cried, throwing herself into a laughing Nick's arms.

The man was always laughing as if hadn't a care in the world. It would be much too easy to love a man like that. She simply had a hard time believing a handsome charmer would have any use for a dour housewife. But if she could dream. . .

Evie flung Jax's rolled-up gift socks like softballs at their guest. "Thaint Nick is putting us all to shame. We either have to kill or keep him."

Apparently bored and looking for amusement, R&R did the same with their socks. Gracie wanted to slide under the couch in embarrassment. The Brit gathered all the sock bombs and blitzed his opponents with their own weapons.

Before war ensued, Gracie wielded her feeble telekinesis and stopped the flying footwear mid-air. Woolly ammunition dropped all over the parlor.

Evie swatted a fallen sock ball under the couch with her foot. "Score!"

A melee ensued, scattering gift wrap where it wouldn't be found until Easter. With a sigh of exasperation, Gracie got up to answer the doorbell, grateful the pets had been confined to the backyard.

Arms piled high, a gift-bearing Larraine in her red velvet Mrs. Claus outfit waited on the porch. Beside her, Toby Block carried the overflow.

"Merry Christmas! We come bearing tidings of great joy and cheer!"

Nick materialized to help haul the load and welcome the newcomers. "Thaint Nick didn't anticipate this," he protested, speaking Gracie's thoughts. "Can I give IOUs?"

"No, no, dear boy, your presence is all the present we need. These are for the kiddies. The good tidings are for the adults." Larraine sailed into the parlor as if she owned it.

"Your bubble is big and silver," Loretta cried, jumping up to hunt through the expensively wrapped presents for name tags. "Are you floating?"

Larraine laughed. "I may be, like a shiny helium balloon." She distributed packages to Aster and the twins after Loretta claimed hers.

"Awesome aura," Evie added in admiration. "Gift-giving suits you."

Gracie wondered if the mayor got rich by blackmailing bad guys. Was she rich enough to buy all their mortgages? That might explain Toby's presence but was Robin Hood behavior a moral answer to their problems?

Perceptive as ever, Pris and Mavis steered the wide-eyed children and their gifts toward the kitchen and cookies. Loretta looked as if she'd resist, but Evie waved her on. For once, Gracie was grateful to her family for their abilities or empathy or whatever in heck they did. Children shouldn't have to worry about whatever Larraine had to say.

A moment later, Iddy returned from checking on dogs, cats, and birds, carrying a tray of mugs and a coffeepot. "Pris will deliver calorie overloads shortly." She took a seat on the hearth, leaving everyone to help themselves. Iddy was good with animals, not so much with people.

Nick leaned over to whisper in Gracie's ear. "Should I stay with you or make myself scarce?"

That he had the courtesy to ask warmed her all over. *Stupid, Gracie, stupid.* And even knowing she was being stupid for wanting him near, she still answered, "Stay. You're one of us. Besides, Mom and the aunts love having the kids to themselves. Pris will be right back." She nodded at Dante, who was engrossed in a book Pris had given him.

With the room reduced by half its energy, the so-called adults found seats on the floor and hearth and anywhere they could find, while the mayor and

Toby took the sofa. Gracie leaned against a stack of boxes probably containing Great-Aunt Val's album collection. She almost melted like hot butter when Nick took the floor beside her.

Pris returned with appetizers. Gracie snatched up a cheesy broccoli. Nick grabbed potato crisps.

Loving the attention, whereas Toby did not, Larraine took a manila envelope from his hands. "Judge Satterwhite, Bill Wright, president of our local bank, and my awesome self were chosen by Tobias Block to execute the reward money for finding his father's killer."

Gracie tensed, almost choking on her broccoli. That could not be a check. . . It was much too soon. They hadn't done *anything*. . .

R&R instantly hit their phones, hunting news they'd ignored because it was a holiday. In the library, Ariel cheered. Jax's sister couldn't handle overstimulation, but she hadn't wanted to stay home alone either. She, apparently, had the presence of mind to stay on top of events.

Reuben stared at his phone and whistled.

Larraine beamed. "That's the reason I couldn't be here earlier."

"You have our full attention," Jax said solemnly. "Reuben, keep your trap shut."

Reuben saluted with his coffee mug and shoved bite-sized omelets into his mouth, letting the mayor have her moment of glory.

"To prevent Rhodes from bailing out, the sheriff expedited the ballistics report based on your evidence of possible blackmail and drug dealing. Ballistics conclude the gun used on Layman was also used on Samuel Walker and Arthur Block. The sheriff admits there was pressure from above to hold Rhodes, but those people don't talk to me, so I can't say who rushed the charges to the DA."

"Governor went to school with Layman and was invested in some of his companies," Roark reported, reading his phone and holding it up. "Ariel is digging."

Nick murmured, "Ouch. The *governor* wanted to steamroller Afterthought?"

"Yup," Gracie whispered back. "He was Block's buddy and hates Larraine. Now he probably hates a useless rat like Rhodes for spoiling his fun."

Larraine waved off their whispers. "I do not indulge in gossip. People gotta hate. I'm here to spread the love. Anyway, with the evidence of blackmail and ballistics, Rhodes has been charged with killing Arthur Block as well as Layman and poor Samuel Walker, as well as assault on *moi*. Since the reward was not set up for conviction, just evidence, we are presenting the Sensible Solutions Agency with the prize of a hundred thousand plus change. With ballistics and the fingerprints on the guns, plus on the vehicle you found, the one Rhodes used to flee after shooting at me, Troy thinks he can get a confession without need of Bertie's ghost."

Even Ariel whooped in the library.

"The answer's always in the aura," Evie said with satisfaction, helping herself to what remained of the omelet appetizers.

Gracie wasn't ready to celebrate yet. Would Nick take his share and go home? She was surprised by how much she hated that thought. She chewed her fingernail and waited while the others shouted and cheered, and Pris popped a Prosecco bottle they'd chilled for dinner.

Toby held out a folder to Jax. "Bill Wright told me to give you this. As soon as dad died, I gave Bill the portfolio of mortgages. Since his is the only bank in town, he's familiar with most of the property and the owners. He's had his employees checking credit files and property reports and so forth. His bank isn't large enough to refinance everyone, but he's making recommendations to larger companies for the loans he can't handle."

Gracie held her breath, watching the folder exchange hands as if it were the Holy Grail. Nick squeezed her shoulders, and she didn't pull away.

Jax flipped the folder open and scanned the top sheet, then glanced up at Gracie. "He can take you, if you can cover the closing costs. Bill isn't doing this out of charity. His bank stands to make a lot of money out of these properties. But his interest rates are considerably lower than Block's. You'll earn the money back in a year or two."

Gracie nearly wilted. Evie and Nick cheered. Iddy and Pris clinked their glasses. Tears welled as she whispered, "Will my share of the reward cover the closing costs?"

"And then some," Jax predicted. "And you can put the amount you save on monthly payments into Aster's college account."

Gracie covered her face with both hands to hide her tears of joy.

"Are you willing to rent a room to a boarder to add to Aster's college fund?" Nick whispered.

Startled, she hastily wiped her eyes. "You have no car. You can't drive to your new job from here."

He grinned in a way that woke all her dormant hormones. "Say yes."

Warily, against her better judgment, she nodded.

He broke into the excited conversation flowing around them. "Do you think Judge Satterwhite might rent the Antique Barn to me and Mr. Patel? We've been talking, and it only seems fair. . ."

Gracie gulped air so fast, she almost fainted.

Recovering, she defiantly floated a glass of Prosecco off Pris's tray. Pointing and cheering, encouraging floating alcohol, everyone lifted their glasses. Even Nick grinned and clinked his glass to hers when she snatched it from mid-air.

He was staying. Oh my. Gracie threw back a healthy swallow—then boldly hugged Nick's neck. "If you are very, very good, you might find a better present under your tree tonight."

He laughed and *snogged* her right in front of everyone.

Lying in Jax's arms that night, exhausted by the day's excess, Evie pressed kisses along his solid chest. "You must be part Native American like Iddy to always be brown."

"And Italian, like Dante. And tenacious, like my parents. You promised to give me a date, Evangeline. I'm no longer poor. Neither are you. Even if your Aunt Val wants her house back, I think we can afford our own place. Give me a date."

Evie fingered her lovely spoon engagement ring. "Beltane." She'd never had a relationship last for a year, and that would be more than a year.

"Beltane," he repeated warily. "And that is?"

She giggled. "You really were raised by wolves, weren't you? May Day. A wedding will distract my mother from lighting bonfires."

She didn't mention all the other superstitions associated with the celebrations for a fertile summer. Her mother wanted more grandchildren.

"May, a year after we met. I like that." He propped himself on his elbow and kissed her thoroughly.

Evie threw herself into the moment with enthusiasm. Kissing led to many pleasant activities.

The covers were on the floor and the schnauzer leaping up from her puppy bed before they heard music drifting from below.

"Don't," Evie said sleepily as Jax prepared to exit the bed to do his protector-of-his-fiefdom duty. "Pris and Dante are working things out. And the twins are on the stairs, keeping watch."

"How do you know this?" He returned Morrigan to her bed and the covers to theirs.

"I didn't say I banished all ghosts," she murmured, snuggling under his arm again. "Some of them are rather useful."

It was an old house, always owned by her family. Their spirits lingered, watching, guarding, and sometimes returning.

Evie hoped their target was Pris and Dante tonight. Maybe they could make it a double wedding—if no more mad judges ran loose.

Characters

MALCOLM FAMILY

Evangeline (Evie) Serena Malcolm Carstairs—sends spirits to light, reads auras
Mavis Malcolm Carstairs—Evie's mother; reads crystal ball
Grania Malcolm Carstairs Jenkins (Gracie) —Mavis's elder telekinetic daughter
Aster—age 6, Gracie's daughter
Idonea (Iddy)—Evie's cousin, veterinarian who talks to animals
Priscilla Broadhurst—Evie's cousin; telepathic
Loretta Aurora Post—eleven-year-old heiress; sees souls
Aunt Felicia—Mavis's sister; Iddy's mother
Aunt Ellen— Mavis's sister; Pris's mother
Great Aunt Evangeline Valerie Malcolm Brindle—Aunt Val, Civil War re-enactor

BOOK FIVE:

Damon Ives Jackson (Jax)—fraud and family lawyer; Evie's significant other
Ariel Ives Jackson—Jax's sister
Roark LeBlanc—hacker friend, former military intelligence
Reuben Thompson, PhD—Roark's engineer partner

CHARACTERS

Dante Alfonso Ives Rossi—archeologist; distant Italian cousin of Jax
Nicolas Gladwell—British marketing expert
Albert (Bertie) Walker—homeless man in attic
Samuel Walker—Bertie's older brother, runs Antique Barn
Louise Walker—their mother
Verity Janus—artist; mother owns gallery
Matthew and Mark Shepherd—own farm, may grow pot
Theodore Turlock Sr.—attorney
Teddy Turlock Jr.—Theodore's son; runs sporting goods store
Tobias Block—former mayor's son, ecologist
Judge Hugh Satterwhite—white-haired judge (father **Kenneth**)
Charlotte Satterwhite—judge's mother
Judge Ralph Rhodes—went to school with Mayor Larraine
Franklin Layman—Developer, wears cowboy boots
Patel—Pakistani fruit store owner
Mrs. Janus—gallery owner, Layman's girlfriend
Philomena Marquette—black policeman; went to school with Evie
Mayor Larraine Ward—fashion designer and business owner

The Aura Answer
Patricia Rice

Copyright © 2022 Patricia Rice
Cover design © 2022 Killion Group
First Publication: Book View Cafe, July 2022
ISBN 978-1-63632-080-9 ebook
ISBN 978-1-63632-084-7 print

Published by Rice Enterprises, Dana Point, CA, an affiliate of Book View Publishing Cooperative

Book View Café
304 S. Jones Blvd. Suite #2906
Las Vegas NV 89107

BOOK VIEW CAFE

About the Author

With several million books in print and *New York Times* and *USA Today's* bestseller lists under her belt, former CPA Patricia Rice is one of romance's hottest authors. Her emotionally-charged contemporary and historical romances have won numerous awards, including the *RT Book Reviews* Reviewers Choice and Career Achievement Awards. Her books have been honored as Romance Writers of America RITA® finalists in the historical, regency and contemporary categories.

A firm believer in happily-ever-after, Patricia Rice is married to her high school sweetheart and has two children. A native of Kentucky and New York, a past resident of North Carolina and Missouri, she currently resides in Southern California, and now does accounting only for herself.

Also by Patricia Rice

About Book View Café

Book View Café Publishing Cooperative (BVC) is an author-owned cooperative of professional writers, publishing in a variety of genres including fantasy, romance, mystery, and science fiction — with 90% of the proceeds going to the authors. Since its debut in 2008, BVC has gained a reputation for producing high-quality ebooks. BVC's ebooks are DRM-free and are distributed around the world. The cooperative is now bringing that same quality to its print editions.

BVC authors include New York Times and USA Today bestsellers as well as winners and nominees of many prestigious awards.